Remembering You

by

Barbara A. Luker

DORRANCE
PUBLISHING CO
EST. 1920
PITTSBURGH, PENNSYLVANIA 15238

Dorrance Publishing Co
585 Alpha Drive
Pittsburgh, PA 15238
Visit our website at www.dorrancebookstore.com

ISBN: 978-1-6453-0997-0
eISBN: 978-1-6461-0255-6

For my grandmother Lillian Moore Smith, the first writer in our family; and to Mr. Harvey, a gentleman and a scholar who taught me more in ninth grade English than just how to structure a sentence; and finally, to the one who first inspired the dream that has become the story...

Thank you all.

Prologue

"This wait to see you is killing me, Paige. How much longer till you're here?" Jake asked.

The sound of power tools and hammering nearly drowned out his question, but I could tell how impatient he was. He had just recently undertaken his newest house renovation project and for a moment I wondered if my presence would be enough to draw him away from his work. Renovating old houses back to their original splendor was something he was passionate about, and I sometimes questioned if his devotion to his work was even greater than his devotion to me.

It wasn't just Jake, though. I was equally anxious for our long-awaited reunion. Each of us had grown more frustrated with the delays that had kept us apart the past few weeks, but the day was finally here and I couldn't wait to feel his strong arms around me again.

"I'm just a few blocks away, baby," I assured him, knowing I was doing all I could to get there quickly. A promise of an extra healthy tip for the cabbie had brought about a death-defying trip from the airport and I had to keep reassuring myself all the near collisions we had experienced on the trip would be worth it when I finally saw Jake.

In some respects, our reunion was like starting all over again. It had been weeks since we had seen each other in person and it was happening back where it all started: Chicago. Only this time we were a long way from the strangers who caught each other's eyes across a crowded group of people at an architectural conference.

As the large diamond on my ring finger caught the sunlight streaming in through the cab's windows, I twirled the ring slightly and thought about the man who was waiting for me at the end of my harrowing ride. He was everything I had ever dreamt about in a man and then some, and I couldn't wait for our lives together to officially start, but work commitments had kept me from even considering a wedding date, and Jake was getting frustrated by the lack of progress on our trip to the altar.

If he had told me once he had told me a thousand times: All he wanted was for the two of us to say vows in front of a judge. But it wasn't what I wanted. As children my sister Jen and I had spent hours daydreaming about our perfect weddings. I would wear a big white princess dress while Dad walked me down the aisle in a church decorated with more tulips than all the fields in Holland. The details had changed as we have grown up—that princess dress morphed into a sleek and sexy off-white dress for me, and white calla lilies as my flower of choice over the tulips—but I still wanted the wedding of my dreams and that would take months and months of planning. That was time I just didn't have when we became engaged.

The biggest solo project of my architectural career had been offered to me the same week we got engaged and it was an opportunity I couldn't pass up. Jake, bless his heart, had been supportive of putting the wedding planning on hold while I attacked the project with every fiber of my being, but now that the church project was well underway, his patience was wearing thin and I knew that this weekend he would press me to set an actual wedding date so the planning process could begin. If I had my druthers, planning would wait until the church project was completely finished, but I had put him off long enough and knew that by the time I went back to Minneapolis, we would have agreed on a date. After making him wait so long, I owed him at least that.

It wasn't as if I didn't want to marry him, because I did—more than anything else in the world. In fact, many sleepless nights were spent worrying that if I didn't get a ring on my finger as soon as possible, he would suddenly realize he had made a mistake and start looking for a way out of our relationship. The man was incredibly handsome with a smile that could melt the polar icecaps, and he was the sweetest person in the world. It also didn't help my confidence that his looks attracted a lot of attention from other women, but there wasn't a vain or mean bone in his body. He loved everyone and everyone loved him, so what was he doing with me?

There was nothing special about me and, if I was being honest with myself, I had no idea what attracted him to me, but something between us sparked. That first day, seeing each other across the large auditorium, I felt an intense attraction to Jake. There's no doubt in my mind that practically every other woman in the room felt the same, but from the moment we locked eyes on each other and he smiled at me—tentatively at first as if he wasn't sure he should, but then widening until the smile encompassed and changed his entire face—I couldn't look away.

Was it love at first sight? Jake always said it was for him, but I was a different story. I fell in love with him—eventually—but not until my feelings for the man began to build and multiply and suddenly I was in love.

So here we are, desperate to reach out and touch each other, and suddenly the cab is slowing down as we entered a construction zone.

"Rats," I said into the phone, "we're still a few blocks away, but there's construction everywhere and we've almost come to a complete stop. It might take a little bit longer."

"Have the driver pull out onto a side street and maybe you can avoid it," Jake suggested, the frustration of yet another delay evident in his voice.

"Oh wait," I told him. "It's okay now. We're moving again." The cab accelerated again as a smile appeared on my face. Just a few more blocks to go. I picked up my small suitcase in preparation for making a quick exit from the cab as I juggled the phone at my ear.

The sound of power tools had now been replaced by the gentle chirping of birds and I knew Jake had exited the house and was impatiently standing at the curb, most likely covered in drywall dust.

"Can you believe this day is finally—"

I never got a chance to finish my sentence.

Chapter One

"Your speech is already on your laptop, but I also put it on this flash drive just in case," Casey told me as she patiently waited to hand over both the drive and my briefcase as I struggled into my coat.

As usual, I had become so wrapped up in work I was running late and in danger of missing my plane to Chicago for the conference. It was my first time speaking in front of a group of fellow architects and I was more nervous than I had expected. Thank goodness Casey was there to take care of me. In addition to being an excellent assistant, she was also a friend and I counted on her more than anyone else in my life to keep all the balls I was juggling in the air.

With my coat finally in place, Casey handed everything over to me and followed as I began to walk swiftly to the elevator.

"And you won't forget to water my plants and collect my mail while I'm gone, right?" I asked for the umpteenth time.

"You know I will, so stop asking," Casey said, a little out of breath from her efforts to keep up with me on my race to the elevator. "Just concentrate on your speech and letting the AIA see how talented you are."

The AIA, more formally known as the American Institute of Architects, had honored me as keynote speaker for this year's conference on historical restoration—something I was becoming well known for across the country. The fact that this honor also spotlighted my firm was welcome publicity for the senior partners. A good showing in front of the association might just put me a step or two closer to my own partnership.

"I'm just going to concentrate on not making a fool of myself," I told her as I impatiently stabbed again at the elevator button. I was used to speaking in front of groups of clients, history buffs, and even state and local officials, but they weren't my peers and didn't have the decades of knowledge that most AIA members had. Even though I had a master's degree, I had only been a licensed architect for a few years and I hoped they wouldn't hold that against me.

As the elevator doors finally opened, I turned to Casey. "Wish me luck?" I asked.

"You don't need luck, Paige. You're a rock star!" Casey said, giving me one last smile before the elevator doors closed between us.

Although I didn't feel like a star most of the time, I had to admit that on occasion I could show brief flashes of brilliance. Certainly the partners in my firm must have agreed, judging by how they trotted me out every time they wanted to impress a new client. My work in the field of historical architecture had attracted a lot of attention from others in the profession and resulted in a lot of business for the firm. While Minnesota didn't have as many historical buildings as some of the east coast states, those we did have were carefully preserved and many times lovingly restored to their former grandeur.

Architecture had interested me since first seeing a building under construction. With the layers of paint and plaster peeled away, even the most basic design fascinated me. But it wasn't until my hometown nearly lost all of our historic structures after a tornado ravaged the community that my more-specific interest in the historic preservation of old buildings took hold.

Even though I was still only a child, the century-old buildings in town had always held a special place in my imagination as the old-world charm and the fine details of their design filled my head. Where others just saw a decrepit old building that no longer worked for current uses, my day dreams were of the old theaters and the bars and hotels and the people who lived and worked on those buildings in the 1800s. The craftsmanship on these buildings gave them character that transgressed the ages.

In my hometown, the owners of those historic properties had made some modifications to make the buildings more useful for current day operations, which resulted in some of the original details of the architecture being lost, but it was nothing compared to the damage done by the tornado. Many of those property owners wanted to restore their buildings, but the cost to restore the original architecture was more than most could handle, and building after building was soon slated for destruction.

In the midst of all the drama of the tornado recovery efforts, a small groundswell of community members fought to stop the demolitions and raise public awareness. Their outrage grew until eventually the State Historical Society stepped in with offers of money and professional guidance on the restoration work. While it was too late for a couple of the buildings that had already been torn down, many more were saved and the final result allowed the entire business district to be placed on the National Register of Historic Places, a designation that not only attracted tourists to town but ensured that the buildings—and the history that went along with them—would forever be preserved.

Without realizing it at the time, the effort to preserve the historical significance of my own community had a profound effect on my future. I had continued my interest and education in historic preservation and now, not only did I design new buildings, but I had become well known for designs that incorporated modern-day amenities and structural soundness in new buildings that looked and felt like they had been there for hundreds of years.

That's what I would be talking about when I stood before hundreds of architects from around the country as the opening keynote speaker at the conference, "bringing history into the future"—a topic I was passionate about and expert in. I only hoped the topic would resonate with at least some of the audience.

By the time the short flight landed at O'Hare International, I was nervous about the presentation. I had reviewed my speech notes several more times even though the speech was already perfect, but once in the cab on my way to the hotel I finally relaxed and soaked in the architectural splendor of the Chicago skyline. My mind critiqued every building I passed, enjoying the beauty of the design or thinking about how I would have changed things, and the ride passed quickly.

The lobby of the designated conference hotel was filled with some familiar faces and those I knew stopped to chat and offer congratulations on being the keynote speaker. One of those I spoke with mentioned attendance at the conference was higher than it had ever been—a fact that served only to heighten my trepidation about speaking to the group—but the friendly faces and words of encouragement from those I visited gave me the boost I needed, leaving me once again looking forward to the next day.

The next morning, after a surprisingly good night's sleep, I looked into the mirror before leaving my room. With just a light application of makeup, deep chocolate eyes sparkled back at me and it was easy to see the royal blue of my dress complemented my complexion and dark wavy hair and I was glad I had chosen it. My knees were shaking ever so slightly, but I looked good and it made me feel confident that it would be a good day.

With one last lipstick touch-up I made my way to the elevator, where the color of my dress stood out like a sore thumb against the dark-hued suits worn by the other conference attendees. For a moment I wondered if for this one appearance, at least, I should have dressed more conservatively, but if I had to stand in front of hundreds of professionals, I wanted to feel like myself.

Previous attendance at AIA conferences had taught me the majority of attendees, both men and women, would be in suits. Dark, drab, and boring suits. It was hard enough to stand out in a male-dominated field let alone to dress like them, and, blessed with a nice figure and being more comfortable in feminine attire, I often wore stylish dresses to work. Being unusual in our field, this sometimes resulted in visitors to the office assuming I was clerical staff. Still, I was proving to be a trendsetter as more of the women architects in the firm started to sport their own more feminine attire. That may not be the case today, but even if I was the only one in the room with a pop a color, at least they would remember me for something.

The McCormick Place Convention Center was located on the south side of Chicago by Lake Michigan—close enough to the river walk to provide plenty of sightseeing for conference goers, but distant enough from downtown and the loop to avoid some of the problems tourists encountered there. Winding my way through the congestion of the lobby, I followed the signs to the main ballroom where my AIA contact, a woman named Sandy, had asked me to meet her at the registration table. Although we had yet to meet in person, she recognized me immediately, due in part, I suspect, to the large posters of me propped on easels on either side of the main doors.

After a brief review of the program, Sandy led the way to the front of the ballroom where sounds in the room continued to increase as conference attendees filed in to find their seats and greet old friends. The nerves I had thought were so under control suddenly threatened to overwhelm me as my stomach erupted in somersaults. Pacing back and forth to calm my nerves, I palmed the flash drive Casey had given me before I left. It was supposed to serve as a backup should the emailed presentation fail, but instead I was using it as a talisman to calm my nerves as I twirled it around in my fingers, trying to release some of my pent-up energy. A few deep breaths helped to calm me again and I looked over the crowd in an attempt to find at least a few familiar faces I could concentrate on once the presentation began.

In the sea of dark suits, two men, seated at a nearby table, stood out in the crowd. Sans suits, in dress shirts and ties, the pair looked ill at ease—certainly nothing like the rest of the crowd—and I wondered if they were new to the profession. Recognizing my judgement of the pair as an unspoken bias that they didn't look like architects, I wondered how many of the men in the audience were thinking the same of me.

Of the two, the older man appeared especially uncomfortable wearing a tie. He reached up over and over again to adjust the knot at his neck before smoothing his thinning hair back in a nervous gesture.

The other man, turned slightly away from me and offering only a very handsome profile, had a good six inches in height on his friend. He seemed to be younger, but his age was difficult to ascertain. He offered words of greeting to people sitting nearby and those passing his table. Just as I was turning my attention back to the stage, the younger man suddenly locked eyes with me and what I saw was so surprising I almost dropped my notes.

The most brilliant, soul-searing smile ever offered to me from a man was directed my way. Although the man was indeed handsome, once that smile hit full wattage, his looks rocketed from ten to twenty in a heartbeat, and my heart seemed to stop beating as he looked at me and mouthed the word "hello." For a minute I could only stare at him until he mouthed the word again, causing me to look backwards, convinced there must be someone else he was talking to. But there was no one.

As I turned back once more in confusion, he pointed at me and mouthed, "Yes, you." I wasn't a lip reader, but it didn't take one to understand his meaning. A shy smile on my own lips, I acknowledged his greeting with my own "hello" back.

"Paige, we're going to get started in just a moment," Sandy said. "Is there anything else I can get for you before we start? Paige?"

Being so distracted by my interaction with the man, I barely registered Sandy asking the question.

"What? No, I'm sorry," I said, hurriedly bringing my attention back to the reason I was there. "I'm fine as long as I don't throw up."

"You'll be just fine," Sandy said with a smile. "I've seen your presentation and they're going to love it. Just be yourself, take your time, and remember to enjoy yourself."

"That's easy for you to say," I told her with a smile.

My legs suddenly felt a bit wobbly and I knew I'd be grateful for the podium to lean on. Moments later I heard my introduction.

"Please help me welcome a rising star in our profession, Paige Cooper from SNK in Minneapolis!"

Making my way to the stage amidst the applause, I caught a brief glimpse of my mystery man with the charming smile and knew I'd have to avoid looking his way during my speech. The look he had given me made my heart skip a beat and my cheeks flush—something to be avoided if I wanted to look professional. With a steady voice, I began my prepared words.

Nearly an hour later my moment in the sun was done. Hands in the crowd immediately started going up before the applause had died down, and with a small thrill I noticed the first hand that shot up was from my mystery man. A question and answer period had not been incorporated into the program and I looked to Sandy for further direction, expecting that the full slate of programs for the conference on the first day most likely left no room for extending my presentation. After a brief conversation about options to address the questions in the audience, Sandy stepped to the microphone.

"Wasn't that a great presentation, folks?" she said as another round of applause began. "We can see that Ms. Cooper's presentation has generated a lot of discussion that unfortunately we don't have time for this morning. However, Paige has agreed to give us an hour or so of her time later today for those who have questions. Once we find an available room, we'll post notice on the bulletin board near the registration table. Let's give Paige one more round of applause for getting this year's conference off to a terrific start. Paige Cooper, everyone!"

The presentation over, my pulse returned to normal. All my preparation had paid off. I hadn't stumbled over one word or said one incorrect thing, and if the silence in the room during the presentation had been any indication, everyone had been paying attention. It had gone better than I had expected.

As the crowd began to vacate the room, I caught the eye of Jerry Nolan, one of the three founding partners of my employer Smith, Nolan, and Kline, more commonly known in the industry as SNK. While it wasn't unusual for him to attend the conference, I hadn't known he was going to be in Chicago and was surprised to see him. His enigmatic smile and thumbs-up were all I needed to know things had gone well and I beamed with satisfaction.

Standing in front of the hundreds of conference attendees all morning meant I was recognized throughout the day, and offers of congratulations on not only the presentation, but my work with SNK as well, followed me throughout the day, leaving little time for me to really learn anything. Still, having that kind of recognition from my peers was invaluable to my career and, of course, to the firm.

Sandy and I had agreed that I would skip the perfunctory social hour scheduled for the end of the day to meet with those who had questions about my presentation. Not being much of a drinker, I didn't mind, but since a lot of people enjoyed indulging during the conference I expected scheduling my Q&A at that time would cut down on the people participating. But that wasn't the case and the room was packed when I arrived as everyone jostled to find a place to sit. Flattered that so many people had interest in my point of view about historical preservation issues, I faced the room with confidence.

"Please help us welcome, once again, Paige Cooper," Sandy said as she introduced me to another round of applause. "Paige, the floor is yours."

"Thanks, Sandy. Wow, I didn't expect to see so many people here, especially with a free bar just down the hall." What I thought was a weak attempt at humor elicited a hearty laugh, putting me more at ease. "Let's get started."

Without even realizing I was doing it, my eyes scanned the room for the man with the electric smile before locking eyes with him as he stood at the very back of the room. His hand was already up.

"Let's start in the back," I told the crowd as I pointed at the man captivating my attention.

"Thanks, Paige. First of all, great presentation this morning," he said to a smattering of applause before continuing. His deep baritone voice made my heart beat a little faster and I could already feel the warmth spreading across my face. "For those of us dealing with smaller projects, like renovating old homes in the inner-city, how do you get buy-in from the property owners who can't afford the expensive costs that come with historically accurate restoration?"

"Great question," I told him, and it was. Property owners of the big budget projects I usually worked on faced the same issues. "I'd start with looking at the overall cost comparison before construction and the expected market values after renovation. Return on investment figures is sometimes all it takes to convince a property owner to fund higher costs on the front end of a project. Granted, even with that information, not everyone is financially able to do so. However, there are state and federal grant programs that offer low-interest and sometimes even no-interest loans to property owners interested in restoring a historically significant property. I can get you a list of those sources next week if you give me your email when we're done here."

As the group erupted into discussion about the possibility of free or low-cost money for their work, I realized that offering to send the information meant my interaction with the handsome stranger wouldn't end when the conference was over. Casey would be proud of me. For years she had pushed me to flirt with one good-looking guy after another.

The Q&A continued for almost an hour before it seemed I had answered every question put to me. With a last round of applause, the crowd headed for the door as I gathered my belongings, and a very handsome face appeared in front of me.

"Hello," he said as I tried very hard to remember my own name. He definitely had that impact on me. "I have to say, your wealth of knowledge about historic renovation is quite impressive. I probably learned more from you in one day than I have in ten years in the business. My name's Jake. Jake Baxter," he said, extending his hand to me.

The features that had been so attractive across the room were even more so close up. Sparkling hazel eyes looked back at me from under dark brows that were offset by high cheekbones and full lips. He sported a stubbly beard covering his jaw that didn't quite hide the small scar just below his chin. Taking his hand, I caught a quick whiff of a very intoxicating cologne that was still evident even this late in the day.

"Hi Jake, I'm Paige," I said as we shook hands, even though he had heard my name several times already today. "Are you an architect?" I asked. It was the question I had been wondering about all day.

"Actually I'm not. I'm licensed as an architectural designer, but really I'm just a contractor at heart. That's my business partner Charlie standing in the back in the blue shirt. We own a small company that renovates houses on Chicago's south side. One of our latest projects is not far from here, actually."

"That's interesting," I told him. "How many projects do you work on each year?"

"It varies depending on finances. Right now we have three houses undergoing renovation. That's about all our crew can handle at once. I'm sure that's not much compared to what you do."

"That might be true, sometimes I only have one project underway at a time. Granted, those are on a much bigger scale..." Seeing no need to belittle his work, I didn't have the heart to brag about the multi-million dollar projects that had become the norm for me.

"I can only imagine," he said with a chuckle. "I wonder...are you doing anything tonight?" At the look of surprise on my face, he continued. "There's just so much more I wanted to discuss with you and I wonder if you might like to have dinner with me."

There was that flip-flop of my heart again as the smile that had been on my face since Jake approached me grew even bigger before remembering it wouldn't work.

"That's so nice," I started as his smile got a little wider also, "but unfortunately I have to work tonight. I've got a proposal for a client that is due to be presented on Monday and I haven't had a chance to look over all the revisions I asked my staff to make on it yet. If you want to shoot me an email," I said, handing him one of my business cards, "I would be happy to answer all your questions when I get back to the office."

His smile disappeared in a flash and the thought occurred to me that he may have been asking me out on a date.

"Ah, okay, sure," he said as he looked down at my business card in his hand. "I'm sorry I bothered you. Have a good evening."

Without a backward glance, he turned and walked back to where his business partner was waiting. Jake said a few words before both men turned and looked at me once again before leaving the room.

Standing in the now-empty room I wondered if I had missed something in our conversation. He seemed to have some interest in me that morning when he caught my eye before the speech and he had sought me out after the afternoon session, but guys who looked like him didn't go out with women who looked like me. Hot guys always ended up with hot women and there was nothing special about me. In my younger years I had dated now and then, but it wasn't like guys were clamoring to ask me out. Any interest the man had in me was most likely professional. I was the person with the answers he needed and that's the only reason he had sought me out.

With a last sigh, I headed back to my hotel, anxious to have a shower, a tepid room service dinner, and finish up the client presentation for Monday. Nevertheless, visions of a pair of hazel eyes ran through my dreams that night.

Chapter Two

*A*fter dreaming of Jake most of the night, I found myself looking forward to talking to him again, but the next two days he was nowhere to be found. Of course a conference with hundreds of attendees and dozens of sessions made the odds of running into a virtual stranger throughout the day nearly impossible. One sighting of his partner was the closest I came and I headed back to my hotel, surprisingly disappointed.

"Ms. Cooper," said a deep, gravelly voice I had feared when I first started with the firm. Jerry Nolan was the most senior of all the firm's partners and I had quickly learned that he was not a fan of women architects. Even in my first week with the firm, I learned that to hear his voice on the associates' floor most likely coincided with an invitation to the partners' offices, which had proved to be an almost surefire precursor to being ushered out the door. I could only hope that having given a well-received address at the conference, I had gained a smidgen of respect from the man.

"Mr. Nolan," I said as I slowly turned to face my employer with a cheerful smile plastered on my face. "Are you enjoying the conference?" I asked.

"As much as one can when you have already heard everything most of the presenters have to say."

Did that apply to my presentation? I wondered. "Still, it must be nice to visit with your peers," I offered.

"Trust me, after fifty years in the business, I'm tired of most of them too," he said with a chuckle. "But I must say, I was quite pleased with your keynote address. I believe it's the first time the association has had a woman deliver that address. Quite a feather in your cap, and it shines a positive light on the firm."

"Thank you, sir. It seemed to be well received." His words were as close to a compliment as I had ever heard him utter.

"Exceptionally well received," he said. "In fact, maybe too much so."

Now that was unexpected. "In what way, sir?" I asked, confused by how it could be a negative thing.

"It's like football. Do you follow football?" he asked without waiting for me to answer. "When your star quarterback's contract is up, he has lots of teams trying to sign him. I've been approached by several firms around the country wondering when your contract is up. Good team owners do what it takes to keep their quarterback. We're a good team, just so you realize it."

"It's nice to be wanted, certainly, but I hope you know, sir, that I'm very happy where I am and have no intentions of looking elsewhere."

"That's my girl," he said before giving me a condescending pat on the shoulder and walking away. As unexpected as our conversation had been, I got his point and realized that my dreams of making partner might just be closer than I had thought.

That night in my hotel room, checking the dozens of emails that had started to pile up in my absence, I was surprised to find an email from Jake Baxter. He certainly hadn't wasted any time getting back to me with his questions. Although he previously made it seem as if he had numerous questions, the reality was quite different and his questions were easily answered.

Ready to hit "reply," a thought struck me. The conference was over the next day, but I had planned to spend the weekend in Chicago, taking in some of the sights before flying home on Sunday night. Convinced that Jake had indeed been asking me out on a date, I gathered my courage and gave the phone number included in his email a call.

"Hello," said a very masculine voice I remembered all too well.

"Jake Baxter, please."

"This is Jake. Can I help you?"

"Hi Jake. I hope you remember me. My name is Paige Cooper and we met a couple days ago at the conference." If he didn't remember me, this would turn awkward quickly.

"Of course I remember you, Paige. I don't know many men who would forget such an attractive woman."

Good lord! What a smooth talker.

"Well, I wonder…I mean, you don't have to if you don't want, but…" The words were tumbling out of my mouth faster than I could think. Why didn't I plan what I would say in advance? Pausing for a breath, I started over.

"Sorry. Let me start over again. I wonder if you might be available for dinner tonight?" Finally the words were out.

"I'd like that very much, but unfortunately I can't. I have a business meeting I can't get out of. I suppose you're going home after the conference ends tomorrow?" Was it just me or did he actually sound disappointed to be turning me down?

"Actually, I'm not," I admitted, relieved that I would be staying the weekend and maybe have another chance to meet with Jake. "I'm not going back until Sunday. Thought I would stay a few extra days and do some sightseeing."

"Would you like a tour guide? I've lived here all my life," he told me.

Suddenly the embarrassment of calling and asking him out wasn't so bad, especially if it resulted in spending the day with Jake.

"That would be great if you think you can spare the time," I said as casually as I could. Deep down my heart was beating a mile a minute at the thought of spending the day with him.

"How about if I pick you up at your hotel around ten on Saturday morning? We can make a day of it and I'll show you all of the regular tourist spots and a couple of places I like that most tourists never see."

"As long as you let me buy you dinner that night, you've got yourself a deal. I'm staying at the Hyatt Regency near the convention center."

"I'm not so sure about you paying, but it's a date. I'll see you Saturday morning and until then, enjoy the rest of the conference."

The short conversation affected me more than I would have expected and I was more excited than I had ever been for a date. But the more I thought about it, the more self-doubt began to fill my mind as I wondered, not for the first time, what he could possibly see in me. Trying not to let my excitement get the better of me, I finished going through my emails and finally went to bed where thoughts of a dark-haired stranger filled my dreams yet again.

By the time the conference wrapped up at noon on Friday and, having already decided to save the sightseeing tour for the next day with Jake, I had the whole afternoon to myself. After a little shopping on Chicago's Magnificent Mile, I booked a massage at the hotel spa and spent the rest of the day being pampered.

The masseuse worked her magic on my tight shoulders and back while my thoughts drifted once more to Jake. Never for a moment did I think I would come to Chicago and meet such an attractive man. Not only was he gorgeous, but he seemed to have an understanding and respect for what was important to my work. The world of architecture encompassed all forms of design, but there weren't many of us in the profession with the desire to restore the oldest buildings. These days the money was in building newer and better and more spectacular, and most people just didn't see how spectacular the past was.

But Jake was different. Although I was disappointed that he took the wonderful old homes and renovated them to modern tastes, at least he seemed interested in the work I was passionate about and that gave us a place to start if tomorrow was going to turn into more than just a sightseeing tour.

By the time the massage was over, I found I needed to share my excitement about the next day with someone.

"Hey Paige," my sister said excitedly when she answered the call. "So how did your speech go?"

Besides Casey, Jen was the only other person I had turned to when nerves about giving the speech had threatened to overwhelm me. Unfortunately, she and her new husband had recently moved to Arizona, and with the time difference and my late hours at work, our calls have been less frequent than either one of us would like.

"Actually, I don't think it was too bad. Of course I was scared to death and it didn't help that one of the senior partners was in the audience," I told her.

"I think you need to stop being so scared of them," Jen said. "From the sounds of it, you are one of their rising stars and they are lucky to have you."

Jen knew all about my successes at work even if she didn't understand the politics of working in a big firm. She and her husband had recently moved from Sacramento to Phoenix to open a real estate firm, and while they were becoming successful, it was still just a small office.

"Too bad they don't see it that way," I said with a laugh. "But maybe after the conference I am a little bit closer to making partner. Anyway, that's not why I called."

"What's up?" she asked.

"I met someone."

"Are you kidding me? Way to go, Paige!"

My feelings were just a bit hurt that she sounded so surprised, although I guess I couldn't blame her. Although I had been dating a guy from the firm for a few years now, Jen was no fan of David, and he felt the same way about her. She had made it perfectly clear to me that she wanted to see me with someone else.

"Don't get so excited, Jennifer," I told her with mock sternness.

"I'm wondering why you don't sound more excited? Finally! Someone other than David Dawson! You know I can't stand that man and I don't know why you waste your time with him. There is something too smooth about him. Like a used car salesman."

"Jennifer! I know you don't like David, but he's been nice to me and it's nice to have him in my life. If he wasn't, I would probably have no social life at all."

"You would have a social life if you didn't spend so much time at work and you know it. You always had more boys interested in you than I did. You just never took your head out of your books to realize it. Anyway, enough about David. Tell me about your new guy."

"Jen, he's not *my* new guy. He's someone I met at the conference, actually."

"So, he's not from Minneapolis?"

"No, he's from Chicago."

"Oh," she said dejectedly. "So you met him and then went home, is that what you're saying? I know you, Paige. He probably asked you out, you said no, and you don't even know his name."

"That's where you're wrong, beloved sister. I'm still in Chicago, his name is Jake Baxter, and we're actually spending the day together tomorrow. He's going to show me around town."

"Paige Lillian Cooper! Get out of here! I can't believe you're actually going for it. I'm proud of you, girl!"

Jen's excitement was contagious and we spent the next half-hour talking about the little I already knew about Jake, what I would wear for the date, and how I felt about the whole thing. Truth be told, I felt a bit guilty going out with Jake because of David. My view of our relationship had changed recently and I was wondering if it was time to end things between us, but I also knew David didn't see the problems between us like I did. He had been with the firm longer than me and at first I thought, based on what he told me, that he was an up-and-comer in the firm. However, that had proved to be patently untrue as time and again he was passed by for projects and promotions that went to less seasoned architects, including myself. The fact that he wasn't as talented as the rest of the architects wasn't the problem—it was him lying to me about it.

When he had first asked me to be his date for a dinner hosted by the partners, I didn't think much of it. He was attractive enough and able to make intelligent conversation, but I wasn't interested in dating a coworker and had made that perfectly clear to him. Still, I let him convince me that it was beneficial for each of us to be in a stable relationship should the partners consider making offers of junior partnerships and I believed him. After that first dinner, we were together more frequently, and although I didn't have any feelings for David other than friendship, it was nice to go to a wedding or a party and not be there solo.

Eventually everyone, including me, began to think of us as a couple, and I did nothing to dissuade that thought. Dating him had become a habit more than something I seriously wanted, and with no one else in the picture it was easier to continue than to be alone. But my feelings for him were not love and when I got back to Minneapolis I was going to end it. However, there was one thing holding me back. Rumor had it that David had more than a bit of a temper and I expected him to be upset when he learned I wouldn't be going out with him again. I wasn't afraid of him exactly, but it wasn't a situation I relished putting myself in either.

"Promise you'll call and tell me all about it when you get back, okay?" Jen asked.

"Of course I will, but don't get your hopes up. It's just a date. Don't start buying your maid of honor dress quite yet," I told her.

"I'm not going to jinx it, but you never know. It's been a very long time since you've been this excited about a guy and that makes me think there's something special about him."

"Can we at least get past the first date before you start planning the wedding?" I said with a smile. While it wouldn't pay to get ahead of myself, there definitely was a spark each time I thought of Jake. Only time would tell, though, and we were still a very long way from where Jen wanted us to be.

"Talk to you next week. Love you," Jen said before she clicked off.

The next morning dawned sunny and windy and I could see the whitecaps on Lake Michigan from my window. A shiver of excitement ran through me at what the day might bring before a quick look at the clock brought me back to reality. Putting the finishing touches on my makeup, the knock on the door startled me. With one last look in the mirror, I took a deep breath before opening the door and being greeted by a low whistle.

"Wow," Jake said as he looked me up and down. "You look fantastic!" He was holding one single red rose. His compliment brought a bit of unexpected color to my cheeks.

"Why, thank you, kind sir, and you look pretty terrific yourself."

He did indeed look even more handsome than I remembered. In a black V-neck sweater and black jeans, he looked dashing and fashionable all at once. His black hair was spiked, but not in a pretty-boy way, and he again had just a hint of stubble on his face—something I had always found attractive in a man and something I rarely encountered in the corporate world.

"Is that for me?" I asked, indicating the flower in his hand.

"Oh yeah," he said as he handed it over. "I would have brought a whole bouquet, but figured you wouldn't have anything to put them in."

"Thank you and you're right," I said before finding a coffee cup to hold the rose and turning back to him. As I did, I turned right into his arms, startling us both, and for a moment neither of us spoke.

"I know the first kiss is supposed to come at the end of the date, but would you mind very much if I kissed you right now?" he asked softly as his eyes burned into my soul.

At my briefest nod, his lips slowly lowered to my own, lingering there for just a moment before pulling away.

"I've wanted to do that from the first moment I saw you," he said. "I'm so glad you didn't go back to Minneapolis."

"Me too," was all I could say, although the smile on my face said it all. Never in my wildest dreams did I think this was the way our day together would begin.

"Ready?" he asked before taking my hand.

As we walked together, I realized that holding the hand of a virtual stranger should feel more awkward to me, but it didn't. Even the gentle kiss, as brief as it had been, felt right somehow, as if we had known each other for years. Jen might just be right. There may be something special about this guy. Whatever it was, I had a feeling he was going to change my life.

Making the way out of the hotel, I was surprised to see a well-used pickup truck out front—a rare sight, I would imagine, in the front of the Hyatt. Less surprising was the fact that Jake steered me toward the truck with no apologies for the vehicle. My clients were all pretty well off and while I made a very handsome living and drove an expensive SUV back home, I had grown up in a family that drove vehicles until the wheels fell off before buying another secondhand car. Jake's pickup reminded me of home and I looked at him with another smile as he helped me into the truck. While it may have had a few dents and scrapes on the outside, the inside of the truck was immaculate.

"So, Mr. Tour Guide, what's the plan for the day?" I finally asked as we pulled away from the hotel into traffic.

"I thought you might like to tour a couple of the historic homes in this part of town," he said as he expertly weaved in and out of the heavy traffic.

"I would love that!" I said excitedly, wondering if the homes we would visit were the ones I had planned to tour before meeting Jake.

"Then, I hope you like baseball, because I have tickets for a Cubs game at Wrigley Field and then dinner after that."

"Sounds like fun."

"The house we'll tour first is the John J. Glessner House. It's a national historic landmark."

"Wasn't it designed by H. H. Richardson?"

"You know your architecture," Jake exclaimed.

"It's hard not to be in this profession without knowing Richardson's work," I told him. "In fact, he's one of my favorite residential architects."

"Chicago recognized the significance of the Glessner house and worked to designate it as historically significant well before its ultimate designation as not just a Chicago landmark, but placement on the National Register of Historic Places. It was named a National Historic Landmark in 1976," Jake told me. Apparently he had also done his homework.

As we drove up to the property my excitement grew. Studying the design in school, I remembered the newly constructed house was considered substantially different from the abutting properties and there was backlash among the neighbors, who found the design distasteful. But what I saw was stunning architecture. The exterior of the house was made of a course of granite with a handsome arch constructed over the front entrance and a series of carved capitals on the second floor columns. But what was unusual for this area of Chicago was the placement of the home on the property. Where other homes in the area had been set back from the roadway, the walls of the Glessner house seemed to be have been built almost at the property lines. While not an uncommon occurrence in bigger cities, at the time the Glessner house was constructed, the other homes in the neighborhood had been set back, providing for a higher level of privacy from all the activity on the street. I wondered what the architect's thought process had been that led him to deviate from that norm.

From the time we entered the house until we left, I could hardly contain myself. Everywhere my eyes landed something new and beautiful caught my attention and I had question after question for the tour guide before I realized I was monopolizing the time for everyone else in our tour group and kept the rest of my questions to myself. But toward the end I just had to ask about the house placement. The tour guide seemed surprised by the question, but actually had an answer.

"Richardson did so to allow for the interior courtyard, which gave the family private space to enjoy nature, as well as providing an abundance of natural light within the main rooms of the house. The long corridor on the north side of the home was used by the servants and served as a buffer between the noise and dirt of the street and the winter winds."

As with many older mansions, it turned out that upkeep and maintenance on the home proved to be too expensive after the family's fortunes changed and the Glessner house had ultimately been slated for demolition. It was a group of architects that had stepped in to save this architectural jewel.

Jake hadn't said much during the tour but had been watching me intently, and eventually I called him on it.

"You don't seem to be getting much out of this tour," I said with a smile as we lingered behind the main tour group.

"I've been here several times before," he admitted. "Besides, it's more interesting to me to see your reaction to it."

"So, am I being too much of an architecture geek?" I asked sheepishly.

"Not at all!" he assured me. "It's great seeing how much enjoyment you're getting out of the tour."

Studying him, I looked for any telltale hints he was making fun of me but found none, and we hurried to catch up with our group for the rest of the tour.

As much as I could have spent all day wandering the rooms of the house, Jake enticed me to leave with the promise of a visit to the Robie house on the University of Chicago campus. The home had been designed by the one and only Frank Lloyd Wright and was known as the premiere model of prairie school style of architecture—the only style of architecture that is uniquely American.

Having been in many Frank Lloyd Wright homes, as I suspect most architects have, my favorite had always been Fallingwaters in Pennsylvania. The style of that home was substantially different than the prairie school style, but as it turned out I became as enthralled with the Robie home as I was with Fallingwaters. Wright had designed everything in the home, including the interiors, windows, lighting, rugs, furnishings, and even the textiles that were used, believing that true design shouldn't stop at the outside.

Wright had been a brilliant architect, but it was said he was a devil to work with and never liked anyone's designs but his own. Unfortunately for architects alive at that time, he never associated with the AIA, deeming most of his colleagues as being beneath him, even though so many could certainly have learned from the man.

As with the Glessner house I was rendered nearly speechless at the wonder of everything he had created that had been lovingly restored. Jake held my hand throughout the tour and once again seemed to be enjoying my reactions to it all more than the tour itself.

"I'm so sorry I seem like a star-struck teenage girl," I told him as we walked back to his truck after the tour had ended.

"Don't ever apologize for what you're passionate about," he told me as we stopped at the truck door before he brushed a stray lock of hair out of my eyes. "Seeing the houses through your eyes has been fun for me."

As he gently touched my face and we looked at each other, I wanted more than anything for him to kiss me again. Not the gentle kiss of the morning, but a deep, soul-searing kiss. For a moment I thought he was thinking the same thing, before he reached around me to open the truck door and helped me in. As he went around the truck to get in his own side, a wave of warmth surged through my body and my hands covered my cheeks to hide the blush that had appeared. The man definitely had an effect on me!

Once again on the road Jake said we were headed to Wrigley Field. As we pulled up to a parking lot near the stadium, Jake greeted the attendant by name.

"You know the parking lot attendant?" I asked in surprise.

"Yeah. Charlie and I have season tickets and Hector and I have become friends. He always saves me the same spot."

I had noticed the reserved sign at the front of the space we pulled into. Season tickets and a reserved parking spot? Jake must be more successful than I thought.

As we each got out of our respective doors, I walked around the truck to see Jake holding out a Cubs cap to me. His own well-worn model was firmly in place on his head.

"Did you just happen to have an extra cap hanging around, or do you buy one for all your dates?" I teased.

"None of the above," he told me. "You're the first girl I've brought to a game. Charlie is usually my date."

"Why don't I believe that?" I said in surprise.

"It's true. Cubs games are kind of like a religion to me. It would be sacrilege to take just anyone to a game," he said in all seriousness.

"Then I consider it an honor. Just so you understand, though, I'm a Twins fan at heart and I feel like a traitor wearing a Cubs hat, but I'll make an exception when I'm with you."

Taking the hat from his hand, I gave the bill a bit of a crease to make it look more worn and put my hair into a quick ponytail before donning the cap. With a bit more adjustment and a final look in the side mirror of the truck, I turned back looking for Jake's approval and was rewarded with a smile. Taking my hand in his, we started toward the stadium, stopping only to grab a pair of Chicago dogs and a couple of beers before making our way to our seats a few rows behind the first base dugout.

Wrigley Field is iconic in the world of major league baseball and the Cubs have loyal and dedicated fans that far outnumbered the Pittsburgh fans in the stands. With no vested interest in either team, I spent most of the game watching Jake from behind my sunglasses and his excitement over his beloved Cubs rivaled even my love of architecture. With the sun shining on our faces and a light wind blowing, it was a perfect afternoon for baseball.

Every now and again, at an especially exciting part of the game, Jake would reach for my hand or put his arm around my shoulders. To anyone watching us, we must have looked like a long-time couple, and for some reason it gave me a thrill. All the other first dates I had been on had been awkward, stilted affairs, with neither of us knowing what to say or how to move. But things were different with Jake. We interacted as if we had known each other for years and from that first gentle kiss in my hotel room, it felt natural for us to be together. That had to mean something, right? But what?

Used to quick, low-scoring games from the Twins, it was exciting when the Cubs and Pirates game became a slugfest. As dusk approached, the stadium lights came on and, catching a glimpse of the watch on Jake's wrist, I was surprised to see it was almost seven o'clock. It was the bottom of the ninth and the Cubs were losing. Not wanting to see Jake's team lose, I took off my cap and turned it around in the universal rally cap superstition as others in the crowd began to do the same.

Jake leaned forward, elbows on his knees, hands clasped nervously together under his chin, and looked at me in surprise when he noticed what I had done with the cap.

Pointing to my rally cap, I told him to have a little faith. "Rally cap works every time, my friend," I said knowingly, while praying the rally cap gods wouldn't let me down. After such a fun day I wanted Jake to be happy.

"From your mouth to God's ears, Paige," he told me with a smile as he hurried to turn his cap around and the first Cubs batter came to the plate to face the Pittsburgh closer.

It was a tense few pitches as the Pittsburgh pitcher seemed to lose all control of his pitches leading to not one but two walks. With two men on base, the Cubs' power hitter stepped into the batter's box as the crowd sensed what was to come. Everyone was on their feet and Jake held my hand tightly.

First pitch…high and wide, and it looked like there might be another walk to load the bases. The Pirates' skipper held a conference with his players on the pitcher's mound as the crowd quieted. As the manager walked back to the dugout, I was surprised the pitcher remained in the game, although I didn't know which team would benefit from him not being pulled.

In the end it didn't matter. By the next pitch it was all over. With one mighty swing of the bat, the ball went flying out to deep center field and dropped with both runners coming home to score as the crowd exploded. Complete strangers high-fived each other, and my small hands were slapped so often they hurt. But the pain was quickly forgotten when Jake took me in his arms and finally gave me the true kiss I had been waiting for all day, leaving my toes curling and my knees weak as the celebration continued around us.

When he finally pulled back, both of us were breathless and the desire I had begun to feel for the man was reflected back at me in his own eyes.

"I think I'm falling in love with you," he whispered into my ear before the moment was interrupted by celebratory claps on the back by those around us, and I stood there, too stunned by what he had told me to move.

Joy at hearing him say the words washed over me, followed quickly by excitement and fear, and worry that all of this was happening too quickly.

Jake was everything I had ever wanted in a man and I felt 100 percent at ease around him, but no one falls in love that quickly.

By the time we eventually made it back to the truck, it was dark outside and had begun to get chilly. My stomach was also now growling loud enough for Jake to hear and we shared a laugh at the less-than-lady-like sound.

"I had plans for a nice romantic dinner at a restaurant I like along the lake, but the game lasted so long we blew past our reservation. What do you say we get takeout and just talk?"

"You mean back at my hotel room?" I asked hesitantly. Although we had shared more than one kiss already, I wasn't yet ready to share my bed with him.

For a moment Jake raised his eyebrow at the thought, but then realized I wasn't making an offer.

"No, but we could go to one of the houses I'm renovating right now. It's not too far away if you want a tour before dinner. I should warn you, though, to expect a little bit of saw dust mixed in with your food," he joked.

"I'd love to see it," I told him.

After a quick call to order pizza, we hopped back in the truck and made our way to his job site, and as we drove further from the area abutting the stadium I began to notice the changes in the residential homes. The further we drove, the more significant decline in the condition of the properties with more and more homes boarded up and abandoned. Here and there a light was on, but those were few and far between until we came to a neighborhood that was obviously lived in. Lights were on in the homes and a few people strolled up and down the sidewalks talking to their neighbors. It was as if an imaginary line had been crossed from wasteland to civilization. We didn't go much further before pulling into the driveway of a home that was very obviously under renovation with a large dumpster taking up most of the street in front.

"This is it," Jake said with a more than a touch of pride in his voice.

The house was a brick design two-flat, a style that was quite common in the early 1900s in Chicago. Originally built as multi-unit houses with the owners living on the first floor and the second floor being a rental, the original designs were identical on both floors. Beautiful, large front-facing bay windows on both stories of the home were made of leaded glass with a transom featuring stained glass designs. The one thing setting this home apart from others of the same design was Victorian ornamentation on the exterior.

"It's beautiful," I told him, although being under construction it would be difficult for a layperson to see the gem underneath all the clutter and debris.

Only the hazy lighting from the corner streetlight half a block away provided illumination, and Jake took my elbow to help me through the maze of debris in the front yard as we walked up to the heavily padlocked front door. Noticing my gaze fall on the lock, Jake explained, "Although every house we put a family into makes this area a bit safer, we're still pretty close to some of the seamier parts of the city. If we don't have everything locked up tight, it tends to walk away in the middle of the night."

As we entered the house, Jake reached for the light switch and suddenly the entryway came to life and all my fears about Jake and his partner destroying the historical character of the house immediately disappeared. They had done no such thing and although there was still work to do, what lay before me seemed to include all the original details of the house. They had spared no expense in this renovation and it showed.

Running my hand along the smoothness of the finely carved wood of the staircase, I marveled at the detail the original craftsman had put into the balusters. The deep shine of the wood told me someone had spent hours staining and varnishing to bring out the original luster, and that was just one example of the attention to detail that had very obviously been lavished on this home.

Jake said nothing as I wandered from room to room taking everything in. An occasional answer to my question about a fixture or flooring material was all he offered.

When we had finished the tour and were once again in the downstairs living room, I turned to him with a huge smile. "It's simply stunning," was all I could say and it was no exaggeration. I knew clients back home who would pay well over a million dollars for a house like this.

"I hoped you would think so," he said. "When I first told you what I did for a living, I got the impression that you didn't think much of me."

"Let me apologize for that. I thought, mistakenly, that you were renovating these houses to make a quick buck and taking out all of the historical character. Obviously you realize from my speech at the conference that's the exact opposite of who I am and what I'm passionate about. It was sad for me to think that you might have been destroying it all. I'm sorry I was so wrong about you."

"Apology accepted," Jake said as he moved toward me with outstretched arms. Whether he was going to kiss me or not I would never know, as a knock on the door signaled the arrival of our pizza.

As he answered the door, I found a relatively clean drop cloth and spread it on the floor of the living room before also grabbing a roll of paper towels I found nearby. Eating deep dish pizza was going to be messy at best, and by the time we finally sat down to eat, it didn't take long before we were laughing at ourselves and our faces were covered with sauce.

"I thought the Chicago dog was going to be the best thing I ate on my trip," I told him. "But this pizza wins hands down!"

"There must be a hundred different pizza joints in Chicago, but this is my favorite. It's not as popular as the others, but that's because those of us who know it keep the secret to ourselves. Would you like a beer? I know there's some in the fridge. It's the only appliance working right now."

"I'm not sure my stomach could hold anything else. How can you eat more than one piece of this?"

"Some of us are just more practiced than you are," he said with a smile before downing the last bite of his second slice.

Noticing that I had begun to shiver in the cool house, Jake excused himself before coming back with a hooded sweatshirt he carefully placed around my shoulders. As he settled in next to me again, he put his arm around my shoulders.

"Tell me about your life in Minnesota," he suggested. We had talked about so much during the day, but most of it was about work.

"What do you want to know?" I asked, not sure where to start.

"I want to know everything, but let's start with where you grew up."

"Okay, well, I grew up in a small town, about eight thousand people. Our family was small—just me, my big sister, and Mom and Dad—but I had lots of cousins and aunts and uncles and lots and lots of friends. There was never a shortage of kids to play with which was good, because Mom didn't believe in kids spending the day in front of a computer screen or television and we spent all day outside playing baseball, or hide-and-seek, or building a tree fort. That's probably where my love of architecture started," I said with a laugh. "'Course that probably wasn't the way it was in the big city, right?"

"Actually I spent the first seven years of my life in a little suburb of Chicago. It might have been a bit bigger than your hometown, but it was pretty much the same childhood for us."

"Why did you move to Chicago?" I asked.

"My dad got a job here and he worked really long hours. Asking him to drive an hour each way was too much, so Mom made the decision to move all five of us to the city."

"So you have brothers and sisters?" I asked.

"One sister, Holly. She's a nurse at Mt. Sinai Hospital here in town, and my brother Ian, who lives in Oregon. He's a plant manager there."

"And your parents?"

"They're still here, although they talk occasionally about moving to Arizona in the winters. What about your mom and dad? Still in your hometown?"

"I wish," I said wistfully. "Dad died a couple years ago from cancer and we lost Mom a year after that. It was so hard on her when Dad died and I think she ended up dying of a broken heart. The doctors never could give a firm cause of death. They just claimed it was heart failure, even though she had no previous heart problems."

Even with all this time since their deaths, thinking of my mom's heartbreak was still fresh in my mind and tears sprang to my eyes before I quickly brushed them away. Jake took my hand in his and gave me a moment to compose myself.

"And your sister? Are you close?" he finally asked.

"Geographically, no. She lives out west, but we're as close as sisters can be. We talk at least once a week and share everything."

"I'd like to meet her one day," he told me and my heart skipped a beat knowing he was thinking into the future.

"I'd like that too," I told him before he pulled our still-joined hands to his lips and carefully kissed mine.

"Paige, I've never met anyone quite like you and I want to be honest with you. Something happened to me the moment I first saw you. I wasn't looking for it and I wasn't expecting it. My life was going along just fine, but then I met you and now I can't stop thinking about you, and I just know that nothing will ever be the same for me without you in my life. What I'm trying to say is I want you so much."

There was such pain and intensity in his statement. Combined with the look in his eyes, it was both exhilarating and a bit frightening at the same time. No man had ever looked at me with such obvious desire and I had to look away. Not sure what to say, I pulled my hand from his and busied myself cleaning up the remnants from our dinner.

"Paige, please look at me," he asked before once again taking my hands in his own. "Say something, please."

"Jake, I like you, I really do, but this is all moving way faster than I'm used to and it scares me."

"I get that, but you need to know, I've never felt this way about any woman before and I have to admit I'm a little scared by it too. It feels like I've known you forever and not just for a few days, but I'm afraid if I don't tell you what I'm feeling you'll just walk away and I'll never see you again."

His words swirled in my mind as I realized I was feeling the same thing, but I had always had a harder time expressing my feelings to a man, afraid that if I did so I would be rejected.

"Can we just take things a little slower and see where it goes?" I asked.

"So you're saying there's a chance you might feel the same way about me?" he asked with a look of hope in his eyes.

"I'm saying let's get to know each other a bit better before we take that next step."

"I won't tell you I'm not disappointed, but I understand what you're asking. As long as I know the door is still open."

"It's still open," I assured him. If I had been a bit more willing to take a risk, something I rarely if ever did, we might have ended up in bed together. It was obvious even to me that the man was interested in me, but I didn't know him well enough to tell if he was just feeding me a line to get me into his bed. It was better to say no and leave Chicago without regret than to acquiesce and have to leave with the knowledge that he would never call me again.

28

"So, I guess I'll take you back to your hotel then," he offered, although he looked anything but happy about it.

"It's still relatively early and there's one thing I planned to do on this trip that I haven't done yet," I told him.

"What's that?" he asked with a bit more interest.

"I have always wanted to walk on the beaches along Lake Michigan, and there's a really nice one just across from my hotel."

"That we can do," he said as he pulled me to my feet.

Placing the leftover pizza in the fridge, we locked the house up tight and hopped back into the pickup for the relatively quick drive to the hotel before walking across the street to the beach access. Removing our shoes, we walked hand in hand down the length of the beach in the moonlight, continuing our stories about our childhoods.

The intensity of our discussion at the house seemed to have disappeared and we both were content to just talk and walk and laugh until we finally arrived back at the hotel. With the doorman watching us surreptitiously from his post, I turned to Jake to say goodnight.

"Thank you for what has probably been the best day of my life," I told him as we stood face to face, mere inches apart.

"Why don't I walk you to your room?" he suggested as he pulled me closer and kissed my forehead.

"That would be nice, but I'm not so sure I'm strong enough to leave you at the door," I told him.

"Would it be so bad to invite me in?" he asked.

"As tempting as that is, it's a little too soon for me," I told him with regret. Sometimes having morals sucked.

"What about tomorrow?" he asked. "Can we get together before you leave?"

"Tomorrow is actually today," I told him with a laugh. "The sun will be up in a couple of hours and I have to leave for the airport by one."

"Holly and I always go to my mom and dad's for brunch on Sundays. Why don't you join us? I'll pick you up here and we can eat, and then I'll drive you to the airport in plenty of time."

"But your family doesn't even know me. Won't they be upset if you just show up with a stranger?"

A laugh escaped his lips and as tired as we both were, his eyes sparkled at the thought.

"Are you kidding me? My mom would be thrilled. She wants nothing more than to see me settled down. Say you'll come? Please?"

There was no way I could deny him.

"Yes, I'll come for brunch."

"Great! I'll pick you up in the lobby at eleven. How's that sound?"

"It's a date!"

With the next morning sorted out, it was time to say good-bye and I found myself having a hard time actually saying it.

"Thank you again, Jake," I said as he held me in his arms and I let my body melt against his before I realized what my touch was doing to him and quickly backed away.

Leaning down once more, Jake gave me a gentle kiss on the cheek, ever mindful of the doorman's gaze, before saying a quiet goodnight.

As he drove away, I realized I missed him already.

Chapter Three

Sunrise came much too early after such a late night, and as much as I wanted to see Jake again, the thought of meeting his family was a bit daunting. Standing in front of the mirror, I tried on outfit after outfit. After a week at the conference, most of my clothing was dirty and I had planned on wearing jeans and a button-down shirt for the flight home. Left with no other choice, I pulled on the jeans and buttoned the shirt before hurrying to finish packing so I had time to check out of the hotel before Jake arrived. When he finally walked in to the lobby, I was relieved to see he was dressed as casually as I was. Walking toward each other, it was hard to tell who had the bigger smile on their face.

"Good morning, gorgeous," he said as he placed a gentle kiss on my cheek before taking the suitcase from my hand. "Did you sleep well?"

"Yes, thank you. It was a short night, but a restful one. How about you?"

"Truth be told, I don't think I slept much at all. I couldn't get you out of my mind," he admitted, although he didn't look too broken up about it. Any worries I might have had about his interest in me waning overnight were swept away as he reached for my hand and we got into the truck and drove away from the hotel.

"So tell me more about this weekly brunch," I asked. As he drove I was able to study his profile as he confidently guided the truck through the heavy Chicago traffic.

"It was my mom's idea to start this. We never did it growing up, but when Holly, Ian, and I moved out, Mom started brunch as a way to get us back home at least once a week. Now that Ian is on the west coast, it's just Holly and I, but every Sunday we show up."

"It's a lovely tradition and I'm sure your parents like the chance to catch up with you both," I told him. "If my family went anywhere on a Sunday, it was usually to a pancake breakfast put on by one charity group or another. Dad worked so hard all week and Sunday was the only day he had to relax, so we didn't do much other than church. I feel bad though that I haven't brought a gift for your mom."

"No worries there," he said with a smile. "You're the first woman I've ever brought to their house. You're the best gift she could get."

"Seriously?" I asked. "You must date a lot of women. You're too good-looking not to." The boldness of that statement took even me by surprise. "I mean, you've probably had lots of girlfriends."

"I'm not sure how you would define 'lots,' and I have dated a few women over the years, but until you came into my life, there was no one I wanted my family to meet."

Once again I realized how quickly whatever was between us was moving. From the corner of my eye I could see him stealing glances at me as I looked straight ahead, wondering how to react to his statement, before he reached for my hand.

"I said it last night and I'll say it again, Paige. I'm falling in love with you. I know that scares you and you think we're moving too fast, but I'm a patient man when there's something I really want. I can wait until you realize you love me too."

Something told me I was well on my way.

Exiting the highway, we turned into a residential area where I took in the beauty of the neighborhoods. Unlike the area near Jake's project house, these homes were obviously owned by those with money. The well-manicured and landscaped lawns offered a pleasing view for those pulling up to what could only be described as estates, and it wasn't long before Jake turned into the driveway of a large colonial. The gardens surrounding the home were bursting with color.

The house had obviously been well designed, but to me, at least, it lacked the charm and character of the smaller homes in the less-advantaged neighborhoods we had already visited.

"This is a huge house. What exactly does your dad do for a living?" I asked.

"Didn't I mention that?" he said, innocently enough. "He's the CEO and founder of an investment bank."

"So, you're rich?" That seemed to me to be something that he might have mentioned before.

"No, my parents are rich. I'm not," he clarified. "You're not a money snob, are you?" he asked with a laugh.

"Certainly not, but look how I'm dressed. You could have warned me to dress up," I suggested as I looked up once again at the massive house.

Rather than feeling sorry for me, he actually laughed at me!

"Honey, please don't worry. I guarantee you that when we walk in the house, my folks will be dressed as casually as we are, and most likely Holly will have on shorts and a T-shirt. You'll fit right in."

"Are you sure?" I asked, still unsure if he was just trying to make me feel better.

"Positive, and don't worry, I'm never going to leave your side."

Jake helped me out of the truck as I smoothed my now-wrinkled shirt the best I could.

"Don't be nervous," he told me. "They're going to love you."

"That's easy for you to say. You know, I think this is the first time I've ever met a man's parents. Well, at least since high school."

We had barely reached the front door before it was thrown wide open and someone who could only be Jake's sister gathered me into her arms. It didn't escape my notice that she was indeed dressed in shorts and a T-shirt from some rock concert or another.

"Paige, it's so nice to finally meet you," she said as she hugged me tightly. Her unexpectedly boisterous greeting caught me off guard and I wondered what she was talking about. How did she even know who I was and what did she mean about "finally" meeting me?

"Good morning, Holly. You could at least let us get in the house before accosting my girlfriend," Jake teased before his sister finally released me and we were able to make our way into the house for proper introductions. "Paige, this is my little sister, Holly. Hol, this is Paige."

"And we're Jake's parents," said a very handsome older man as he and a lovely woman walked toward us. Jake was right. They were dressed as casually as I was and I finally relaxed.

Offering me his hand in a less rambunctious, but no less sincere, welcome, Jake's dad introduced himself. "I'm Luke, and this is my wife Karen. Welcome to our home."

"I'm pleased to meet you both," I told him.

Jake's mom also welcomed me with a hug. Jake's family were definitely huggers.

"I'm so happy to meet you, Paige," she said. "Jake has obviously been keeping you a secret from us."

Giving her son a stern look, she put her arm through mine and steered me toward a large sitting room streaming with light from floor to ceiling windows before we sat on the sofa together, Mom on one side of me and Holly on the other as a maid walked into the room.

"We'll eat in a bit, but would you care for something to drink, Paige?" Mr. Baxter asked.

"Coffee would be wonderful," I told him as the others provided their own orders to the maid.

"Tell me all about yourself. How did you and my son meet?" Mrs. Baxter asked.

"Mom, why don't we give Paige a chance to catch her breath before you start with the inquisition?" Jake suggested as he sat with his father on the matching sofa across from us. He seemed amused by his family.

"We only just met this past week at the AIA conference."

"Jake says you're an architect," Luke said. "Wonderful profession. No shortage of work with the economy these days, I'll wager."

Exactly how much did his family already know about me?

"That's true. My firm is busy and all of us are working pretty hard to keep up."

"Paige gave the keynote address at the conference," Jake told them. "She spoke about bringing historical properties into the future."

"An interesting concept. My bank has several investments in historical properties, but they seem to be money pits." His take on the issue was one a lot of investors struggled with, and yet I knew just how profitable that side of the business could be.

"I've found that although the initial investment can be substantial, if the project is well managed and all of the age related structural issues are addressed at the beginning, the properties oftentimes sell for substantially more than the investment. There is definitely a market out there for restored properties and, at least in Minnesota, they are snapped up pretty quickly."

"Hmm, what you're saying makes sense. Maybe I need to do a little more investigating of how our properties are being managed. Would you mind if I reach out to you for some more advice on the issue?" he asked.

"I'd be honored, sir," I told him as the maid returned with drinks for everyone.

"Enough work talk," Karen interjected. "I want to know about you, my dear. Tell me how you charmed my son. I don't know if he told you, but you're the first woman he's ever brought to meet us. I was beginning to think that we'd never see Jake settled down."

With a quick smile Jake's way, I realized that everything he had told me about his family was completely true. With all eyes on me, I gave them a bit of background about my family, answering a question here or there, and they listened with rapt attention before Mrs. Baxter directed everyone into the dining room where a sumptuous brunch was laid out.

My concerns about what I would say to these people evaporated as I became a spectator to the discussion. Story after story was told, most designed to embarrass Jake, but he took it all in stride and laughed along with the rest of us as stories from his childhood and high school years came out. The affection and love shared by everyone was plainly evident, and I realized that was most likely why Jake had developed such strong feelings for me in such a short amount of time. This clearly was a family that loved freely.

As the meal concluded, Mrs. Baxter offered me a tour of their home and Holly joined us.

"Your home is quite lovely," I said as we toured one spectacular room after another. "Did you have a professional designer?"

"Oh boy, Paige, you really gained brownie points with that one," Holly said with a smile and a glance at her mother, who was beaming from ear to ear.

"What do you mean?"

"Mom fancies herself an interior designer and this was all done by her. She's just too modest to tell you herself."

"You should be proud to claim this work," I told her. "I've worked with many interior designers and rarely see such attention to detail. It's really stunning."

Although the formal style of the home didn't suit my more-casual tastes, the interior was indeed exquisite. Mrs. Baxter, who I suspected deep down was intensely proud of her accomplishment, put her arm through mine as we continued the tour. There was something about the way she looked at me that told me I had already been accepted by her.

"Paige? Are you guys up there?" Jake asked from the bottom of the stairway. "We need to get going to the airport if you're going to make your flight."

A quick glance at my watch told me he was right and we hurried down the stairs as the family gathered once more in the massive foyer.

"Thank you for a lovely brunch. It was a pleasure meeting you all," I told them as Jake put his arm around me. I offered my hand to Mr. and Mrs. Baxter, but was quickly enveloped in a hug instead.

"I always knew Jake was particular in his choice of women and now I see why," Mr. Baxter told me. "You're lovely, and I'm glad he waited until he found you."

His words made me blush.

"I hope you will come and visit us again very soon," Mrs. Baxter told me. "I'd love to talk design with you."

Even Holly gave me a quick hug. "Maybe next time you're in town we can go shopping or something."

"I'd like that very much," I said with a smile, and I meant it. Jen was so far away and I missed spending time with family.

Jake gave his dad a hug and his mom a quick kiss on the cheek before we took our leave. As he helped me into the truck, he stopped for a moment and looked at me in that strange way I was becoming so fond of.

"What?" I asked.

"Oh, nothing," he said with a smile. "Just thinking about how well that went. My family loves you already."

"Wasn't that the plan?" I teased.

"Okay, you got me there, but still I'm happy. It couldn't have gone better, right?"

"You're right, and they were all so nice…just like you." Without even thinking, I leaned in and gave him a kiss. It just seemed natural and as he kissed me back, I realized how very much I had wanted it. Getting on the plane was going to be harder than I expected.

"As much as I hate you leaving, I guess we better get going," Jake said before giving me one last quick kiss and closing the door.

The drive to the airport was quiet, each of us lost in our own thoughts. Wondering how someone I had just met could mean so much to me, I realized with a start that we had reached the airport. As Jake pulled slowly to the curb, I turned to him, unsure what to say as he reached for my hand and gave it a squeeze.

"God, this is harder than I thought it would be," he said as he turned to look at me. "Paige, I—"

"Don't say it, Jake. I never expected to come to Chicago and meet someone. Heck, a week ago the only thing I was worried about was forgetting my speech! But then I saw you and, well, I guess what I'm trying to say is this has been wonderful."

The look of surprise on his face took me by surprise. "Are you saying good-bye to me?"

"I, no, I…weren't you going to say good-bye to me?" I asked, sure that was what was coming from him.

"Absolutely not. I told you: I'm falling in love with you. I've never felt this way about a woman before and I know you're not quite where I am as far as feelings go, but I'll make you fall in love with me if you just give me a chance."

The look in his eyes broke my heart because I could see the fear there.

"You're not going to be able to keep me away from you Jake," I said shyly. "I don't know how to describe what I'm feeling and I'm not sure it's love, but there is definitely something drawing me to you and I want to see where this goes too."

"Promise?" he asked.

"Cross my heart," I told him as I did indeed cross my heart and we sealed our promise with another kiss.

"I guess this is it, then," he finally said as an airport policeman approached the truck with a stern look on his face and we both got out of the truck. Jake handed me my suitcase and gave me one last lingering hug and kiss. "Call me when you get home, okay?"

Chapter Four

Going back to work on Monday was a challenge for me. Although I loved my job and couldn't wait to get back to the projects I was working on, thoughts of Jake kept running through my mind, making it hard to concentrate on anything. As promised, I had called him when I got home the night before and we ended up talking until the wee hours, leaving me bone weary this morning. Only the never-ending supply of coffee Casey kept handing me kept me awake.

Hiding in my office after the early morning client presentation turned out not to be an option as meeting after meeting came up and colleagues dropped in unannounced to congratulate me on the conference presentation. Word had spread quickly about how well it had gone.

Casey soon discovered the source. According to her, the office grapevine was abuzz with Mr. Nolan singing my praises to anyone who would listen. A feather in my cap? Definitely. But before long all I wanted was a little peace and quiet. By late afternoon I couldn't resist closing my door and turning my chair to stare out the window at the hazy skyline.

"Should I call maintenance to widen your door frame?" Casey asked with a laugh as she came up behind me. "With all the attention you've been getting today your head must be swelling!"

"Ha-ha," I told her before swinging around to face her as she sat in the chair opposite my desk. "I sure as heck didn't ask for this and you know it."

"You're right, but I also think that it's about time you get the recognition you deserve, Paige. The amount of money you have brought to this firm is probably ten times that of any other associate, and it's about time someone recognizes that. I'm happy for you."

Casey had always thought my accomplishments didn't receive the same recognition a male architect would have gotten, and although I wouldn't admit it to anyone, at times I felt the same way.

"All that aside, what else happened in Chicago? There's something different about you today that I just can't put my finger on," she said as she settled back into her chair.

"I don't know what you mean," I told her. "I already told you everything about the conference."

"No, I don't think you have," she said as she leaned forward to study my face a bit better. "Are you blushing?" she asked. "You are! Paige Cooper, what is going on? Did you meet someone?"

"Well, yeah, I did. But how did you know?" Casey was an excellent assistant, but she wasn't a mind reader.

"Maybe it was this," she said as she pulled a pink phone message from behind her back and waved it at me. "So, spill. Who's Jake?" she demanded as she handed the message to me.

"Okay, so you got me," I admitted. "I met him at the conference."

"And...?" she prompted.

"And he asked me out."

"And?"

"And I said yes." Even though it was more than just a date, I wasn't ready to share that I had basically spent the weekend with him.

"O-M-G, Paige, I'm so happy for you! What's he like? He sounded handsome on the phone."

"As brilliant as you are, Casey, even you can't tell that from a phone conversation."

"But I'm right, aren't I?" she asked.

"Yes, you're right. He's very good-looking and he's smart and funny and caring and successful." As the words came out of my mouth, I didn't realize a dopey look was spreading across my face, but Casey didn't miss it.

"Wow, you really like this guy, don't you?" she asked.

"Yeah, I guess I do," I admitted.

"So, when are you going to see him again?"

"If you'd stop playing twenty questions, maybe I could return his call and find out," I teased.

"Then I'll just walk myself back to my desk and leave you to it," Casey told me. Halfway to the door, she stopped once more. "Paige, I'm really happy for you."

"Thanks, Case."

Having been so distracted all day, I hadn't had a chance to catch up on the mountain of emails and phone messages that had welcomed me back to the office after the conference. Even though I knew I should start with the business messages first, I didn't hesitate to pick up the phone and dial Jake's number.

"Hey there, beautiful," he said in greeting. "How's your day going?"

"Pretty good, but it's better now that I've heard your voice," I told him. "How are you?"

"Lonely for you."

"I'll bet you say that to all your girlfriends," I teased.

"Only the ones that look good in a Cubs cap. What are you doing this weekend?"

"Working probably. After a week out of the office, I am seriously behind on everything and I've gotten nothing done all day. Why?"

"I thought maybe I'd fly up for the weekend. That is, if you'll have me," he said.

"Of course I will, if you don't mind if I put in some work hours too," I replied. As much as I would love to spend the weekend with Jake, there were deadlines I just had to make on a couple of projects. "I'll work as late as I can each night to try and minimize work this weekend, but I won't be able to avoid going into the office."

"I'll settle for whatever you can give me if it means I can see you again," he said, and I could hear the smile in his voice. Even though I just left him yesterday, I was excited about seeing him again too.

"I'll do my best, and now that I have something to look forward to, I better get back to work. Call me with your flight arrangements and I'll pick you up at the airport," I told him.

"Don't work too late tonight, Paige. Talk to you tomorrow," he said before ending the call.

We had known each other less than a week and already were talking to each other every day. If that had been David, I would be feeling overwhelmed with it all, but something about it just felt so right and natural with Jake.

David was another matter. He had appeared in my office first thing that morning. We definitely needed to talk and I had spent several days thinking about what I wanted to say to him, but it was a conversation that needed to wait until the end of the day. The smile on his face when he agreed to meet me later left me wondering if he was expecting a different type of discussion, but I hadn't had much time to dwell on the thought and now he was due any minute. After the thrill of Jake's call, I knew my discussion with David would be the exact opposite.

Turning once again to stare out the window, I didn't hear David approach until I felt his hands massaging my shoulders and I flinched in surprise.

"Wow, Paige, it's just me. Someone could sure use a massage," he said before I turned my chair to get away from his touch.

"Thanks for coming down, David," I said, indicating the chair in front of my desk, hoping he would take the hint and give me some breathing room.

"Rumor has it that you were quite the hit at the conference," he said with what I realized I had come to think of as his car-salesman smile. "Heard old man Nolan talking about it when he got back last week. That's my girl!"

"I wanted to talk you about that," I said.

"What do you mean?"

"I don't think this is working for me."

"Don't be stupid. We're great together," he said, looking at me with a bit of surprise.

"David, please don't call me stupid. I know we've had some good times together, but I just don't have feelings for you anymore." The tone of my voice was very measured as I waited for a reaction from him. All I received in return was a confused look before he got angry.

"What the hell is going on?" he asked angrily. "It was all right with you to be with me before you went to Chicago, but then you come back a superstar and now suddenly you want nothing to do with me?"

"David, it has nothing to do with Chicago. You know as well as I do that whatever was between us at the beginning is gone. It's time for us to go our separate ways and maybe you'll find someone who's better suited for you."

For a moment he just stared at me and I felt a moment of fear as his eyes grew darker and his lips pursed together. Casey had already told me several times that David was known to have a hair-trigger temper, but having never seen any sign of it myself, I thought it was just an exaggeration.

"Fine," he finally said. "If that's the way you want it, then that's fine with me. But I promise you're going to regret this. No one treats David Dawson like this and gets away with it." His nostrils flared as he spat the words at me.

"Are you actually threatening me?" I asked. Although I didn't think he would dare threaten a colleague, his body language indicated otherwise.

"Just making a promise. You might have the senior partner's ear, but don't think for a minute that the rest of us will put up with your grandstanding. The associates have had enough of watching you take all the good projects and leaving us with the crap designs no one else will touch. You better watch your back if you know what's good for you."

With barely contained fury, he rose from his chair and stormed out of the office, slamming the door in his wake before Casey came running in.

"What the heck was that?" she asked with a look of concern on her face.

"It was nothing," I assured her, even as I tried to control the sudden shaking of my hands.

"It didn't sound like nothing to me," she said before casting a quick glance back at the doorway. "Are you okay?"

"I'm fine. I simply told David that I didn't want to see him anymore. He didn't take too kindly to the thought is all."

"Paige, you need to watch your step with him," she said before sitting down in the same chair David had recently vacated. "I know you don't believe it, but there's something off about him that gives me the creeps. I'd hate to have him as an enemy."

"Unfortunately, from what he said to me, I think I might have done just that," I told her. "In fact, I think he actually threatened me."

"Oh my gosh, Paige, you need to go to HR and file a complaint."

"That would only make it worse, I'm afraid. It's one thing for him to be mad at me because I won't go out with him anymore. It's a whole other thing if I did something that would put his career in jeopardy. From what I've heard, he's already on shaky enough ground with the partners. If I file a complaint, they might actually let him go, and I don't want to be the cause of someone losing their job. If he does anything, then I'll reconsider going to HR, but for now let's just keep this between the two of us."

Casey studied me for a bit and I could tell she wanted to argue the point, but finally she agreed. "Let's hope not reporting it doesn't come back to bite you in the butt!"

"One can only hope," I told her. "I'm going to be here for several more hours, but why don't you go home? No sense in both of us burning the midnight oil."

"If you're sure," she said. I knew her well enough to know she was hoping she wouldn't be asked to say.

"More than sure. I'll see you tomorrow, okay?"

By the time Casey had closed down her computer and grabbed her things, I could see lights going off in offices all over the floor. Working by myself wasn't my favorite thing to do, but knowing the reason why I would be working late certainly made it easier to accept and I turned my attention back to my work.

The rest of the week was a whirlwind of activity as I worked late every night so that I could spend every moment with Jake during the weekend. The only flight he could get on such short notice was scheduled to land just after eleven on Friday night and I had promised to pick him up from the airport. At least having such a late flight would allow us to avoid traffic, although with a concert just letting out at US Bank stadium just a few blocks from my office building, I needed to allow extra time to navigate through the streets that were suddenly swarming with concert goers. Even with the early start I was late arriving at the airport.

As I pulled up to the congested lower level baggage claim area, I could see Jake's handsome profile as he scanned approaching cars looking for me before checking his watch and pulling out his phone. My phone immediately started ringing on the seat next to me.

"Hello," I said as casually as I could, although my heart was pumping wildly as I eased the car into the parking space just in front of Jake. With the tinted windows on my SUV, he obviously didn't know it was me in the vehicle.

"Hi," he said as he continued to look at the oncoming cars, even though I was right in front of him. "I'm here already. Where are you?"

"Look to your right," I said, reaching for the button to roll down the passenger window as he finally spotted me.

"Boy, you are a sight for sore eyes," he said tiredly as he leaned down to look into the car while continuing to talk into the phone.

Quickly putting the car in park and throwing my own phone down onto the seat, I raced around the car and threw myself into his arms before we locked lips.

"Welcome to Minnesota," I told him when we finally came up for air. "Sorry I was late."

"You can be as late as you want as long as that's the kind of greeting I get," he said with a laugh. "I've missed you."

"I missed you too," I said. Even though we had spoken by phone more than once a day since I got back, more than anything I missed the feel of him next to me.

By the time we got his single carry-on tucked into the back seat and were headed away from the airport, it was already quite late and even though Jake didn't say it, I could tell he was as tired as I was. Holding hands, we were comfortable not saying much and a quick twenty minutes later we were walking in the door of my converted loft apartment in downtown Minneapolis. Throwing my keys on the table near the door, I waited for Jake's reaction to the space.

The four-story building had originally been a factory back in the early 1900s and had been carefully converted to large apartments, four on each floor. The developer at that time had worked hard to ensure all of the architectural details were not only preserved but in fact featured in the space, which was why I loved it so much. Living in an apartment was something I never thought I would consider, but once I saw the space I never looked back. The fact that it was an easy ten-minute walk to my office didn't hurt either.

Jake placed his bag down on the floor and began to look around as I stood in the corner and watched. Being a contractor, it didn't surprise me when his hands reached out time and time again to touch the exposed brick of the focus wall in the living room or run across the millwork framing each of the doors. The doors weren't original to the space, which had originally featured a completely open design, but they were all pieces from other structures built during the same time period. Finally Jake found his way to the doors leading onto the large balcony overlooking the Mississippi River. As he walked out to take in the view, I joined him and he put his arm around my shoulder and pulled me close to him.

"I don't know why I'm surprised that you have such a fantastic place with an even better view," he told me. "But this place is spectacular."

"Glad you like it. Are you hungry? Can I make you something to eat?"

"Thank you and yes, I am hungry," he said as we walked arm in arm back into the kitchen and I opened the fridge to see what I could whip up quickly as he settled onto a stool at the breakfast bar.

"Hmm, I haven't really had much time to shop, so options are kind of limited. I know this sounds weird, but when it's late and I'm hungry, all I can think about is breakfast. How do you feel about pancakes and eggs?"

"One of my favorite late-night snacks!" he said.

As I cooked, Jake told me about his week, but I found my mind wandering with a question I had been concerned about all week: What would our sleeping arrangements be? As much as I wanted him to make love to me, my puritanical upbringing told me it was still too soon. Still weighing the pros and cons of sleeping with him, I didn't realize Jake had stopped talking and was staring at me as I stood with a spatula in one hand, ignoring the pancakes that needed flipping.

"Are you okay?" he asked.

"What? No, sorry. I'm fine. Just lost in thought," I told him as I quickly tended to the pancakes, relieved to see I hadn't burned them.

"About what?

"Hmm? What?" I asked, still kind of not keeping up with the conversation.

"What were you lost in thought about?"

"Um…it's nothing, I guess," I told him as my cheeks began to turn crimson.

46

"Paige, you might not realize it yet, but you can tell me anything. What's on your mind?"

"This is embarrassing, but I was thinking about the sleeping arrangements," I said nervously, suddenly unable to look him in the eye and realizing that we should have sorted the situation out long before he arrived.

"Is that all?" Jake said with a smile as he came around the counter to take me into his arms. "Paige, I'm not going to pressure you to sleep with me. As much as I want you, and I really do, I want our first time to be something we both remember. If you're worried that it's too soon for you I'm okay with that. I can just sleep on the couch."

"You don't have to do that," I started to say, relieved that he understood what I was worried about.

"No, really," he insisted. "I'm sure your couch is very comfortable." The way he said it told me he was less than sure about the couch.

"That's not what I was saying," I told him, now much more comfortable with the discussion. "I have a wonderful guest room with a comfy queen-size bed, but I just don't want you to think that I lured you here with any false promises."

"I won't tell you that I'm not disappointed, but I understand how you feel and I respect you for it."

"Thank you," I told him as I gave him a kiss on the cheek. As much as I would have loved a different kind of kiss, it seemed too much to ask for after telling him we wouldn't be sleeping together.

By the time Jake finished his meal, we could both barely keep our eyes open and I showed him to the guest room. Although he had readily agreed to the sleeping arrangements, I could see the longing in his eyes as I said goodnight and slowly closed the door behind me before making my way to my own bed.

Exhausted from a very long week, the look on his face as I left him in the guest room haunted me and my own longing for the man began to build. The debate between how much I wanted him in my bed and knowing it just shouldn't happen raged within me until I finally made my decision.

Clad only in the oversized concert T-shirt I usually slept in, I got out of bed and slowly crept down the hallway to the guest room. I would leave it up to fate—a quiet knock on the door—and if he was already asleep I would just go back to my room and the decision would be made for me. If he answered…well, that would be okay with me too. Softly I knocked. Hearing nothing and suddenly filled with disappointment, I turned to go back to my room, only to hear the creak of the door hinge behind me. I turned around and looked at him shyly.

Without a sound, Jake pulled me into his arms and kissed me with all the built-up passion I had seen in his eyes as he lifted me from my feet and placed me gently down on his bed. As he towered over me, he asked just one question: "Are you sure?"

Unable to answer him, all I could do was nod my head in agreement before he lowered his body to my own.

Chapter Five

Our first night together was everything I had hoped it would be, and long after Jake was sound asleep I had lain in bed wondering at whatever bit of fate or luck or whatever had brought him into my life. Any lingering doubts I may have had about whether sleeping with him was the right thing to do had been long forgotten. Instead, I now found myself wondering how I could ever survive without him in my life.

By the time I finally woke up after only a few hours of sleep, I felt a bit unsure. Spending the night with David had always happened at his apartment. It was the first time a man had spent the night in mine and I wasn't sure what to do. Should I lay there and wait for him to wake up, or get up and make him breakfast in bed? The uncharted territory of it all was a bit unsettling. Finally, not knowing how long Jake would sleep, I quietly eased out of bed and went to take a shower in my own bathroom.

Emerging from my room fully dressed, I found Jake in the kitchen making coffee. Clad only in a pair of jeans, muscles bulging everywhere I saw skin, my heart stopped at the sight of him. He had obviously found his own way to the guest shower, judging by his wet hair, and as I leaned against the wall watching him, desire for the man washed over me yet again. Walking quietly behind him, I wrapped my arms around his waist and kissed his back gently before he turned in surprise and took me into his arms with a quick kiss on the lips.

"Good morning, my love. I was disappointed when I woke up and you weren't next to me."

"I woke up early and thought I would make you breakfast, but I see you beat me to it," I told him.

"Just coffee, I'm afraid, but it should be ready in a minute. I'm not sure I want to know the answer to this, but you don't have any regrets about last night, do you?" he asked as he scanned my face for any telltale signs.

Smiling shyly back at him, I quickly reassured him. "Not a one. But you need to know that what happened last night is a first for me."

The look of surprise on his face caught me by surprise until I realized he might think I was telling him I had been a virgin and I started to laugh.

"No, not that first time," I said, still laughing. "I meant it was the first time I have ever slept with someone so soon. Maybe my parents' sex talk really worked with me, but making love was always something I save for someone I really care for."

"And does that mean...?" he asked. I could see where his mind was going and he was expecting me to tell him I loved him.

"It means that I care for you very much, Jake. I know that's not the response you were hoping for, but you're definitely growing on me."

"As I said, Paige, I'm a patient man. Even if you can't see it yet, I know what the future holds for us and I'll wait because you're worth it."

"How can you be so sure?"

"Sometimes you just know," he said firmly before giving me another kiss and a swat on the butt. "Now, are you going to cook breakfast for me or what?"

Even though we had just had breakfast a few hours ago, I quickly put together another one while Jake left to finish getting dressed, and by the time he returned food was already on the table.

"What would you like to do today, sweetheart?" Jake asked as we ate.

"Sorry to say, but I do have to go into the office. I have about three hours of work left before I can enjoy our weekend together," I told him. Even having worked until midnight or later each night wasn't enough to get caught up after the conference.

"What if I go with you?" he suggested. "I can watch you work and I'll answer some work emails on my phone and then we can explore Minneapolis."

"Are you sure you won't be bored? I can always come back and pick you up when I'm done," I suggested. Not wanting to miss a minute we could be spending together, I didn't want him to just sit and stare at me either. On top of that, I wasn't so sure I would be able to concentrate on my design knowing he was watching every move I was making.

"I promise you won't even know I'm there," he assured me as if he had been reading my mind. "If you don't want me to come with, I understand, but I want to know everything about your life, and that includes your work."

There was no resisting that sad puppy-dog look he gave me as I stood there debating the issue in my mind.

"Fine, but I hope you have lots of emails to check because watching me sit in front of my computer or drafting table is going to be pretty boring," I warned him. "If you're ready, we could go now. That would give us more time for fun stuff."

Minutes later we were on our way out the door. Unlike the previous evening when we were both tired and dialogue came at a premium, conversation came easily this morning. It was as if we had known each other a lifetime already, and without a break in our conversation we finally made it to the fourteenth floor and my office.

"Wow, this is a pretty snazzy office," Jake said as he looked around the large spacious office. It wasn't a corner office, but it was one of the bigger ones on the floor—one that was highly coveted by the other associates.

"Thanks, but my favorite part is the view. Take a look at this," I told him while steering him to the bank of windows behind my desk. The entire Minneapolis skyline was laid out before us, including the relatively new U.S. Bank Stadium, which immediately drew his attention.

"Is that the Vikings stadium?" he asked.

"Yup, and I can't tell you how disappointed SNK was to lose out on that job," I told him as we stood side by side looking at the striking design of the stadium. "It sure would have been a feather in our cap to be the designers. But HKS did a good job on it. I thought we would walk over there and take a closer look when I'm done here. It's only about five blocks away."

"That would be great, but I better let you get to work. Okay if I just sit on the couch?"

Jake was referring to the small sitting area where I sometimes met with clients. As he settled in a spot where he had a good view of me at my drafting table, I unrolled the plans I had been working on the night before and went back to work. Although my computer was loaded with software that would allow me to design the building electronically, I still enjoyed the tactile feel of working with pencil, ruler, and all the other tools I had first learned to use when making my designs. At first I was nervous knowing that Jake was watching me, but it wasn't long before I became engrossed in the fine details of the building I was designing and I completely forgot he was even in the room.

"Ahem," came a deep, gravelly voice.

Lost in my work, it took a moment for me to realize it wasn't Jake making the sound. Instead, I looked up to see Jerry Nolan standing as big as life in the doorway to my office.

"Mr. Nolan, hello," I said as I quickly stood up to greet him while noticing from the corner of my eye Jake doing the same before walking over to my boss and extending his hand.

"Mr. Nolan, pleasure to see you again," Jake said as the two men shook hands.

Again?

"Hello, my boy," Mr. Nolan said as he clapped Jake on the back. "I didn't expect to see you here with my favorite up-and-comer. Miss Cooper, why didn't you tell me you knew this man?"

"I'm sorry, sir, I didn't know the two of you were acquainted," I said truthfully, still bewildered that they knew each other.

"We met at the conference," Jake told me as he and Mr. Nolan sat together on the couch.

"We did indeed, but I've known Jake's father for years. Are you...?"

"We're friends," I hurriedly told him as Jake looked back at me with a smile and a raised eyebrow. Of course by now we were much more than mere friends, but I couldn't actually get into that with my boss. What would I say? We're lovers? We're boyfriend and girlfriend?

"We're very good friends and I'm visiting Paige for the weekend. She just had a bit of work to catch up on first."

Mr. Nolan looked at me as I stood there, not sure what to do.

"Well then, I better let her get back to it. I just stopped in to grab a file myself and saw the light on. Jake, nice to see you again, and please don't hesitate to stop in next time you're in town. You and Paige must come over to the house for dinner."

With a final nod my way, he left and I quickly walked to the door and closed it softly behind him.

"Nice man," Jake said before going back to his phone.

"Nice man? Jake, do you realize that was the senior partner of this firm?" I asked, still a bit in shock by the whole interaction.

"Isn't he nice?"

"Of course he is, but he's my boss."

"And?" The sly smile on his face finally gave it away. He was teasing me.

"Oh you," I exclaimed before finally joining him on the couch as he put his arm around me.

"Sorry, I couldn't resist. You looked so panicked when he walked in, like a kid caught with their hand in the cookie jar." As he laughed at my obvious nervousness over the interaction, I finally relaxed.

"Do you know the man has never been in my office before? I wasn't even sure he knew what floor I worked on, and then he walks in here on a weekend when I'm supposed to be working to find I have my boyfriend with me."

"Say it again," Jake said as he turned to look me in the eye, suddenly all serious.

"What?"

"Say I'm your boyfriend. That's the first time you've admitted we are more than friends."

"You, Jake Baxter," I said as I took his face in my hands and stared into his eyes, "are my boyfriend."

The kiss we shared was passionate and soul-searing, and when it ended, I realized with that simple declaration my life's path had been forever altered.

"Let's get out of here and have some fun," I told him before jumping up to pack up my briefcase and power down my computer.

We spent the rest of the day touring Minneapolis, starting with the Vikings stadium and the Mill House Museum, a quick lunch near the Farmer's Market, and ending in the late afternoon at Minnehaha Falls where the water was flowing strongly as it cascaded over the falls into the pool below.

A longtime favorite spot for amateur photographers, it was stunning in the fading light of sunset.

Walking hand in hand back to the car from the falls, my empty stomach rumbled.

"What would you like to do for dinner?" I asked. "There are a couple of really good restaurants nearby, or I could cook something for you."

"You don't have to cook for me. I know you're tired," Jake said.

"That's because you kept me awake most of the night," I teased. "But I'm not complaining at all!"

"You better not be," he teased back. "How about if I buy you dinner? You pick the spot."

"Well, there's a great food truck with real Irish fish and chips, my personal favorites. It's usually parked outside of a popular brewing company. How about we go there? We can get great food and every possible kind of beer, including, if you're brave enough, a local beer made out of cereal!"

"You're kidding, right?" he asked.

"Nope," I assured him. "Want to give it a try?"

"Lead the way."

The line that greeted us at the brewery was lengthy, but having been there before I knew it would move quickly. We were lucky enough to snag a table on the patio and with food and a sampler of different beers, it didn't take long to see my choice of dining establishments was a hit with Jake.

"How did you discover this place?" he said as he finished one of the large pieces of fish in front of him.

"Actually I had a date bring me here once," I told him as I wiped beer foam from my lip. "I was never much of a beer drinker, but started to like it after sampling some of the different types they offer here." The pale ale that was in front of me showed I still wasn't a fan of the stronger beers.

"A date, huh? So have you dated many guys?"

There it was. The obligatory past-lovers conversation.

"In high school I dated just one guy, Michael Snyder, but his family moved away when we were juniors and I never saw him again. In college I went out a lot, but usually it was just a couple of dates and that was it."

"Why?" he asked.

"In case you haven't figured it out yet, I'm kind of a nerd. College was really important to me and I wanted to concentrate on getting my degree, so I spent most of my time studying. I wasn't much of a party girl and the guys that asked me out were more interested in seeing how much they could drink then actually building a relationship."

"I get that," he told me. "I'm not proud of it, but I was guilty of that behavior myself. When I enrolled I had no idea what I wanted to do with my life, and my first couple of years at college I wasn't such a good student."

"What changed?"

"Dad threatened to stop paying for college after my sophomore year. He said I was throwing away good money and he was tired of it. I spent that summer working construction for one of my dad's friends and after that I was hooked. But as much as I enjoyed working with my hands and being outside, I didn't want to just do manual labor the rest of the my life. Then I discovered the world of architectural design and I never looked back."

"Good for you," I told him.

"Of course, now I am doing manual labor, but I'm also the boss and the final design is mine. It's the best of both worlds for me. But back to your past boyfriends. There must have been someone special in your life since college."

"Not really. Once I got out of college and started work, I've just been too busy. I do get asked out, quite a bit actually, but really don't have much time to date."

"So you're not seeing anyone else?" he asked casually.

"After last night can you really think I would be? I hope you realize that I don't just hop in and out of men's beds."

"Sorry, that's not what I meant. I'm just surprised that someone as beautiful as you are isn't already taken."

"Thank you for that," I said, accepting the compliment. "There was one guy...David Dawson. He works at SNK too."

"But he's not your boyfriend, right?"

"Not any more. We broke up when I got back from Chicago," I told him.

"Was that because of me?" he asked with a look of victory on his face.

"Partly," I admitted. "But more so because I really didn't have any feelings for him. He was more someone to see a movie with or go to dinner every once in a while. So when I got back from Chicago, I told him I wouldn't see him anymore. He didn't take it too well."

"What do you mean?"

"He was angry. In fact, angrier than the situation called for, if you ask me. He didn't hesitate to let me know that there might be consequences to my having dumped him."

Just remembering the fury in David's eyes made the hair stand up on my arms. But nothing had happened all week and I figured they were just empty promises.

"Are you telling me he threatened you?" Jake asked angrily.

"Not in so many words, but I guess you could say he implied it. Honestly, he's harmless. He's like a used car salesman, all bluster and no substance, and now he's out of my life. Other than passing him in the hallway at work, I have no contact with him."

"Paige, I don't think you should assume that he won't do anything. Did you report it to your boss?"

That was the same thing Casey had suggested, but neither she nor Jake knew David like I did and I believed his reaction was probably no more than hurt feelings about my dumping him.

"No, and I truly don't think he was threatening me. He was just hurt and he's probably well over it by now."

Taking my hand from across the table, Jake cautioned me against complacency. "Please be careful. Guys can do really stupid things when they feel emasculated. From the sounds of this David, he might be someone to watch out for."

"I appreciate your concern, but I really don't think it will be a problem," I assured him. "But now that I've given you my dating history, it's your turn. Let's hear all about your relationships."

As sexy as Jake was, I settled in for a long story, certain that he had had dozens of girlfriends, but was surprised by his answer.

"You're it," was all he said.

"Come on, don't tease me," I asked with a smile. "Let's hear it."

"Seriously, Paige, you are the only woman I have ever had a relationship with. Don't get me wrong, I've dated a lot of women, slept with a few of them, but those weren't relationships. You are the one and only woman I have ever seriously cared for."

"How can that be?" I asked.

"Like you, I dated quite a bit in high school. But when you come from a wealthy family, it was always hard to tell if the girls liked me for me or because my family had money, so I never let myself get close to anyone. Back then, being the star of the football team, no one seemed to think it was strange when I went from girl to girl, but I always wanted to have someone that I could be close to. It just never happened. When my family told you that you were the first girl I ever brought home, that was the truth."

"What was different about me?" I asked. I wasn't just fishing for compliments. It was hard for me to imagine what was special enough about me to make him change his pattern with women.

"Honestly, I don't know. But the minute I looked into your eyes, I just knew that you were the woman I was meant to be with for the rest of my life. It's like you triggered a switch in my heart. I can't explain it any better than that. I just knew and now I can't imagine my life without you in it."

Humbled and just a bit frightened about the intensity of his feelings for me, I looked down at my lap, afraid that if I looked at Jake, I might burst into tears. Placing his hand gently under my chin, he lifted it until I was looking directly at him and I could see the tears in his own eyes.

"Paige, I am in love with you, and even if you never love me back, there will never be another woman for me. You have my heart forever, my love."

Rising from the table, he gathered me into his arms for a gentle kiss. The boisterous conversations of those around us were drowned out as the only sound I could hear was the thunderous beating of my own heart. I knew that I was falling for Jake, but having known each other just over a week, I just couldn't bring myself to tell him I was in love with him yet.

"Come on, let's go home. It's way too crowded here for my tastes," he whispered softly in my ear before taking my hand and leading me to the car for the short drive back to my apartment, where we made our way straight to my bed.

That night as we made love, the passion that had been building in me throughout the day was unleashed. There was no doubt in my mind that Jake was sincere in everything he had told me about his feelings, and with all doubts about the man now erased, I gave myself to him fully and without reservation.

Sunday morning dawned gray and wet as large raindrops pelted the windows in the bedroom in stark juxtaposition to the joy I felt waking up with Jake next to me—something I found I quite liked.

As he lay sleeping on his belly next to me, arms above his head, his face turned toward me, I had an uninterrupted opportunity to stare to my heart's content and could find nothing that wasn't sexy as hell about him. His skin was well tanned, and even in sleep, every muscle in his back and shoulders was well defined, leaving me with a lingering desire to run my hands over him. While I contemplated doing just that, his eyes slowly opened and a smile turned up the corners of his mouth as he realized I was watching him.

"Good morning, my love," he said softly before reaching over to kiss me.

"Good morning to you also." Now that he was awake, I snuggled over next to him as he wrapped his arms around me and pulled me closer.

"Were you watching me sleep?"

"Guilty as charged," I told him. "Did you know you snore?"

"Only when I'm super tired and believe me, you wore me out last night!"

"That's not a complaint, is it?"

"Not a chance," he told me as he rolled us over so that he was looking down at me. "I won't ever get enough of you."

My laughter was soon drowned out by the kisses he lavished all over my face and it was much later before we finally got out of bed. Finding our way out to the kitchen for some much needed food, we talked about the day.

"I need to be at the airport by seven tonight, so that gives us the afternoon together. What would you like to do today?" Jake asked.

"I had originally thought we could take a walk around the lakes and maybe have a late lunch or early supper at one of the lakeside restaurants, but it looks like it's going to rain all day. Do you have anything you want to do or go see? I know you've been to Minneapolis before, but probably not as a tourist."

"Honestly, I'm perfectly happy just staying in and spending time together. You know I can't get enough of being with you," he said as he came around the counter to take me into his arms.

"I'll bet you say that to all your girlfriends," I teased, although by now I knew there was no one else in his life but me.

"Only the hot ones," he assured me before he leaned in to give me a kiss. I could feel his passion growing and before I knew it, he had swept me up into his arms and carried me back to the freshly made bed.

"This is how I want to spend the day," he told me with a smoldering look that set my blood on fire.

"Your wish is my command," I told him before being lost in a wave of passion.

And that's how we spent our Sunday. Each time we came up for air, we'd lay in each other's arms talking even more and getting to know each other even better. It was the most perfect day I had ever spent with a man, but it was over much too soon.

Jake hopped in the shower as I searched the kitchen for something to feed him before he had to leave. I had seriously neglected grocery shopping. Over BLTs we talked about when we could see each other again.

"I can fly down to Chicago on Saturday," I suggested.

"Or I can take Friday off and come up to give us a longer weekend," Jake proposed.

"Are you sure? Didn't you say you're under a deadline on one of your houses?" He had indeed told me that time was tight to get one of their project houses on the market with an open house scheduled the following weekend.

"Charlie can handle things without me for a change," Jake assured me. "All he has to do is sit there and make sure no one is goofing off. He's good at that."

"I don't want this to cause any problems for you at work," I told him. My dad had owned his own business and I knew the only way small businesses made money was when the owner was directly involved.

"It won't be a problem, I promise," he said. "Charlie owes me one anyway, and I'll remind him of that if he complains about me being gone."

"If you're sure."

"I'm positive. I'll send you the details of my flight when I have it."

Suddenly the smile that had been on Jake's face from the moment I picked him up at the airport was gone and he took me into his arms.

"It's going to be a very long week without you," he said softly.

"For me too. You've become very important to me, Jake Baxter."

"And I love you and can't wait until you can say it back to me," he said wistfully.

God but it was hard to look at him and know that all he wanted from me was to hear me say I loved him, but I didn't want to say it if it wasn't true.

"I know that's what you want, but I'm just not there yet. Would it help if I told you I've never felt this way about another man?" I asked in an effort to help ease his sadness.

"It's a start," he said with a smile. "But I can see I'll have to work harder to win your heart, and I look forward to the challenge."

For me at least, it was a sad ending to an otherwise exciting weekend we had shared together, and when I dropped Jake off at the airport for his flight home, my heart was breaking that I couldn't say the one thing that would have made the weekend perfect. He tried to put on a happy face, but I could feel the sadness in him as he kissed me good-bye and walked into the terminal with one final wave.

On the drive home, I searched my soul for the answers, but as much as I cared for Jake, I just couldn't believe what I was feeling was love. Love just didn't happen in a couple of weeks. On the other hand, the thought of my life without Jake in it was terrifying and a part of me worried that unless I told him what he wanted to hear, he would move on to a woman who could say the words to him. My heart was telling me one thing while my mind was saying another, but with such an important decision, there was no room for error. With a heavy heart that night, I went to bed while thoughts of Jake filled my dreams.

Chapter Six

"Paige? Earth to Paige!"

Casey's words barely cut through the fog I found myself in this morning. Turning my chair around to face her, I tried to concentrate on what she had been saying to me.

"What? Sorry, Casey, I guess my mind was somewhere else," I told her as I accepted the cup of coffee she was holding out to me.

"Ten bucks says I can guess where that was—or should I say with whom?" she teased. "Could you have been daydreaming about your handsome house-guest perhaps?"

Mr. Nolan wasn't the only one at work who knew Jake has spent the weekend with me. Casey had figured it out almost from the start.

"Yeah, I guess I was," I admitted. "Tell me something...how long did you and Bruce date before you realized you loved him?"

Bruce was Casey's husband and they had been together since college.

"Are you in love with Jake?" she asked excitedly as she quickly sat down in the chair in front of me.

"No, I'm not...At least, I don't think so. Geez Case, I've only known the man for a couple of weeks!" I said to try and calm her down. "I was just asking a question. I guess I'm not really sure what love is."

"You've never been in love before?"

"No."

"Well, Bruce and I probably aren't the best couple to use as your sounding board. I hated that man when I first met him."

"What changed?"

Casey leaned back in her chair and stared out the window over my head, seemingly lost in her memories.

"He wore me down," she finally told me. "Every time he tried a cheesy pickup line on me I said no, but he kept coming back and eventually I felt sorry for him and agreed to go out with him."

"And then what?" I asked.

"And then I discovered that he was nothing like I first thought. He was kind, and funny, and considerate, and when I realized that all the pickup lines were just insecurity on his part, I guess I fell for him. It was obvious he needed someone to tell him how wonderful he was and that someone was me, I guess."

"So there was no big thunderbolt of emotion where you suddenly woke up and thought, 'I'm in love'?"

"Nope. Not for me. When I finally told Bruce I loved him, it just came out of my mouth. I didn't intend to say it, but as soon as the words were out, I knew it was true."

"I guess it's not like in the movies, then," I said absentmindedly.

"Paige, I'm not saying every couple is like us. I think everyone's experience is different and if it happens for you—I mean, *when* it happens for you—you'll know it. You might not see it in yourself, but something has changed in you since you met Jake. Maybe you are in love, but just not ready to see it."

Standing once again, Casey looked at her watch. "Don't forget you have a client meeting in the conference room at ten."

"Thanks. I didn't forget, although I'm not looking forward to it. David will be part of that meeting."

"Oh yeah, how's that going? Has he contacted you since you dumped him?"

"No."

"You really need to be careful around him. I've said it before, there's something odd about that man and I don't trust him."

"Thanks for your concern, but it'll be fine," I told her before she walked back to her own desk. Casey was a good judge of people, but in this instance, I thought she was wrong.

By the time I had walked into the conference room for the meeting, I had already forgotten Casey's words of caution. My arms were overloaded with the materials I had brought for the meeting and just as I was about to put them down on the table, someone bumped me from behind, causing the whole pile to spill onto the floor in front of me. With an embarrassed look at the client already seated at the table, I apologized as I hurried to collect everything.

Kneeling on the floor, I looked up just in time to see David as he brushed by me to find his seat. From the smug look on his face and the fact that he didn't offer to help me, I suspected he had been the one that caused me to drop everything.

How childish could he be? Did he really think playing tricks was going to make me change my mind about him? Vowing not to let him get to me, I finished collecting everything and began the presentation as my client watched with rapt attention. The smile on her face as I explained my design for her new twenty-thousand-square-foot home on previously undeveloped lakeshore property told me I had finally hit a homerun with my ideas.

Then David opened his mouth.

"Sorry, Paige, but I think you might have overlooked the fact that the soil samples indicate an inferior substructure at that site. If you build a house that size, the whole thing might eventually implode."

The client wasn't the only one who looked at David in stunned silence.

"Is that true, Ms. Cooper?" Mrs. Nelsen asked when she could regain use of her mouth. We had been working on the plans for this home for almost a year now and this was the first time she had been happy with the design. David might have torpedoed it all.

I hurried to assure her. "Not at all. Mr. Dawson must be confused with another study," I said, casting him a stern look. "The report I commissioned—if you remember we reviewed it together almost a year ago—shows the exact opposite. Your land is extremely stable and if anything, we may incur some higher excavation costs due to the amount of rock. Mr. Dawson must have made a mistake."

"Maybe. Sorry about that," David said without any hint of real remorse. "If you'll excuse me."

As he exited the conference room, Mrs. Nelsen still looked back at me in doubt.

"Maybe I should ask someone else to check your work, my dear," she told me. "It's not that I don't love working with you and I really do love this design, but you understand. It's a lot of money and I want to be sure of the facts before we go ahead."

How could a whole year's relationship with this client suddenly be in jeopardy because of one stupid comment by David?

"I understand your concern, but please don't let what just happened worry you. I assure you that I personally contracted for the soil samples and I have gone over that report with a fine-toothed comb. There is nothing to worry about. Of course I can't stop you if you decide to engage someone else, but I hope that won't be the case. If you like, I could certainly provide a copy of the soil study to a geotechnical engineer to give you an opinion, but I hope that we can continue to work together."

Short of begging, there wasn't much else I could say to convince her to go ahead with the project. Mrs. Nelsen was an extremely wealthy and long-time client of SNK, and Mr. Nolan had personally asked me to design her new home. He would be very unhappy if I screwed this up.

"Well," she finally said, "if you're sure." She looked anything but sure about her decision, and I wondered if I would receive a phone call firing me as soon as she left.

"I'm positive," I told her with as much confidence as I could muster. "I'll give you a call next week and we can set up our next meeting and sign the contracts."

"Thank you, Paige."

As she left the room, I plopped down into the nearest chair and thought about what had happened since I entered the room. Was David really petty enough to sabotage a client meeting? Maybe Jake and Casey were right and I needed to be more careful.

It wasn't long before fear that I had lost Mrs. Nelsen's project began to be replaced by anger at David. Obviously I should address what he had done to me, but would that only make matters worse? Gathering my things, I headed back to my office, glad to see that Casey wasn't at her desk. The look of fury on my face would have tipped her off that something had happened and I needed to calm down a bit before talking about it.

Finding the soil sample report, I went over it word for word to make sure I was right. As expected, there was nothing to be concerned about. It wasn't just a case of David being confused; he was downright wrong and intuitively I knew he had done it on purpose to make me look bad in front of a client. The question was, what should I do about it?

The ringing of my cell phone interrupted my thoughts.

"Hello, sexy," Jake said as I answered the call.

"Hi."

"Hey, what's wrong?" he asked. The man could already read me like a book.

"I'm not sure. I just had the strangest client meeting of my career and I'm not sure what to do about it," I told him.

"Are you okay? Tell me what happened," he asked.

As I relayed the story, I continued to have doubts that David had done it on purpose.

"I must be reading it wrong," I told Jake. "Nobody would do something so stupid and jeopardize not only me, but the firm. Would they?"

"Paige, you're being too nice. I think you need to go with your first instinct. The guy already threatened you and now he's trying to undermine you in front of a client. You need to go to Jerry and tell him what's happening."

"But it's only speculation on my part. Maybe David didn't bump into me and maybe he really did get the reports mixed up. What if I'm wrong?"

"If you're wrong, then you can apologize, but he could be dangerous. Maybe this is just the start of what he has planned. Do you want me to talk to him for you?"

"I appreciate your support, but I think that would only make matters worse. There has to be a way we can work together without any drama." I wished I had ended things with David differently.

"You just let me know if you change your mind."

Putting David behind us at least for now, we sorted out the details for picking Jake up at the airport on Thursday night. Just knowing that it was only a couple more days before we could be together again made the problem with David seem less important, and by the time the call ended, a smile was back on my face for the rest of the day.

"I'm sorry to cut this short, but I better see what kind of damage control I can do with Mrs. Nelsen," I told him.

"Please don't worry about it, sweetheart, I'm sure you can convince her that everything will be fine and there won't be any harm done. I'll call you later tonight."

As we ended the call, I realized not for the first time that I was beginning to look forward to hearing Jake's voice every day. Even seeing his name on caller ID could bring a smile to my face and the little problems I faced every day were somehow eased by having him in my life. Although it was a wonderful thought, it was offset by fears that if I couldn't tell him I loved him he might walk away from me. But for now at least, things were good between us and once again I couldn't wait for the weekend.

The week passed by quickly and by Thursday night not only was I on time, but I was also inside the terminal so I could greet Jake as soon as he landed. The surprise on his face at seeing me there was more than worth the effort I had put into leaving work early, and he dropped his bag before picking me up and twirling me in the air. Greeting each other with a kiss, we were oblivious to the stares and smiles of the other passengers weaving their way around us as we embraced.

"Hello, stranger," I said into Jake's ear as we hugged. "You smell so good!" One of the things I missed most when we were apart was the smell of his cologne.

"Hello yourself, my love," he whispered back before lowering me back to the ground and picking up his bag.

Holding hands, we made our way out to the parking ramp chattering non-stop about our day. After a quick stop for Chinese takeout, we made our way back to my apartment and spent the rest of the night catching up before bed.

"I have a surprise for you," I told Jake as we lay snuggling together in the dark.

"A good one or a bad one?" he asked.

"I'll let you decide," I teased. "I took tomorrow off!"

While he might not grasp the significance of my taking a day off work, it was a big deal for me. Since starting with SNK, the only days off I had taken were for my parents' funerals and once when I was sick, but for once in my life I was putting myself first and what I wanted was to spend as much time as possible with Jake.

"Good for you," he told me.

"No, good for us," I assured him. "And there's more," I said, pausing for effect. "We're going fishing!"

"Seriously?" Jake asked. I could see the excitement written all over his face. "I love fishing, but I never would have figured you for an angler."

"I'm not really, but I saw all those photos of you and your dad on fishing trips when your mom was giving me a tour of their house and I thought you might like it. Casey's husband Bruce is going to be our fishing guide on Lake Minnetonka and he promises I will like it."

"Oh you will," he promised me. "But what about our gear?"

"Bruce has it all covered. He even has a boat and we're going to meet him at the boat landing at 6:00 A.M. We'll stop and get fishing licenses on the way."

"But that's in three hours," Jake pointed out after a quick look at the bedside clock. "Are you sure you want to get up so early?"

"Hey, I thought real fishermen are used to getting up at the crack of dawn?" I teased.

"We are, but not usually after wearing ourselves out the night before. Fishing! I never would have expected it from you."

With a quick kiss, we both settled down and it wasn't long before we drifted off.

The next morning, after quick introductions at the boat landing, we were on the lake in the pre-dawn hours. My carefully chosen outfit was soon covered by a life jacket and although disappointed that I had suddenly become less than the fashion model I had hoped to be, the size of the lake was daunting and I was happy to have some form of protection as the large waves hit the side of the boat. Bruce told me the waves were called "walleye chops" and he assured me it was a good sign for fishing.

Of course Jake and Bruce were at ease on the water and they soon began an exchange of fishing stories. The pure joy on Jake's face was worth being relegated to the role of spectator as we motored to Bruce's favorite spot where the guys set about getting rods and reels ready to go. When I noticed Jake starting to put together a third rod, I had to step in.

"Is that mine?" I asked.

"I'm just getting you set up, sweetheart," Jake told me.

"I can do that myself," I said. Bruce and Jake both stopped what they were doing to cast doubtful glances my way. "What? You think a woman can't do it?"

"It's okay, Paige," Bruce said. "Casey told me you're not much of an angler." Jake nodded his head in agreement.

"Maybe so, but that doesn't mean I can't learn," I insisted as I held out my hand for my rod, hoping beyond hope that I wouldn't make a fool of myself.

The look of amusement that passed between the two men before they passed the rod to me made me determined to show them I could do it. As Jake prepared his own rod, he carefully explained to me what he was doing and how to do it. By the time he was done, I was ready to go—or so I thought.

"Great, now how do I throw it in?" I asked.

"Sorry, honey, but you're not quite ready to cast yet," Jake said with a laugh. Bruce was also sporting a big smile. "First you have to attach the bait. Would you like me to put it on for you?"

When I was a kid fishing from shore with my dad, we had used minnows and I knew I could handle that.

"Jake, why don't you get the leeches out?" Bruce asked with a smile as a look of revulsion crossed my face.

"Leeches! Oh no, there's no way," I said as I backed up in fear. There wasn't enough room on the boat for me to get away from leeches.

They erupted in laughter while I tried to figure out what was going on before Jake finally took pity on me.

"Paige, it's fine," he said as he pulled a large minnow out of the live bait well. "See, no leeches!"

Not sure whether to throttle the pair of them or simply be grateful for not having to handle a leech, I finally relaxed and joined in the laughter as I attached the bait to my line and released my cast over their heads.

"Boy, you should have seen the look on your face," Bruce said. "Wait until I tell Casey about this!"

"Ha-ha!" I told him in mock anger. "I admit you got me, but we'll see who catches the biggest fish."

"Sounds like a bet to me, Bruce," Jake said as they clapped each other on the back. "What should the stakes be?"

"Leave me out of it, friend," Bruce said with a smile as he busied himself putting a jig on his line and casting out.

"Chicken," Jake told him. "That leaves you and me, Paige. What do you say if I win, you come to Chicago next weekend?"

"I can live with that, especially since you're not going to beat me. And if I win...Let's see...If I win, you have to wear a Twins jersey at the game tomorrow night."

I already knew that Jake had packed his Cubs jersey to wear to the game even though the Cubs weren't playing the Twins.

"It's a bet, but don't expect to see any Minnesota logo on my chest tomorrow, my love."

"Looks like I already have a bite," I told him with pride. Quickly casting a glance at my now bent rod, he hurried to my side to offer advice on landing what appeared to be a large fish. After a brief struggle and feeling like my arms were going to be pulled out of their sockets, the fish surfaced near the boat and it was big.

"Look at the size of that walleye," Bruce said excitedly as he handed Jake a net. Leaning over the side of the boat, Jake appeared ready to net the fish when it suddenly disappeared just as my line went slack. I almost toppled over backward.

"What happened?" I asked in disappointment as Bruce grabbed for my now-dangling line.

"Fish cut the line," he said. "Happens sometimes. Sorry, Paige. It was a nice fish too. I'll get you set up again."

"Sorry, honey," Jake said with a mixture of sadness and relief.

"I saw that fish and all I could see was myself in a Twins jersey."

"It's okay," I told him, although I was disappointed. Catching sunfish with my dad had never been as exciting as this. If this is what true fishing was, I wouldn't mind going again. "But I've got a bet to win," I said with a smile as Bruce handed me my now-repaired line and I cast it out, hoping for another chance at the large walleye. My competitive nature had definitely kicked in.

We fished for several hours and were hauling in a lot of fish that were then released due to their size. While we weren't keeping many, it was fun. Bruce and Jake were getting along like best buddies while I was mostly just content to sit and watch the waves, only occasionally paying attention to my line. As much as I wanted to win the bet, even if I lost it would be a win for me because I welcomed the opportunity to go back to Chicago. In fact, I had already booked my flight without telling Jake.

"Well folks, it's about time we think about heading back to shore," Bruce finally said after hours in the boat and the fishing having grown cold.

"I guess," Jake told him with disappointment. He had obviously enjoyed the day on the lake. Of course, the fact that he was the only one of the two of us with a fish in the live well didn't hurt either.

Just as I began reeling in, something struck my line, hard and fast, nearly pulling the rod out of my hands. Quietly I started reeling in whatever was on the other end of my line as Jake and Bruce continued bringing in theirs on the other side of the boat.

"Honey, do you need…?" Jake started to ask before noticing the pull on my line. "Paige, do you have a fish on?"

"Boy, does she!" Bruce said with excitement as Jake came to my side and Bruce worked to turn the boat slightly.

"Easy does it, Paige. Keep your rod tip up," Jake told me. I could tell he would have loved to take the rod from my hand, but he limited himself to offering advice as Bruce came up with the net and I tried to keep my mind on bringing the fish in.

"Good job, Paige. Keep reeling in," Bruce said.

The struggle continued for several minutes until finally we had our first glimpse of the fish. It was even bigger than the one I had lost at the start of the day and my heart started to pound in excitement.

"Holy crap, that's a big fish," Bruce said excitedly. "Jake, I'd say you'll be in Twins gear tomorrow."

"I think you're right," Jake said with a laugh. "Keep it up, Paige. He's getting tired now."

"He's not the only one," I told him. My shoulders and arms were on fire. How could one fish be so strong?

"Keep reeling, Paige. That's right, bring him in now," Jake told me as the fish came close enough to the boat for Bruce to lean down and slowly lower the net around it. As he hoisted it into the boat, I collapsed onto the seat in exhaustion. The fish flopped around inside the net, still struggling for its life, before Bruce attached it to a scale and hoisted it up.

"Thirty-two pounds two ounces," he proudly exclaimed. The fish was as long as his arms and those in nearby boats had stopped to watch with a smattering of applause.

"We need to take a picture of you with your trophy, Paige," Jake said as he dug his phone out of his pocket. "Can you hold it up yourself?" he asked.

"I think so," I told him as Bruce carefully handed me the heavy fish and I tried to hold it up for the picture. The thing was a monster and slippery as heck, but with a great sunburnt smile on my face and hair blowing every which way, Jake took photo after photo.

"Guys, he's getting heavy," I said, suddenly realizing I was losing my grip. With one last powerful flip of its tail, the fish flew out of my hand and landed back in the water. The three of us stood at the side of the boat, watched it for a moment before it glided deeper into the dark water, and was gone.

Casting a glance on either side of me, I thought I was about to watch two grown men burst into tears as they stared at the water where the monstrous fish had been.

"Well, I guess I win the bet," I finally said with a laugh. Maybe I should have been more disappointed that the fish got away, but deep down I was glad. Something that has lived to be so big didn't deserve to end up as shore lunch.

Finally coming around from their stupor, Jake and Bruce joined in my laughter.

"Holy cow, Paige, I've never caught a northern that big. I'm sorry," Bruce told me finally.

"I'm sorry too, sweetheart," Jake said. "We should never have let you hold it by yourself. That fish was almost as long as you are tall!"

"Guys, don't worry. I'm not upset. Actually, I'm kind of glad he's back where he belongs." Reaching out to poke Jake in the chest, I said, "But I can't wait to see you in your brand-new Twins jersey."

"Oh no," Jake countered as he backed up just a bit. "You didn't win that bet. You couldn't even keep your fish in the boat, so it doesn't count. Tell her, Bruce."

"Don't drag me into it," he said with a chuckle.

"Okay, I'll give and let you win. Guess I'm coming to Chicago," I told Jake with a kiss. "But I want a rematch!"

"Definitely," he promised with his most charming smile.

The rest of the weekend was as pleasant as our day on the lake. The Twins finally won a home game and Jake eventually conceded I had caught a bigger fish and wore the Twins jersey to the game along with his favorite Cubs cap. We spent Sunday afternoon with Casey and Bruce and their kids grilling the few fish we had been able to keep and telling stories of our day on the water.

The story of my monster fish sounded like just another fish story to Casey until Jake brought out his phone and showed her picture after picture, with all of us getting a big laugh at the last photo of the northern in mid-air on its quest for freedom. Even I had to admit the look on my face was priceless as the fish slipped from my hands. I only wish I had similar photos of Bruce and Jake when they watched the massive fish land back in the water.

When it was finally time to leave once again for the airport, Bruce and Jake exchanged promises for many more fishing trips together as Casey and I stood arm in arm watching them become BFFs.

"You are really lucky, you know that, Paige?" she told me quietly.

"In what way?"

"You're the smartest woman I know, you're gorgeous, you have a fantastic job doing what you love the most, you have a charming and totally wonderful assistant, and now you have that man. If there is something that isn't charmed about your life, I can't imagine what it would be."

She didn't have to convince me. I had been thinking the same thing ever since I met Jake.

"I think I'm pretty lucky too—especially about the wonderful assistant. Thanks so much for inviting us over today. I think Jake has found a great friend in Bruce and I'm happy for both of them. Of course it might be hard to get them off the lake this summer!"

"Don't say I didn't warn you. Bruce would fish every day if he didn't have to work. Still, I'm glad he found someone who enjoys it as much as he does. Sometimes I feel badly that I uprooted him from his friends back home because it's taken him a long time to make friends in Minnesota, but now he has Jake. Well, at least as long as you have Jake I suppose."

"What's that supposed to mean?" I asked her, a bit surprised by her negativity.

"Nothing, it's just Jake seems much more taken with you than you are with him. Or am I reading you wrong?"

"I don't know," I said, shaking my head.

"What do you mean by that?"

"Oh, it's not what you think. I care more for Jake than anyone else I've ever met, but all this is moving so fast, I just don't know how I really feel."

"Something tells me you do," she told me as we walked arm in arm out to the car. "You just need to admit it to yourself."

Surprised by her comment, I was saved from a response when Jake and Bruce appeared behind us.

"Ready to go, Paige?" Jake asked. "Thanks again for a great weekend," he told Bruce and Casey as they shook hands.

"Next time you're in town, we can try some river fishing," Bruce suggested before Casey gave me a knowing look.

"Thanks for everything, Casey. See you tomorrow," I told her before we got in the car and started the drive to the airport.

For the first time in my career, the thought of going back to the office wasn't something I was looking forward to because it meant another long week without Jake. Pulling up to the drop-off area at the airport, I eased slowly up to the curb and put the car in park.

"So, I'll take a cab in from the airport and meet you at your job site," I told Jake. The day after I was scheduled to arrive was their first open house event on the newly remodeled house and I knew he and Charlie needed every minute possible to finish in time.

"Thank you for the best weekend I've had in a long time," he told me as we held hands in the car.

"I'm glad you enjoyed yourself, and I'm glad you made a new friend."

"Yea, Bruce is terrific. So, I'll see you in Chicago on Friday night right?"

"Definitely, and I'll have my painting shirt ready to go to help with whatever is needed." Knowing they were worried about finishing in time, I had volunteered to help where I could.

"Guess I better get going or I'm going to miss my flight," he finally said. "God, I love you, Paige." He held my face in his hands and gave me a lingering kiss.

"Travel safely, sweetheart," was the best I could offer back, and I felt like an absolute heel.

"Bye."

As Jake grabbed his bag and walked away from the car, I felt a sense of déjà vu and realized that instead of getting easier, it was getting much, much harder to say good-bye to the man.

Chapter Seven

Once again it was a very busy week, which helped somewhat to ease the loneliness I felt without Jake. But I also had David to deal with. While Mrs. Nelsen hadn't fired me, she had insisted on a geotechnical engineer's opinion, which would delay groundbreaking on the project, and there wasn't a thing I could do about it.

But that wasn't the only issue with David I was dealing with. Still hard pressed to provide any concrete proof, it appeared he was trying to undermine me in other ways. Meetings that had been set up with clients suddenly started being cancelled at an alarming rate. When Casey questioned the client about the cancellation, more often than not they indicated they had changed their mind about the project, or worse yet, were considering other architects. None of them would provide more details about their decision, leaving me to wonder what had gone wrong.

In the beginning the possibility of David being involved never entered my mind, at least until Casey wandered by his office at just the right time to see one of my long-time—and very wealthy clients, I might add—exiting David's office. Suspicious about their interaction, Casey followed Mr. Warren to the elevator, where his surprise at seeing Casey next to him elicited a tell-tale look of guilt.

"Miss Cooper was really disappointed you had to cancel your appointment this morning," Casey told him casually as they waited for the elevator.

"Uh, yes, well, it was unfortunate," he stammered, trying to avoid her gaze.

"I know she's free right now and since you're already in the building, how about you just follow me and I'll get you right in?"

"Uh, no, that's okay," he continued to stammer as his face turned a deep shade of red. "Mr. Dawson is helping me now."

The elevator doors opened in front of him and he hurried inside as Casey watched before hurrying back to report her findings.

"It's David," she said as she burst into my office.

"What's David?" I asked without looking up from the plans I was working with.

"He's stealing your clients. All those cancellations? Orchestrated by him!"

Now that got my attention.

"How do you know that?" I asked as I looked up, not quite ready to believe that David could be that devious and spiteful.

"I just saw John Warren coming out of his office."

"That doesn't mean he's stealing my clients," I told her sensibly, although my suspicions were also starting to lead me that direction.

"That's true," she admitted. "But I followed Mr. Warren to the elevator and told him you were free to meet with him now and he told me that David is now his architect."

Standing with hands on her hips in a look of victory, Casey waited for what she assumed would be my look of outrage. Instead she got a deep sigh.

"I just can't believe he would be so underhanded," I finally said.

If David was indeed behind all the recent cancellations, he might just force my hand about going to HR. But we didn't have any actual proof and at this point anything I could report would be circumstantial. I wasn't willing to get him in trouble without more proof, but I knew just how to get it.

"Casey, how well do you know David's assistant?"

"Paula? I know her enough to know she's as untrustworthy as her boss," she said. "But, I also know Jackie, who works at the desk across from Paula. If Paula knows something, Jackie does too, and I'll bet I could get her to spill what she knows."

"Why don't you invite Jackie to lunch and see if you can get more information? David is so arrogant about everything, I'm willing to bet he's talking about what we suspect he's up to. If we can get someone else to confirm what he appears to be doing, then I'll go to HR."

"And in the meantime?" Casey asked.

"In the meantime, we'll keep doing what we're doing. But if we have any more cancellations, I want to talk directly to the client. Maybe I can try and undo whatever David is up to before it gets too out of hand."

"Will do. But Paige?"

"Yes?"

"Stay away from David, please. I think he's dangerous."

For whatever reason, the cancellations tapered off the rest of the week and my normal busy schedule resumed, leaving little time to finalize my birthday present for Jake's dad. The family had planned a special birthday celebration for him on Saturday night and I was invited.

Struggling to find a gift for a man who had enough money to buy whatever he wanted had been difficult until I finally hit on something really unique. The City of Chicago's Department of Building still had the original set of 1910 architectural plans for Mr. Baxter's bank. All the handwritten notes from the architect were still mostly visible on the four-sheet set of plans, and with Casey's assistance I had arranged for everything to be copied and the originals mounted in a series of four framed prints that I hoped Mr. Baxter would want to hang in his office. The framing company was having them wrapped and delivered to the Baxter residence the afternoon of his party, and I couldn't wait to see the look on his face when he opened his gift, hoping it would be the perfect ending to a family weekend.

Arriving in Chicago late Friday afternoon, I took a cab directly to the project house where Jake and I had shared our first meal together. Hair pulled back into a ponytail, well-worn Twins cap covering my hair to protect it from any stray splatters of paint, I pulled my painting shirt out of my suitcase and was ready to go to work. My shirt was splattered with so much paint from previous jobs I looked like a Jackson Pollock painting. Entering the house, I spotted Charlie first.

"Hey Charlie," I said as he stopped what he was working on to look at me.

"Can I help you, miss?" he asked in confusion. Obviously he didn't recognize me in my work clothes.

"Charlie, it's me. Paige Cooper," I told him as I took off my hat so he could see my face.

"Oh, Miss Cooper, I didn't recognize you for a minute there," he said in embarrassment. Actually, we hadn't formally met each other at the conference and this was the first time we were face to face, so I shouldn't have assumed he would know me.

"Please, call me Paige. Is Jake around?"

"He just ran out to buy some supplies, but he should be back any minute. He told me you would be here much later."

"I caught an earlier flight to surprise him," I admitted, although I guess the surprise was on me. "Did he tell you I'm here to help?"

Looking at my well-stained clothes, I could tell by the look of derision on Charlie's face he didn't think I would be much help. "I might not look it, but I am a pretty good painter," I quickly assured him.

Embarrassed again when he realized I had figured out what he was thinking, Charlie hurried to find me a paint brush and led me to an upstairs room where the trim had already been painted and the walls and millwork were taped off. With a few instructions of what colors they wanted where, he left me to it with just a single backward glance and a shake of his head.

So, he still didn't believe I would get the job done. Guess I'd just have to show him, I thought with a chuckle. Without further ado, I started to paint and by the time I finally heard Jake's voice drifting up the stairs, I was about halfway done with the room.

"Hmm," came the sexy baritone voice I was so enamored of. Jake was leaning against the door frame, arms crossed in front of him with a massive smile on his face. "If all of my crew had a shape like yours, I'd never get any work done."

"If all of your crew had a shape like mine, I don't think I'd want you to go to work," I responded as a tingle swept through my body at the sight of him.

Carefully putting the wet paint brush down, I made my way through the mess in the room and greeted him properly.

"God, I've missed you," I told him between kisses.

"I've missed you too, but how'd you get here so early?" he asked. "I wasn't expecting you for a couple more hours."

"I caught an earlier flight. I know you're worried about getting the house done in time and I thought you could use the help."

"We sure could and thank you," he said. He looked so tired. He and Charlie had been working really long hours this week and it was taking a toll on him. Looking around the room at my paint job, I waited for his verdict and I wasn't disappointed.

"I might have to hire you permanently. You're pretty good at this."

"Thank you, and I don't think I've gotten any paint on my shirt yet. That's kind of a record for me."

"How can you tell?" he asked with a laugh. "Seriously, Paige, I was really worried we weren't going to get done in time, but with your help I think we might just make it. Thank you so much. Now, I've got to finish tiling in the downstairs bathroom, so I'll let you get back to it. Let me know if you need anything."

"How about another kiss?" I asked before I was enveloped in his arms with kisses being planted all over my face.

By the time it was dark outside, I had finished painting two rooms and was almost done with a third. Hearing a knock on the door, cheers suddenly went up from the crew downstairs and I put down my brush and wiped the sweat from my forehead.

"Paige, come down here, please," Jake yelled up the stairs.

Walking down the stairs, I realized why they were cheering. The dinner I ordered from one of Jake's favorite burger joints had just been delivered and the crew had already started to dig into the bags of burgers, onion rings, fries, and drinks spread across the kitchen counter.

"Did you do this for us?" Jake asked as we walked hand in hand into the kitchen.

"I didn't think you'd have time to stop to eat and I thought you might be hungry," I told him.

"And you were so right. Everyone, this is Paige Cooper, and you should thank her for all this," Jake said by way of introduction.

In between bites, the guys on his crew introduced themselves and thanked me for the dinner. Minutes later, they went back to work and Jake left the room to make a call, leaving Charlie and me to finish up our own meals.

"That was awful nice of you, Paige," Charlie said.

"I'm just happy to find a way to help," I told him. "I'm almost done with the painting upstairs. What else can I do?"

"Jake says you have a pretty good eye for interiors. In a couple hours or so we'll start cleaning up this mess and start staging the house. The trailer out front is full of everything we rented for the staging. Can you give us a hand deciding where everything goes?"

"I would love that," I assured him. Finally something that would be fun!

"Great! Well, I better get back to what I was doing. Thanks again for dinner." The man didn't say much, but for the first time since I arrived, I think I was finally winning him over.

"You're very welcome," I said as I began to clean up the mess before Jake returned to wrap his arms around me from behind. Leaning into his embrace I couldn't prevent the yawn that escaped as he nuzzled at my neck. It was barely seven o'clock, but already I was beat. It had been a tiring week.

"Thank you again for supper. You made ten guys very happy tonight," he told me.

"I was happy to do it. What time do you think you'll finish up tonight?"

"Maybe by midnight if the staging goes well."

"Charlie asked me to help with that," I told him as I turned around to face him. "You look so tired."

"It's always like this just before an open house. Something always goes wrong that sets us behind schedule and then it's a mad dash to get the house show-worthy. But this isn't so bad. By tomorrow afternoon, it will all be over and we can just wait for offers to pour in. At least, that's what we hope."

"I wish I could be here with you tomorrow. I could walk around the house when buyers arrive and sing the praises of the renovation."

"While I appreciate your enthusiasm, I think that might be a little deceptive. Besides, I think this house will go fast. It turned out well," he said as he looked around.

"I agree, and you should be proud of what you've accomplished. Well, I better get back to my painting."

"Love you," he told me with a smile before I wandered back to the netherworld of upstairs where I continued to work on my own.

Listening to the easy banter between Jake and his crew once again, I felt badly that I couldn't tell Jake I loved him. I knew it wasn't his intent to make me feel guilty when he said it, but I did and it was getting harder to ignore while my feelings for him were getting even stronger. But I just wasn't ready.

It was midnight before the staging actually began and the crew worked in silence as the neighborhood slept, bringing in load after load of furniture and other household goods all designed to give the house a lived-in look without actually being lived-in. As it turned out, I did have a knack for staging and the work went quickly. By the time all the rented items were brought into the house, most of the rest of the crew was ready to go home after a very long week.

Jake and I stood with arms around each other as he said goodnight to his guys before another yawn escaped me.

"I'm sorry, Paige, but I have just a few touch up items to finish before we go. Do you want to just hang out in the living room until I'm ready? It should just be a half-hour or so."

"Do you want me to help?" I asked tiredly.

"I appreciate it, but unless you know how to hook up a dishwasher, I better do this one on my own."

With a quick kiss he grabbed his tool belt and headed to the kitchen while I dropped to the sofa in exhaustion. It had been a long week for me also and I was beat. Before I even realized it was happening, my eyes closed and I was fast asleep.

"Paige, honey, wake up. Time to go home," Jake said, his voice barely penetrating my mind.

"What time is it?" I asked.

"It's about three."

Helping me slowly to my feet, he grabbed my suitcase and we walked to his truck. While he walked around to get in the driver's side, I took another look at the exterior of the house, remembering the disheveled appearance from just a few weeks ago. With a few security lights still illuminating the property, it now looked warm and welcoming, and I had no doubt it would sell quickly.

By the time we arrived at Jake's house, I was once again wide awake. Grabbing my suitcase from the bed of the truck, Jake took my hand as I prepared to see his home for the first time.

"Oh my God, Jake, this is gorgeous," I told him as we entered the house. The house was an early 1900s design—one of the "four square" craftsman-type homes. Four square meant a second story, an unusual feature in craftsman homes, had been part of the original design. The home had low-pitched roof lines, a gabled roof with a wide unenclosed eave overhang, and exposed rafters under the eaves. Tapered, square columns jutting up from the large porch supported the roof and the columns rested on massive stone piers that extended to ground level. A single, wide dormer stood at the front of the home.

Inside the home featured built-in cabinetry in every room and the living room centered on a large and very prominent fireplace showcasing the craftsmanship of the builder. Double-hung, four-over-one windows and partially paned doors with thick glass panes in the upper third of the door at each entrance provided the telltale hallmark design of nearly all original craftsman homes.

Having seen the care and detail Jake put into the project house, it was no surprise that his own home exhibited the same attention to the little things. Everywhere I looked was a new and exciting surprise for me. I wanted to ask so many questions, but when I turned to look at Jake I could see he was asleep on his feet and knew my questions would have to wait.

"Come on, sweetheart. Let's get you to bed. You can give me the full tour another time."

We headed straight up to bed, both of us too tired to do more than crawl into bed and hold each other as we fell asleep before the harsh ring of the alarm jolted us back awake after what seemed like minutes.

"Five more minutes please," I mumbled at Jake as he reached across me to turn off the alarm before giving me a kiss.

"No can do, sleepyhead," he told me. "It's a big day and there's money to be made. And you have to get over to my parents to help set up for the party."

"Ughhh, you're right," I told him. Rolling over and stretching like a cat, I watched him get out of bed and head into the bathroom for a shower. Debating whether to go back to sleep or get up, it didn't take long before the thought of Jake, naked and soapy in the shower, tempted me to join him.

It was a delicious way to start the day, even if we had less than three hours of sleep, but it was a big day for everyone in the Baxter family and we didn't dawdle too much. Jake needed to be at the project house before I left for his parents' home, and while he got dressed, I put together a quick breakfast of eggs and toast. By the time the coffee was done he had joined me.

"Oh my, don't you look handsome," I told him as I reached to straighten his tie. He was wearing a dress shirt and tie, just as he had the first time I met him. A quick flash of memory from the moment we first spotted each other went through my mind. Attracted to him from the start, those feelings were nothing compared to what I felt now that I knew him and a wave of warmth spread through me. "It's probably a good thing I'm not going to be there today because I wouldn't be able to keep my hands off you! What time do you have to be at the house?"

"Charlie is meeting me there at eight and the open house starts at nine," he said as he sat down to eat. "I should be at my folks' house by five."

"Do you want me to drop off something at lunch time for you both?" I asked as I poured him a cup of coffee.

"Thanks for thinking of it, but Charlie's wife is going to make sandwiches, I guess. Will you be okay getting over to Mom and Dad's on your own?"

"I'll just call a cab," I told him.

"Thank you for helping out, not only with the house last night but with the party. Mom and Holly are thrilled that you're going to be part of it."

"As am I. It sounds like it's going to be pretty swanky and I can't wait to see your dad's reaction to my gift."

"You bought him something?" he asked in surprise. "You didn't have to do that."

"Of course I did. It's his birthday. Although after I ordered it, I have to admit I had second thoughts and realized I might have bought it more because I liked it than he will."

"What did you get him?" Jake asked.

"You'll have to wait and be surprised along with your family," I said mysteriously. "You better get moving if you're going to be there by eight."

A glance at his watch and Jake quickly picked up his plate and placed it in the sink before taking me in his arms.

"Have I told you today how much I love you?" he asked.

"Even if you did, say it again," I suggested.

"I love you to the moon and back!" he said before placing a gentle kiss on my lips. "Wish me luck?"

"You don't need luck. The house is beautiful and I'll bet you don't even make it to lunchtime without an offer."

"From your mouth to God's ears," he said before grabbing his things and heading out the door.

Grabbing my own cup of coffee, I watched from the front bay window as he got into his truck and drove away, all while saying a quick prayer that his day would go well.

Chapter Eight

By the time I made it to his parents' house, the party preparations were already well underway. Several box trucks were parked in the curved driveway as delivery people unloaded their items and made their way to the backyard where the party was taking place. Leaving the hubbub of the deliveries behind me, I walked into the house looking for Holly or her mother.

"Hey Paige, welcome," Holly said as she greeted me with a hug. "Boy, am I glad you're here. This place is a disaster area and Mom is driving me crazy."

"Well, I'm ready to help. What would you like me to do first?"

Noticing the garment bag I was holding over my arms, Holly directed me to an upstairs bedroom to deposit my change of clothes for the party. The bedroom was decidedly masculine and I knew immediately it had been Jake's when he lived in the house. Placing the bag carefully on the bed so as not to wrinkle the dress inside, I wandered over to the bookcase to look at the trophies from Jake's youth. Football, baseball, and hockey. It seemed there wasn't anything Jake wasn't good at.

"Ah, I see you've discovered the shrine," Holly said as she joined me. "Mom refuses to get rid of all of Jake's high school trophies and Jake has no interest in them. I think Mom is hoping that she can pass them on down to Jake's kids."

"Looks like he was quite the athlete," I said as I picked up each trophy to read the inscription.

"He was pretty good, but Ian was even better. The two of them spent their high school years trying to outdo each other. Didn't Jake tell you about that part of his childhood?"

"No, he didn't," I admitted.

"No, I don't suppose he would," she said. "He's never been very interested in the accolades he was given. Jake was a natural athlete and never had to work very hard to excel. Ian, on the other hand, had to work ten times harder. Nothing ever seemed to come easy for him. I think that's why he moved so far away."

"What do you mean?"

"He always felt like he was playing catch up with Jake. Everyone always compared the two of them at school even though Ian was older than Jake. It happened so often Ian began to feel like he didn't match up to his little brother. So when he graduated from college, he moved to the west coast where he wasn't known as Jake Baxter's brother. He was simply Ian. Once he got out from under Jake's shadow, he blossomed and he's built a nice life for himself out there."

"You make it sound like they didn't get along," I said in surprise. Jake seemed to love his brother very much.

"Not at all. As much as Ian competed with Jake, they were best friends and they did everything together. They encouraged each other in everything they did."

"Will Ian be here for the party? I'd love to meet him," I told her.

"He doesn't make it back too often and we thought he was coming, but one of his kids came down with measles so now they can't make it."

"That's too bad. I'm sure your dad would love to have him here."

"You're right about that. It would have been nice to have the whole family together again for Dad's birthday."

"Holly, are you up there?"

"Oops, that's Mom. Maybe with you here she won't be quite the tyrant she's been so far today. Coming, Mom…"

Holly's description of her mom's behavior was anything but accurate, unless she was suddenly on her best behavior because I was in the house. More likely it was simply a case of pre-party jitters and wanting everything to go off without a hitch. Once Mrs. Baxter assigned duties to Holly and me, the three of us worked well together and I started to miss my own mother and Jen. This was the kind of event both of them would have loved being part of.

Holly and I spent most of the afternoon working side by side, talking about her work as a nurse, her relationship with Jake, and ultimately about my relationship with her brother.

"So do you think this is a forever thing with Jake or what?" she asked.

"Holly we've only known each other a few weeks," I said with a nervous laugh.

"I understand that, but you should know something about my brother," she said as she stopped arranging the flowers she had been working with and looked at me. "Jake means the world to me—well, to all of us really—and I know that he's head over heels in love with you. If you don't feel the same way about him, I'm begging you to walk away now. I don't want to see him get hurt."

Tears sprang to my eyes at the love she felt for her brother and I wanted so much to tell her how I really felt about Jake, but I needed to tell him first. So I did my best to ease her worry.

"I'll do my very best to make sure that doesn't happen," I assured her. "Jake is very important to me also."

Holly stared at me for the longest time until finally a smile crossed her face. "Thank you," was her only comment before we went back to work.

It was just after noon when my cell phone rang and I knew without looking it would be Jake.

"You sold the house, didn't you?" I asked excitedly as I walked away to find a quiet place to talk.

"Maybe. We have a couple of offers for full asking price, but how did you know?" he asked in surprise.

"Don't you remember I told you this morning that you'd sell by lunchtime?"

"You did, but as nice as this house is, I didn't think it would happen. 'Course nothing's official yet. How are things going there?"

"Great, although it's a zoo. Your mom insists that it's a very well-orchestrated symphony of preparation—her words not mine—but there are people everywhere."

"Mom's been planning for Dad's fiftieth for a couple of years now. She wants it to be the party of the year when it's all over."

"She told me that almost three hundred people are invited," I told him. "How will they all fit in the backyard?" Their backyard was huge compared to the one I grew up with, but that was still a lot of people.

"Somehow it will all work out," Jake insisted. "Do you need me to bring anything when I come over?"

"No, I can't imagine what else we might need. But I can't wait until you get here," I told him.

"Paige!" Jake's mom was calling for me.

"That's your mom. I better get back to work," I told him. "I miss you."

"I miss you too. Don't let Mom and Holly work you too hard," he said. "I'll be there as quickly as I can. Love you."

"Love you too," I said before clicking off and realizing with surprise what I had just said. Did Jake realize it too, and if he did, how would he react? I stood there for a moment expecting him to call back right away, but he didn't.

Although my response had been rather flip and maybe just a slip of the tongue, I realized it was the truth. I was in love with the man.

The rest of the afternoon passed by in a haze as I did whatever was asked of me while thinking about what I had said. Karen and Holly commented on my lack of attention, but I couldn't explain it to them. Did Jake actually hear what I had said, and if he had, why hadn't he called back?

An hour before guests were to arrive, Karen dismissed Holly and me so we could get ready for the party. Jake still hadn't arrived and I was anxious to see what his reaction to my comment would be, but it would have to wait as I hurried to take a shower, finish my hair, and slip into my dress and heels. My dress was new and I had spent more on it than anything else I had ever owned in an attempt to fit in with the wealthy crowd I expected to see at the party. Even though Jake's family had made me feel more than welcome, it was important to me to make the best impression when I was introduced as Jake's girlfriend for the first time.

My dress was deep violet and made entirely of lace. Once I had seen it in the window, I just knew I had to have it, and it fit me like a second skin in all the right places. I looked sexy and it gave me confidence I might not

88

otherwise have had. Now the only question in my mind was whether Jake would like it.

He still wasn't home by the time the first guests arrived and I wondered if something had gone wrong with the open house since we last talked. Calls to his cell went straight to voicemail, but I didn't have a lot of time to dwell on the thought as the house was soon filled with guests and I made my way out to the backyard tent while the Baxter's greeted the new arrivals.

Worrying about Jake's absence, the glass of champagne in my hand went largely untouched as I wandered through the tent, smiling at people here and there and wondering what had caused his delay. Maybe one more call to his cell? As I turned to head back in for my phone, Jake suddenly appeared in front of me and my heart stopped in my chest at how debonair he looked.

Dressed in a charcoal black designer suit and crisp white shirt with a tie that nearly matched the deep violet of my dress, he looked so sexy it took my breath away. Slowly we walked toward each other until we were inches apart.

"You look beautiful," he whispered into my ear as I melted against him.

"And you look nothing like the working man I spent the night with last night," I told him. "I don't know if I'm going to be able to control myself around you tonight."

"Save that thought for later, okay?" he asked with a wink and a kiss. "Sorry I'm so late. There were so many people at the open house we had to stay an extra hour."

"But it went well?"

"Couldn't have been better. We have multiple offers and unless they all fall through, we'll sell it above list price. It's been a long day, but now I could use a drink and then it's time to introduce you to my friends."

He had said nothing about what I told him on the phone earlier. Knowing him the way I did, if he had heard it, he would have said something and I finally began to relax without even realizing how tense I had become. Deep down I wanted the moment when I told Jake I loved him to be like a scene from a romance novel, candlelight and romantic music and all. Surely not a quick slip of the tongue on a phone call! Maybe I still had that chance. Either way, now wasn't the time to dwell on it, and I pushed it from my mind, determined to enjoy the party.

"Jake, my boy," came that gravelly voice I knew so well from the office. Turning around I was face to face with Jerry Nolan. "And Paige Cooper. I wondered if I would see you here."

"Hello Mr. Nolan," I said as Jake slipped his arm around my waist before extending the other to shake my boss's hand.

"Jerry, glad you could make it," Jake told him. "Have you seen Dad yet?"

"I have, and he's looking awfully young for fifty."

"I hope you told him that," Jake said. "It will make his day!"

"Paige, you're looking lovely tonight," he told me as he looked me up and down. "That color suits you."

"Thank you, sir. Is your wife with you tonight?" I asked him. His comments on my appearance had left me feeling a bit uncomfortable.

"No, Beth is chairing a fundraiser tonight and she's mad as hell I'm not with her. But I couldn't let my old friend Luke celebrate alone, so here I am. Jake, would you please get me another scotch on the rocks?"

Jake took the empty glass from his hand and left to do as requested, leaving me alone with Mr. Nolan and not quite sure what to say to him, but as it turned out, it wasn't small talk he was after.

"What's this I hear about you losing clients?" he asked when Jake was well out of ear shot. We stood side by side looking at the party guests.

"Um, I'm not really sure what you're talking about, sir," I said. The question had come out of the blue.

"My secretary says—and you know she's the eyes and ears of the company for me—Margo says that rumor has it your clients are jumping ship. What do you know about that?"

"Sir, I don't think it's quite that extreme. True, a couple of my clients have decided to switch to another architect in the firm, but that's it."

"And would that other architect be David Dawson by any chance?" he asked. The way he said it I was pretty sure he already knew that.

"Yes, that's what I've heard," I admitted.

"I also heard from Helen Nelsen that Mr. Dawson was involved in a presentation you did for her new mansion and he made a comment that caused her some concern."

"Sir, I've already addressed her concerns and she's fine now," I said, shocked that this whole discussion was happening at the party.

Turning to face me directly, the look on his face was anything but happy and I knew I was in trouble. "Paige, I want you to tell me the truth. Is Dawson the cause of all these problems?"

"Honestly, sir, I'm not sure. It appears that way, but I have no proof," I said.

"And did all this happen at the same time you told him you wouldn't date him anymore?"

My jaw dropped and my mind was spinning. How in the world did he know that? Maybe the office gossip was true and Margo really did know everything that happened in the building.

"Yes," I said softly.

"And he threatened you?"

"Not directly, but it was implied."

"Paige, why didn't you come to me?" he asked with unexpected kindness. "Don't you know how important you are to the firm? That little prick Dawson should have been fired long ago. He's gone too far this time. When I get back to work on Monday, he's gone. You won't have to put up with him anymore."

"Sir, please. I don't want to get anyone fired."

"I appreciate that, young lady, but that's my decision and one that should have happened long ago. I promise I'll keep your name out of it. Now, I'm going to go find that boyfriend of yours and see what happened to my drink."

As he walked away from me, I felt a mixture of relief and dread. Once David was gone, I would no longer have to see him at work, but he was sure to connect his firing to me and I dreaded what he might do in retaliation. One thing was sure, Monday would be full of drama.

It was at least another half hour before I could find Jake in the crowd again and I discovered him surrounded by a group of laughing men. Jake noticed me right away and quickly pulled me to his side.

"Guys, this is my girlfriend Paige. Paige, these guys are my high school buddies." Introductions were quickly made as I shook hands with each of them.

"Where have you been hiding this one, Baxter? She's beautiful," one of the guys said as if I wasn't standing right there.

"And she's smart. Paige is an architect," he said. I felt like I was being judged.

"And I'm standing right here!" I said with a laugh.

"Sorry, sweetheart," Jake said before giving me a kiss on the cheek.

"I hope you're all hungry because they have started to direct people to their tables for dinner," I told the group of friends.

The group made its way to the tent before Jake and I left his friends at their table and we made our way to the family table. By the time everyone had eaten and a round of speeches and toasts had been made to the guest of honor, the staff began to rearrange everything for the music and dancing that had been planned after the meal. Jake and I made our way back to his friends where room was made for us at their table and stories about their high school antics began. Soon we were all laughing.

It wasn't long before smooth jazz music could be heard and people began to join Jake's parents on the dance floor. I waited patiently for Jake to ask me to dance while tapping my foot to the music as he and his friends continued to relive their high school days.

"Would you mind terribly if I danced with your girl?" Jerry Nolan towered over me with his hand out as he addressed the question to Jake.

"Paige?" Jake asked me in response. It wasn't my boss I wanted to dance with, but Jake didn't seem to realize that and it disappointed me.

Taking Mr. Nolan's hand, I let him lead me out to the dance floor to discover he was a surprisingly good dancer. Letting go of the fact that my dance partner was also my boss, it wasn't long before I was enjoying myself.

As the song ended, we stood there clapping with the rest of the guests before Jake came up and wrapped his arm around me.

"I hope you won't mind if I claim Paige for myself," he told Mr. Nolan.

"Not at all, son, but what took you so long?" he replied gracefully before leaving the dance floor as Jake twirled me and the music began again.

"I'm sorry for neglecting you," he said softly as we swayed together.

"It's okay. I figured at some point I would get you back from your friends."

"I won't leave your side the rest of the night," he assured me.

Laying my head on his chest, I could feel his heart beat and a wave of love for the man washed over me.

The rest of the evening was magical and Jake and I spent every moment on the dance floor. He was as good a dancer as he appeared to be an athlete, and even though my high heels were killing me by the end of the night, I couldn't have enjoyed the party more. As we joined the rest of the family in saying good-bye to the guests, I should have been tired, but instead was a bundle of energy.

"Well, that was a fun night. Thank you for all your hard work, Karen," Luke said as he embraced his wife.

"You're welcome, sweetheart, and happy birthday," she told him. It wasn't difficult to see the love they shared after decades of marriage. "But don't forget to thank Holly and Paige. They were a lot of help and I couldn't have pulled this off without them."

"Of course. Thank you both," he said warmly as the whole family moved into the living room while staff worked around us to clean up the party debris that was scattered throughout the house.

Jake and I sat together on the couch holding hands as Jake tried unsuccessfully to stifle a yawn.

"Sorry Mom, but it's been a long day," he said.

"Paige said you got offers on the house," his mother said.

"Several," he told her. "I think it will end up in a bidding war. Look, I'm sorry to do this, but I am just beat and I think Paige and I better head home."

"Why don't you both just spend the night here?" his dad suggested. "You're tired and we've all had a lot to drink tonight."

"And you would be coming back here in just a few hours for brunch anyway," his mother pointed out. After spending the whole day at the house I was surprised they were still planning on brunch on Sunday.

Jake looked at me and I couldn't tell if he was looking for a way out of it or hoping I would agree.

"I'm fine either way," I told him. "It does make sense to spend the night here, but it's your decision, sweetheart."

"I am pretty beat, so I guess it makes sense. But only if you're sure, Mom," he told her.

"I'm sure, and your old room is ready and waiting."

A part of me wondered if it would be more polite to have separate rooms in his parents' house, but it appeared the decision had already been made for us.

"Paige, take me to bed," Jake said with a smile as I got up from the couch and pulled him up. "Goodnight, everyone."

"See you in the morning," I told them as we made our way arm in arm up the staircase to his old room.

As we undressed for bed, Jake pulled out an old Jim Morrison T-shirt of his for me to sleep in.

"Were you a fan of the Doors?" I asked as we crawled into bed and snuggled together.

"I'm a fan of anything from the sixties and seventies," he told me, a fact I should have known if I would have thought more about it. Every time we were in his truck together it was turned to a station playing that music.

"And here I thought I knew everything about you already," I told him.

"Not quite," he said as his eyes closed. "But I'll bet I know everything about you."

"Oh yeah?" I asked. There was no response. He was already sound asleep.

"But I'll bet you don't know how much I love you, Jake Baxter." I said softly before I closed my eyes also.

It was a later-than-normal brunch, as we all slept in the next morning and by the time we gathered in the dining room it was closer to lunchtime. Sunday was officially Mr. Baxter's birthday and before we ate, it was time for him to open his gifts. A quick discussion with Mrs. Baxter directed me to where my gift had been placed after it was delivered, and I brought it in with all the rest of the gifts and placed the large package off to the side.

"My, that's a big present," he exclaimed when he got to my gift. "Is this from you also, Mother?" he asked his wife.

"It's from me," I said softly.

"Well, thank you, Paige, but you didn't have to get me anything," Luke said. "Let's see what we have here. Son, will you help me open it?" he asked Jake.

The two of them worked together to unwrap the package and slide the heavily padded prints out of the box. As he slowly unwrapped each one, he leaned them against the fireplace so everyone could see them.

"Luke, what are they?" Karen asked.

Sliding his glasses a bit further down his nose, Luke studied them carefully. "If I'm not mistaken, they are the original blueprints for the bank," he said as he looked at me for confirmation.

"That's right," I said, waiting for some sign that he liked the gift.

He continued to look at the prints and then back at me before taking a handkerchief from his pocket, removing his glasses, and cleaning them before putting the glasses back on. Finally he leaned down to give me a hug.

"It's a wonderful gift. Thank you, Paige. I love it," he told me.

"Oh my, Paige! That's wonderful," Karen told me as she and Holly got up for a closer look at the blueprints.

"I thought maybe you would like to hang them in your office," I suggested.

"That's just what I was thinking," he said excitedly.

Jake joined me on the couch and put his arm around me. "That was a wonderful gift, Paige. I wish I had thought of it. Just one more reason why I love you."

"Let's eat, everyone," his mother announced, interrupting the moment between us.

Chapter Nine

A wonderful weekend full of family, friends, and love was over, and after yet another difficult goodbye at the airport, I found myself back in Minneapolis, already looking forward to next Friday when Jake had asked me to take the afternoon off work for a mystery road trip. Since one of us was always traveling on a weekend, I was surprised and more than a bit intrigued to learn he wanted to go somewhere else, but as much as I tried to get him to tell me where we were headed, he wouldn't spill.

Jake didn't know it, but Saturday was my birthday. Until I met him, the day would have been spent like the many birthdays before he came into my life: low key, with maybe a few friends or family. Hopefully this year, alone with Jake somewhere, that would change.

But before we could get to the weekend, I had to deal with the drama that was sure to ensue when David was fired. First thing Monday morning I called Casey into my office and told her about my discussion with Jerry Nolan at the party. She wasn't surprised to find out Margo knew what had been going on with David and had passed the information to her boss. One thing everyone knew about Margo, her loyalties were 100 percent to Jerry and to SNK. We waited on pins and needles to see what would happen, but by mid-morning it was apparently over and had been no big deal for anyone except David. There were no threats made and no shouting. In fact, according to those who witnessed him being escorted out of the building, he had no reaction at all and had even smiled as the elevator doors closed on him.

Could it all be that simple? Maybe David had seen the writing on the wall. Maybe David knew that he was on shaky ground and, more importantly for me, maybe he wouldn't connect me to his firing. I felt like the weight of the world had been taken off my shoulders and by the time lunch was over, I had already put the man out of my mind and it was a peaceful, albeit hectic week.

"Hey Paige, you better get going if you're going to make it to the airport in time," Casey said as she walked into my office to hand me a stack of files. "I don't know why you're taking this afternoon off to spend with Jake and taking work home with you."

"It's not like the architect fairy is going to show up and do my work for me!" I told her with a smile as I packed my briefcase.

"True, but you deserve to have a weekend to yourself," she said in return. "Heck, if I had Jake at home waiting for me, I wouldn't even think about working."

"And I hope that's how it goes, but having the files means I can work if the opportunity presents itself," I insisted.

"Oh, almost forgot," she said before darting back out of the office. I could hear her digging through her desk for something before coming back with a small wrapped present in her hand.

"Happy birthday, Paige!"

"Wow, Casey, you remembered! Thank you so much."

"Open it."

Inside was a delicate bird figurine made entirely out of cobalt blue glass.

"Thank you, but I don't get it," I admitted.

"It's the blue bird of happiness," she told me. "I figured that at this point in your life you have everything you need to make you happy—family, friends, good health, a great job, and now a wonderful man. The blue bird is just my way of ensuring your happiness."

"Geez Casey, you're going to make me cry," I told her as tears welled up in my eyes and I walked over to give her a hug.

"I just hope that Jake takes you somewhere special this weekend," she said as she wiped tears from her eyes also.

"He did say we were going on a road trip, but he doesn't know it's my birthday. But even if it's just fishing for the weekend, I'll be happy as long as we're together."

It looked for a moment like Casey knew something I didn't, but it was gone so quickly I wasn't sure what I had seen.

"Now you really better get going. Have a fantastic birthday and I can't wait to hear all about it."

"Thanks, and see you Monday," I told her as I grabbed my briefcase and the box with Casey's gift and headed to the elevator for the quick ride to the airport.

Jake had said we'd leave directly from the airport and I already had a bag packed and in the back of my SUV. It had been pretty difficult to pack since I didn't know where we were going, so my bag had almost double the amount of clothes I would normally bring for a weekend. Along with my jeans, shorts, and T-shirts, I also packed a nice dress and a pair of heels just in case. Surprises definitely weren't my thing and I wanted to be ready for anything.

Pulling up to the curb at the terminal where Jake was waiting with a smile on his face, I quickly got out of the car and ran around to greet him. Throwing myself into his arms, I wrapped my legs around his waist and kissed him for all I was worth.

"Wow!" he said when he could breathe again. "What did I do to deserve that welcome?"

"You're here and I missed you is all," I told him before he put me gently down on the ground to the looks of amusement on the faces of the other passengers around us.

"So where are we going?" I asked as he drove away from the airport, wondering if he knew how to get to wherever it was.

"You'll see," he said mysteriously. "I promise it will be a good surprise."

"But how do you know where you're going?" I asked. "You didn't even program the GPS on the car."

"Don't need to. I have it all up here," he told me as he pointed to his head. "So, tell me about your week."

It seemed like I had so much to tell, starting with my discussion with Jerry Nolan at the party and David's subsequent firing. As I talked, with Jake saying very little except to ask a clarifying question every now and then, I noticed that we were heading north. I still had no clue where we were going, but at least I knew the direction.

"I'm just glad that he's gone. I know you weren't worried about him, Paige, but some guys just can't take rejection, especially when they still have to see the girl every day. But now he's gone and you should be okay," he told me.

"Trust me, I'm fine. I'm sorry you were worried for nothing."

"It wasn't nothing. Don't you know you're the most important person in the world to me?" he said as he reached for my hand.

"I do know, and it means the world to me," I said. Anxious to get the subject on to something more pleasant than David, I asked once again where we were going.

"I'm surprised you haven't figured it out already. We're going to Duluth," he told me with a smile.

"Are you kidding me? I love Duluth!" I told him.

"I know, Casey told me," he admitted. "She also told me about your favorite hotel, the Lake Superior Suites, and I booked a king-size lakefront suite on the top floor for the weekend."

"You are too good to me," I told him before giving him the best kiss I could without making us crash. "Something tells me I'm not going to get any work done this weekend."

"Don't you even think about it," he cautioned. "This weekend is for you and me and nothing else."

Jake had no idea just how true that was. I had decided it was finally time for me to tell him exactly how I felt about him. He might not have heard it the first time, and he might have slept through it the second time, but this weekend he would hear me.

It was late by the time we made it to our hotel room, so we ordered room service and ate our dinner on the balcony overlooking Lake Superior. As usual it was a bit cooler that far north, but after the excessive heat in Minneapolis the past week, it was a nice break and we were both comfortable in shorts and sweatshirts while watching the large ships come into port under the aerial lift bridge Duluth was famous for.

Jake had done research on Duluth in preparation for our getaway, but he had never seen the city in person, and pulling our chairs closer together we held hands as I told him stories from my previous trips to the city.

"My sister Jen used to run in Grandmas' Marathon each June. We'd come up as a family to support her and you can't imagine the madhouse as the population doubles just for the race."

"You never told me she was a runner," Jake said.

"I was too, until I blew out my knee, but I never had any interest in running a whole marathon."

"What else do you like to do here?" he asked.

"You probably won't be surprised, but I love visiting Glensheen Mansion."

"Isn't that where those murders happened?" he asked.

"So you know about it! I suppose that's what draws most people to the house, but my interest is more in the architecture of the mansion. It's gorgeous. I'd love to be your tour guide while we're here if you want to go," I offered.

"It's definitely on the agenda for tomorrow. I knew you would want to see it, although I didn't know you had been there before."

"I would go once a year if I could. There's always something new to see and always more than you can learn in just one tour." The house was truly spectacular and I had been there a dozen times.

"How do you feel about hiking? I heard the Superior Hiking Trail is a good place to go."

"That would be great too. I packed my walking shoes just in case," I told him.

"We'll do that tomorrow morning, then, and we'll have a nice dinner tomorrow night. Only problem is we have to leave pretty early on Sunday to get back for my afternoon flight. It was the only one I could get."

"We'll make it work," I told him. "As long as we spend every minute together, we'll make it work."

The sun was beginning to set and the lift bridge was casting long shadows across Lake Superior as the temperatures were quickly dropping. I had forgotten how chilly the nights could be in Duluth. Heading inside to bed, the sound of a freighter blowing its horn as it pulled into the harbor could be heard echoing across the lake.

"I've missed you so much," Jake said as he took me into his arms. I could feel his desire beginning to build, matching the heat that was suddenly flowing through my body, and the stubble of his late-day beard tickled my skin as he kissed me gently.

"I missed you too," I said, kissing him back. God, how I missed his touch.

Slowly and deliberately he started to remove my clothing until I stood naked before him. Lifting me into his arms, he lowered me onto the bed before quickly removing his own clothes and lowering his body to mine. No further words were spoken as we both satisfied the desire that had been building in us since we were last together.

Each time we reunited after a week apart, it was as if we picked up right where we left off and neither one of us could get enough of the other. I had waited an entire lifetime to find this man and there was no way I would ever let him go. Tomorrow he would know exactly what he meant to me now that I felt secure in what I felt for the man and I closed my eyes and snuggled even closer before sleep overtook us both.

The cries of gulls swooping over the lake looking for their breakfast woke me the next morning and I slowly opened my eyes to the sunlight spilling into our room. Jake still slept and I carefully moved closer, trying not to wake him. The heat of his arm draped across my body made me feel safe and protected, and all the love I felt for him bubbled once more to the surface. Waking to the sight of him was the best way I had ever started a birthday and I said a quick prayer that there would be many more such days in our lives.

Staring at the ceiling daydreaming of our future together, I was surprised when I noticed he was awake and had been watching me.

"Good morning, my love," he whispered as he pulled me even closer to him and kissed me. "Did you sleep well?"

"How could I not with you next to me?" I asked quietly. "I could get used to waking up like this. The sound of the waves crashing on the shore, gulls calling to each other, the distant sound of the ship's horns, and of course you next to me."

"You do realize we have the same thing in Chicago, right?" he asked with a smile.

"True, but your lake isn't 'superior,'" I told him with my own smile before he began to tickle me and I erupted into laughter while trying desperately to escape his touch. A bit of quick maneuvering and I was on top of Jake with his hands pinned above his head. Suddenly the laughter was replaced by passion and soon we were lost in each other.

"We need to get out of this bed soon or we never will," Jake told me as he tried to recover after our early morning love-making session.

"Would that be so bad?" I teased.

"You know I'd like nothing better," he insisted, "but I have a full day planned for us. Why don't you hop in the shower while I make a couple of calls? We can have breakfast downstairs and then get our day started."

"Do you want to join me in the shower?" I offered.

"As soon as I'm done with my calls," he said mysteriously. "Now go."

Crawling out of bed, I walked seductively toward the bathroom, knowing full well he was watching my every move. It wasn't long before he joined me in the shower and the water wasn't the only thing steaming up the room.

The hotel's dining room was almost empty by the time we finally came down for breakfast and we didn't linger over our food. Jake was excited to get started on our hike and I was anxious to start burning some calories. It was a perfect day with sunny skies, a light wind blowing in off the lake, and low seventy degree temperatures. Perfect for tackling the Superior Trail.

The scenic vistas along the trail provided plenty of opportunities to stop for a selfie or two, which we took full advantage of. Surprisingly for such a wonderfully mild day, there were few other hikers, and for most of the hike it felt like Jake and I were alone in the wilderness. We spent the entire morning talking, walking, and laughing with each other before arriving at the end of the trail for a picnic lunch, where I tried as hard as I could to get him to divulge the rest of the plans for the weekend, but the man was a master secret keeper. Finally I just gave up, intent on enjoying each surprise as it came.

As we had been walking, my phone had started to chirp with incoming texts. With busy lives, being interrupted by calls was a common occurrence, but this weekend we had both promised our phones were going to be ignored. I hadn't looked at or responded to a single text that had come in since leaving Minneapolis on Friday, but I didn't need to look. The texts were most likely birthday wishes from friends and family. As we ate, another text came in.

"I don't mind if you respond to your text, Paige," Jake told me as he enjoyed his sandwich. "Obviously someone needs to get in touch with you or they wouldn't keep texting every five minutes."

"No, we made a promise to each other. This weekend is for us and whatever it is can wait," I assured him.

"You should at least look at your phone to make sure it's not an emergency," he said wisely.

"It's not."

"How do you know if you don't look?" he asked. "Go ahead. I won't be mad."

Knowing Jake the way I did, I knew there was no way he was going to let it go, so I stole a quick glance at my phone, scrolled through a few messages, and put it back in my pocket. As I suspected, my phone had been blowing up with birthday wishes.

"Well?"

"It was nothing," I told him.

"Nothing? You probably have a dozen messages just since we started our hike. Doesn't sound like nothing to me."

He really was going to make this hard and I needed to tell him something, but what could I say that wouldn't be a lie?

"It's just Casey and my sister Jen. Just wondering what I'm doing today." That part at least was true.

"That many messages just to find out what you're doing? That seems odd," he said with a funny kind of smile.

He was right—it did, but I couldn't exactly tell him it was my birthday. He would have felt horrible he didn't know.

"I guess, but that's the way they are. I'm just going to turn my phone off so I can concentrate completely on you," I said in an effort to get us off the subject. "Are you ready to head back up the trail?"

With my phone off, there was no more discussion about the messages, and we got back to the hotel in time to change clothes and do some sightseeing around Duluth.

Expecting to tour the mansion, I was more than a little disappointed each time Jake took me somewhere else, and before I knew it, the afternoon was over and we were back at the hotel again.

"Did you have a nice day, Paige?" Jake asked as we relaxed on the balcony with a glass of wine.

"It was very nice, thank you," I told him, trying to keep the disappointment out of my tone.

"But you're disappointed, right?" he asked. Guess I didn't do such a good job hiding my thoughts.

"No...well, kind of. I had hoped that after talking about Glensheen we would tour it today."

"I know, and I'm sorry to have gotten your hopes up and all, but we can still see it tonight before the special dinner I have planned."

"That would have been great, but they close at five and it's almost that now. Maybe we can come back another time?"

"We don't have to. They have extended hours today. I booked a tour at seven."

"Seriously?" I asked. "I didn't know they did tours at night now."

"Good thing I planned this trip, then," Jake told me as he reached over to give me a kiss. "I've arranged for the tour and then we're going to a very exclusive restaurant for a late dinner."

"Wow, that sounds fancy," I told him, suddenly worried that the only dress I had packed wouldn't be formal enough. "But is the dress I brought appropriate for this fancy restaurant?"

"That's my other surprise," he said as we both turned at the knock on our door. Jake got up to answer it as I followed him. The bellhop handed him two garment bags that he placed on the bed before looking at me. "Surprise!" he said as he gestured to the bags.

"What's going on?"

"Tonight's dinner is formal, so I hope you don't mind, but I bought you a dress to wear and the other bag is a suit for me."

"You bought us clothes for dinner tonight?" This was bizarre.

"Well, not for me, the suit is mine and was in my suitcase. The hotel just had it pressed for me. But the dress is for you."

No man had ever bought me a dress before and for a minute I was torn between love for the man and a feeling that something weird was happening.

"Aren't you going to look at it?" Jake prompted as I stood there trying to process the whole situation.

"Okay." Slowly unzipping the garment bag, I realized I was holding my breath. As the dress was revealed, I released it in one long "Wow." The dress was made of black satin in a style that would have suited Audrey Hepburn. Sleeveless with a tight-fitting bodice and a full flowing knee-length skirt, the dress was accentuated only by a slim belt with a jeweled buckle that circled the waist. It was stunning in its simplicity and old-world glamour.

"You bought this for me?" was all I could say as tears gathered in my eyes.

"I'll admit I had an ulterior motive," Jake said as he wrapped his arms around me from behind. "I think you'll look sexy as hell in it," he admitted before kissing my neck. "There's a pair of heels in that bag somewhere too, and a wrap for the cold," he told me.

There were indeed, and after hanging the dress carefully in the closet, I sat down on the bed before Jake helped me slip on the black pumps. They fit me perfectly and I felt like Cinderella.

"But how did you know my size?" I asked him as he sat down next to me.

"Don't you think by now I know this body?" he told me as he put his arm around me and pulled me closer with a laugh. "Well, that, and a little help from Casey!"

"Ah-ha, that explains a lot," I told him. Casey had been acting shady the past week and I guess now I knew why.

"But if we're going to make our tour and dinner, you'll have to wear your new clothes while we tour the mansion. Is that okay with you?"

"More than okay! In fact, wearing that dress at the mansion will make me feel like I live there."

"Great! Well, we better start getting ready."

Of course Jake was ready long before I was, and by the time I finally emerged from the bathroom ready to go, he took my breath away. He stood before me dressed in a black pinstripe suit, striking white dress shirt, and black silk tie with a crisp white handkerchief in his breast pocket. I knew clothes and I knew that his suit was no off-the-rack model. It was designer and most likely expensive as hell. He looked like a model and I couldn't take my eyes off him. He had left a bit of beard stubble, the look that he knew by now really turned me on, and his hair was perfectly styled. The faint scent of his aftershave drew me to his side where I wrapped my arms around his waist and looked into his eyes.

"You are the most handsome man I have ever laid eyes on."

"And you, my love, are more beautiful than ever."

"Thank you for all this," I told him as he leaned down to kiss me gently. "You are full of surprises and I don't know what I did to deserve you."

"The night's just beginning," he said mysteriously. "Are you ready to go?"

"Definitely!"

Placing the wrap around my shoulder, he took my hand and we went downstairs to find a small group of people gathered near the hotel entrance. Jake eased us through the crowd and that's when I saw what everyone had been staring at: a horse-drawn carriage with a driver in livery and a top hat, and a beautiful coal-black horse with four white stockings. The horse shook its head and stamped its feet as we exited the hotel.

"Wow, look at that," I said, expecting Jake to turn toward the parking area and almost running into him when he stopped. "Someone's getting a treat."

"That someone is you," he told me as he held out his hand to me.

"Really?" I asked with excitement.

"Really," he assured me as he helped me up into the carriage.

"Good evening, miss," the driver said. "My name is James and my horse is Poppy."

"Good evening, James," I told him as Jake settled in beside me and placed a light blanket over our laps.

"This is how we're getting to Glensheen?" I asked Jake.

"It is, so settle in and enjoy the ride. We're ready, James."

With a little slap of the reins, Poppy started us out and I snuggled in closer to Jake. Soon we were away from the congestion of downtown on the road running parallel to Lake Superior, the steady *clip clop* of Poppy's hooves the only sound in the night.

My heart was beating with excitement and overflowing with love for Jake, and I wanted to tell him how I felt about him right then and there, but then I caught my first glimpse of Glensheen through the trees.

"The mansion is just ahead," James told us. "We'll go past it and then come back using the same drive the Congdens used to use for their carriages."

"Jake, are you sure it's open tonight?" I asked. There were no cars in the parking lot as we went by, yet every other time I had toured the mansion the parking lot had been full.

"I'm sure," he said, giving my hand a squeeze as James turned the carriage down a driveway I hadn't even known existed.

At night the home was even more magnificent than during the day. Warm lights peeked out from every room of the house, making it seem as if the family was still in residence. As we pulled up to the house, a man and a woman dressed in servants' uniforms came out to greet us. In all the times I had been at the mansion before, none of the guides had been dressed in period clothing, but maybe it was something new this year or maybe it had to do with the late hours.

"I'll be waiting for you here when you're done, sir," James told us.

"Thanks, James," Jake told him as he helped me down from the carriage.

"Miss Cooper, Mr. Baxter, welcome to Glensheen!" the man said. "I am Matthew and this is Sarah, and we'll be your guides for this evening's tour."

"Are we waiting for the others?" I asked in confusion, and then realized he had called us by name.

"You are our only guests this evening," Matthew said as he gestured toward the front door of the house and we walked inside.

"What's going on?" I whispered to Jake.

"This is your next surprise," he told me. "Tonight we are having a private tour of the house. It's just you and I and our tour guides. I know how hard it is for you to have questions about these historic properties and not feel like you can ask during a tour. Tonight you can ask any and every question you want and take as much time as you want. And as long as we don't sit on anything, we can even go right into the rooms for a closer look. There's no velvet ropes to keep us out."

"Really?" I said hopefully.

"Really!" Taking my hand in his, Jake said we were ready to start.

For the next two hours or so, we viewed every inch of the thirty-nine rooms of the twenty-thousand-square-foot house. Matthew and Sarah were not just our tour guides. It turned out they were also graduate level architectural students and were so fully versed in the history of Glensheen, I found myself asking surprisingly few questions.

"The house was originally owned and commissioned by Chester and Clara Congdon in 1905, and it took three years to build. Miss Cooper, I'm sure you know it's done in a Jacobean Revival style, and the house itself was designed by architect Clarence H. Johnson, Sr., with the interiors designed by William A. French Co., and the formal terraced garden and English-style landscape designed by the Charles Wellford Leavitt firm out of New York," Matthew told us.

Sarah continued the story as we explored the house. "The rooms are trimmed or paneled in numerous woods, including Circassian walnut, mahogany, cypress, fumed oak, enameled birch, and American walnut, with the furniture in each room made of the same wood used in the woodwork. The original furniture brought into the house in 1908 and '09 remains in virtually the same place it has been for over 110 years. Some of the wall coverings and upholstery are also original, and the hallways exhibit original stenciling in the Arts and Crafts style as well as beautiful wood carvings. The wall and ceiling coverings are made of wool, silk, filled burlap, and gold leaf. If you look carefully, you'll see that the doors throughout the home are made of two kinds of wood, with oak on the hallway side and the other side made of whatever variety of wood was used in the room."

"Could you imagine having all those materials imported from all over the world and brought in by steamer ship through the Great Lakes or by horse-drawn cart from St. Paul?" I said. "It probably took years for some of the materials to arrive."

"You're right, Ms. Cooper. But once the house was finished, visitors from all over the world were welcomed to Glensheen. In fact, you may have noticed the pineapple carvings on the main staircase bannister and in other areas of the home. In certain areas of the country, a pineapple was a symbol of warmth, welcome, friendship, and hospitality. It was a sign of gracious living that was adopted by Mr. and Mrs. Congdon," Sarah told us.

"In addition to the main mansion, the estate has its own carriage house, gardener's cottage, and a boathouse on Lake Superior. In 1968 the estate was given to the University of Minnesota Duluth, which operates Glensheen to this day," Matthew told us.

"Didn't the Congdons' daughter live here in the seventies, though?" Jake asked. He knew about the murders, and I knew that the tour guides hesitated to talk about that dark time in the home's history.

To my surprise, Sarah didn't hesitate to answer, though. "She did. Her name was Elisabeth and she was the Congdons' youngest daughter. She had a life estate claim to the house, allowing her to live here until her death. You probably know that Elisabeth and her nurse were murdered here in 1977."

"We do know," I said.

"About two years after Ms. Congdon was murdered, the University opened Glensheen to the public."

"It's sad that so many people only visit Glensheen because of the murders. They don't have any appreciation for the magnificence of the home," I said.

"Actually, we think that's changing," Matthew said. "It's been over forty years since the murders and a lot of our guests aren't even aware of what happened that night. For many visitors, Glensheen is simply an example of a life gone by and the kind of wealth that so many will never know."

Another woman dressed in a maid's uniform came up and whispered something in Sarah's ear.

"It seems your dinner is ready," she said. "If you'll please follow me out to the terrace."

Passing by windows on the lake side of the house, I had noticed activity on the three-tiered terrace that overlooked the formal garden adjacent to the lake and I now looked at Jake with a raised eyebrow.

"Surprise number two, Paige. Welcome to our exclusive restaurant," he said as he took my hand and led me out to the terrace, where a candlelit table for two had been arranged with my favorite flowers—calla lilies—and place settings of the finest china. The terrace was lit with tiny twinkle lights in the trees and soft piano music caught my ear. Glensheen had just been transformed into the most romantic moonlit restaurant ever.

Stunned into silence, I let Jake help me to my seat as Matthew appeared with my wrap from the front entryway, and Jake placed it around my shoulders against the chill of the slight breeze coming off Lake Superior.

"Jake, I..."

"Yes, my love?" he said as I struggled to find words for what I was feeling.

"I don't know what to say. This is the best surprise ever and I can't thank you enough."

"So, you like it?" he asked with a smile as he placed his napkin in his lap.

"Like it?" I said. "This might be the best night of my entire life!"

"I wanted to do something extra special for your birthday," he said, leaving me in stunned silence. "Happy birthday, my love!"

Rising from his seat, he leaned over to give me a kiss. I could only look at him in shock.

"How'd you know?" I finally asked as I looked across the table at him.

"You'd be surprised what a promise to take Bruce fishing for the weekend does in getting your assistant to talk," he admitted.

"I should have known," I said with a smile as waiters began to appear with champagne and appetizers. "She was acting secretive all week long."

"Don't be mad at her for telling me. She held up pretty well to all my badgering."

"I'm not mad. In fact, I almost had to tell you myself. Those texts that have been coming in all day? Birthday wishes from friends and family. I was so afraid you'd see my phone and feel badly if you had found out what today was."

Taking his hand across the table, I looked deep into his eyes and knew that even if we had shared this meal at McDonald's, my birthday couldn't have been any better.

As we ate, with course after course coming out to us, we talked about the beauty of the mansion and how difficult it must have been to build such a massive structure in the early 1900s. Occasionally a pleasure boat would pass by on the lake and toot their horns as we waved back. It was truly a magical evening.

The meal finally done, Jake and I wandered arm in arm through the formal gardens under the nearly full moon.

"When we grow old together and are sitting on matching rocking chairs on the front porch of our home, I'll always remember the joy on your face today," he told me before lapsing into an extended silence. "But I need you to know this. You deserve to be as happy as you are right now, and if I'm not the man that can do that for you, I'll step back. It will kill me, but I'll do it. That's how much I love you."

The tears in his eyes were my undoing. I had put the man through hell for weeks as he waited for me to tell him I loved him, and even though we had only known each other such a short time, I knew without a shred of doubt that I was in love with him. Turning to him, I knew it was time.

"I love you," I said softly as I reached up to caress his cheek. "I love you more than I ever knew it was possible to love someone, and the thought of me without you is unbearable. I'm sorry it took me so long to say it, but I'm in love with you, Jake."

The words were barely out of my mouth before he crushed me in his arms. When he finally released me, he dropped to one knee and pulled a small box out of his pocket as I stared at him in shock.

"Jake..."

"Please Paige, let me say this first," he asked as he took my hand in his. "I've been carrying this ring around for weeks now waiting to hear you say you love me. I know you don't believe in love at first sight, but that's what happened to me the first moment I saw you. You stole my heart and as hard as it was waiting for you to realize you loved me too, I would never have given up on winning you over. You have become my life. You're the air that I breathe, the nourishment that sustains me, and more than anything, you are the love of my life. There will never be another woman for me, so, Paige, please put me out of my misery and say that you'll become my wife."

Tears were falling freely down my cheeks as he opened the tiny box to reveal a square-cut diamond framed by smaller diamonds in the same cut. My hands were shaking and my legs felt like they would no longer support me, but there was no question in my mind what my answer would be. I nodded my head, unable to speak.

"I need to hear the words from your lips. Paige, will you marry me?" Jake asked again.

"Yes, Jake, I will marry you!" I finally said as Jake leapt to his feet to pick me up and twirl me around. The waitstaff had witnessed the whole thing and they clapped for us from up above on the terrace.

"Did you hear her?" he shouted. "She said yes!"

Kissing me long and hard before finally remembering the ring in his hand, Jake slipped it on my finger and as everything else about us had been from the start, it was a perfect fit. We might have had the shortest courtship in history, but as we danced in the moonlight reflecting off Lake Superior to the appropriately titled "Claire de Lune," there was no doubt in my mind that ours would be a long and loving marriage.

By the time we had to start our trip back to the hotel, Jake had wasted no time telling everyone we were now engaged. James and Poppy were the first to know, of course, and when the carriage finally stopped and Jake helped me out, I slipped Poppy a couple cubes of sugar I had pocketed from our dinner while Jake tipped James. Poppy nearly ate the large ring on my finger before I convinced her I had no more sugar cubes, and I gave her velvety soft nose a gentle pat before Jake took my hand and pulled me to his side.

"Congratulations to you both. I hope you'll be as happy together as me and my missus," James said with a smile as he tipped his hat and clicked at Poppy to start their trip home.

Jake noticed me staring at the ring on my hand as we walked arm in arm back to our suite. "Do you like it?" he asked when we got inside.

"It's beautiful, but just how long have you really been carrying this around?"

"Don't laugh, but I bought it the morning of our first date before I picked you up," he admitted. "I think I've shown incredible patience waiting this long to ask you to marry me. In fact, I would have asked you at the Cubs game if I thought you would say yes."

"You're kidding, right?" I asked as he took off his suit coat and loosened his tie.

"Nope, and you can ask Holly if you don't believe me. She was with me when I bought it."

"So your family knows already?" It didn't really matter to me if they did. I knew that I couldn't wait to call Jen and tell her I was engaged.

"Just Holly," he told me. "And truthfully, she thought I was a little nuts, but she's come around to the idea after meeting you. She thinks you're terrific. You know, as sexy as you look in that dress, isn't it about time it comes off?" he asked with a voice made deeper by the passion I saw reflected back at me. He had been unbuttoning his shirt as he walked toward me, and soon it was on the floor behind him.

Running my newly adorned hand across the well-defined muscles of his stomach before placing a gentle kiss above his heart, there was only one way to answer that question.

"Why don't you see if you can help me with that," I urged before slowly removing his belt and easing his trousers and boxers to the floor. The belt around my waist was next to go as Jake leisurely unzipped my dress and let it fall to the floor. Nearly naked, he swept me up into his arms and carried me to the bed. Kneeling at my side, he leaned down and began gently caressing my skin, leaving me wild with desire for the man.

"This better be the shortest engagement in history," Jake whispered before we were both swept up in our need for each other.

Finally exhausted by all the excitement of our day and drained of all energy, Jake fell into a deep slumber, his arms securely around me, while I lay with my head on his chest listening to his gentle breathing and re-living every moment of our romantic evening. Twirling the ring on my finger to catch the barest bit of moonlight coming in through our balcony doors, I thanked God for bringing such love into my life before succumbing to my own exhaustion.

Even with all the excitement of my birthday and our engagement, we were both up early the next morning as planned, and after a quick breakfast in the dining room, we headed back to Minneapolis. The ride back was full of discussion about our future and Jake's pleas for a quick trip to the altar.

"I'm happy just going to a justice of the peace," he told me. "Anything to make you my wife as soon as possible."

"Jake, we've only just gotten engaged. Don't you want to savor that?" I asked him, only partly in jest.

Becoming Mrs. Jake Baxter was something I couldn't wait for either. But planning the kind of wedding I had dreamt of my whole life didn't just happen overnight. Admitting that the plans would need to be a compromise between both of us, we agreed that for now, we would put the wedding plans on hold until we had at least talked to our families.

The miles flew by as we talked about our future, but even still the long drive from Duluth took even longer due to the heavy traffic. In the end, we barely made it to the airport in time and once again had to say our good-byes at curbside.

"You know, if we got married in Vegas next weekend we wouldn't have to say good-bye at the airport anymore," Jake suggested.

"Don't even tease about a Vegas wedding," I told him. "Don't you want to see me walking down the aisle to you in a beautiful white dress?"

As I said it, I pressed seductively against him, hoping to distract him from the wedding planning, and wasn't disappointed when his body began to respond to me.

"Keep that up, Paige, and they won't allow me on the plane," he said as he gently moved me away. "I better get going. I'll call you when I get to the house."

"Travel safely. I love you, Jake."

"I'm never going to get tired of hearing that," he said with a smile. "I love you too."

One last kiss and he disappeared into the terminal as I started the short drive back to my apartment and another lonely week without him.

Chapter Ten

Being newly engaged, Jake and I hoped to spend every moment we could together, which for us meant one of us flying to the other for the weekend. Certainly the short flights between Chicago and St. Paul were doable, but as luck would have it, my professional life soon interfered with those plans.

Coming in to work on Monday morning, sporting my new engagement ring, I wasn't expecting to be immediately called into Jerry Nolan's office.

"Paige, thank God you're here," Casey said in a rush as she trailed me into my office without even her usual offering of coffee.

"What's wrong?" I said as she stood nervously looking at me.

"Mr. Nolan called. He wants you in his office first thing, and I told him when he called you'd be here a half-hour ago. Where have you been?"

"Casey, calm down. Remember I told you at the end of last week I was going to meet a client for coffee this morning?"

"What? Oh, that's right. I'm so sorry, Paige. I forgot. Anyway, you better drop everything and get up to Mr. Nolan's office right away. I don't know exactly what's going on, but it's something big. Did I tell you he called himself? It wasn't even Margo. That has to mean something's up. You're not getting fired, are you? Oh Paige, what have you done?"

The words were spilling out of her mouth so quickly I could hardly understand what she was asking.

Taking her by the shoulders, I encouraged her to breathe. "Nice deep breaths. In and out. That's right. Now, what's this nonsense about me getting fired?"

"You know the only time associates get called up to the top floor is when someone is losing their job," she said worriedly. "Are you getting fired?"

She was right. Past history was proof firing was usually what happened on the top floor, but that couldn't be. Mr. Nolan had always been complimentary of my work and he continued to tout me as the firm's newest up-and-coming architect. No, I didn't think I was being fired. But was David somehow involved in this strange start to my Monday?

"It's going to be okay, Casey. I am not getting fired," I told her with as much confidence as I could muster. "I'm supposed to meet with Mrs. Nelsen this morning. Why don't you see if you can push her back an hour? By that time, whatever this is should have sorted itself out and we can both get back to normal. And in the meantime, I'll go find out what's going on."

Leaving Casey to make her call to Mrs. Nelsen, I took a quick look in the mirror, straightened a few wayward strands of hair, and headed upstairs.

"Good morning, Paige," Margo said with her characteristic deadpan look. "Mr. Nolan has been waiting for you. Go right on in."

Conversation suddenly halted and the room became quiet as a tomb when I walked in. My heart dropped. All three of the senior partners were in attendance, as well as my direct supervisor, Bob Sanderson. Maybe I really was being fired.

"Paige, good morning," Mr. Nolan said as he directed me to sit directly adjacent to him. No one else said anything and I took my seat with as much bravado as I had left in me, which wasn't much.

"Did you have a nice weekend?" Mr. Nolan asked.

Should I tell him it was the best weekend of my life? Probably not.

"Yes, thank you. I'm sorry you've been waiting for me. I had an early morning client meeting and I just got back."

"That's what I like about you, Paige. You're always working to generate income for the firm," Jerry said as the other partners nodded in agreement. "I suppose you wonder why we've asked you up here."

"Yes, actually I am," I responded. No sense in denying it.

"It hasn't escaped our notice that you've brought quite a bit of prestige to the firm since you started, most especially with your address to the AIA."

"Thank you, sir." Maybe I wasn't being fired.

"I've also heard good reports from your clients. Everyone seems very pleased with your work. This morning the partners were discussing how well you've been doing in comparison with some of the other associates, and while we don't all agree, we've decided to do something we've never done before."

Holding my breath in anticipation, I realized I also had the arms of my chair in a death grip.

"Paige, how would you like to be the lead architect on the Basilica of St. Catherine's project?"

For a moment I sat in stunned silence. The Basilica project had been commissioned by the Diocese to replace a century-old forty-thousand-square-foot building that, until it was destroyed in a massive fire a year ago, had been the hallmark of the Catholic Church in Minneapolis. The Diocese had been very upfront publically about wanting a new building that looked like it had been there for centuries. The project would most likely take the next two years or more and had been coveted by every member of the firm. Being so new, I could only have hoped to somehow be involved in the project, but here he was offering me the lead position. This one project alone could make my career and catapult me into a partnership.

Suddenly realizing that everyone at the table was staring at me and I hadn't yet responded to his question, I hurried to accept the offer.

"Of course I would love the project! Thank you for even considering me, sir," I told him.

Suddenly the room erupted with conversation as all the men in suits talked excitedly about the project. More than the money the project would bring to the firm, the partners were excited about the prestige it would offer.

"You should know that we didn't initially get the commission for the project, but the other firm wasn't living up to the expectations of the Diocese and they decided to switch to SNK. From what we have gathered in our meetings with church officials, the previous firm was designing something more modern than the Church was looking for and they were way over budget. What's most surprising was as they parted ways, the original architect mentioned that you might be the one to design what they were looking for. Apparently he heard you speak at the conference."

Wow!

Fielding questions from both sides of the table, we spent the next hour talking about who would be part of the project team. Each of the names mentioned was someone I had worked successfully with in the past.

"So there's no mistake, you will be in charge of this project, Paige, and I have every confidence you'll do a smashing job, but Bob here will supervise your work."

Bob Sanderson had been my supervisor since arriving at the firm. He was a very nice man and a talented architect, but most of the time it seemed to me he would rather be on the golf course than in the office.

"It's a huge risk putting someone with such limited experience in the lead position, and while the design will be solely yours, at least in the beginning Bob will sit in on all the project meetings just to make sure everything's going according to plan." Jerry looked down at me with what could only be described as a father's pride. "We expect you'll knock this project out of the ballpark, Paige. If you need any help in any way, don't hesitate to ask. Now, do you have any questions for us?"

"Not now. But I do want to tell you how much I appreciate this opportunity and your faith in me. I won't let you down."

Shaking hands all around, I took my leave and headed back downstairs where Casey was waiting nervously. The smile on my face answered her question, but she quickly realized something else was up when I nodded in the direction of my office and closed the door behind her as she came in and took a seat.

"So, good news, I take it?" she asked.

"Better than good. Casey, hold your hat: They offered me the lead on the Basilica project!"

"Are you kidding me?" she said before erupting in a cry of joy. "Oh my goodness, every architect in the building is going to be so jealous. And you, just an associate! What a feather in your cap!"

"And you could have knocked me over with that feather when they offered me the project," I told her as I leaned back in my chair savoring the moment. "Bob will supervise, but I get the impression that unless I make any missteps, his supervision will be limited to sitting in on project meetings. Oh my gosh, there is so much to do. I'll email you the names of the other team members and see if you can arrange the first meeting for today or tomorrow. The Diocese wants to get moving on the project as soon as possible, so it's going to be a lot of very late nights and working weekends. Wait a minute." Suddenly I realized that Casey might not be thrilled with the idea of putting in so many hours. "Are you going to be okay with all this extra work?"

"Actually, now is the perfect time. The kids leave for summer camp in a week, and then they are staying with Bruce's parents in Milwaukee for a month. Bruce was planning on spending his summer fishing with his buddies, and I was looking at a long summer with not much to do. So, yeah, I'm in!"

With my most important work asset sorted out, I suddenly remembered Jake and my excitement was replaced by a look of sadness. How would he take the news? It would mean we would see very little of each other just when we had gotten engaged.

Casey noticed the change in my demeanor at the same time she noticed the ring on my finger.

"Paige Cooper! What is that?" she asked as she reached across the desk to grab my left hand. "Are you and Jake engaged?"

My frown turned into a huge smile as I looked at her studying my new ring. "It's hard to believe it myself, but yeah, we are!"

Casey came around the desk and hugged me. "I knew it. I knew you loved him. So tell me all about it."

Even though there was so much to do for the church project, I spent the next half hour telling Casey about our romantic weekend.

"Geez, I thought stuff like that only happened in the movies," she said as she looked at the ring once more. "So did you set a date?"

"Well, no, and now with this morning's news, we might have to wait a bit longer," I admitted. "Jake would be happy with a Vegas wedding or in front of a judge, but I have always dreamed of the big church wedding and the fancy dress. I just don't see how I can plan a wedding while working on the biggest opportunity of my career. He'll understand, won't he?"

"Probably," she said without much conviction. "But my guess would be that a man who falls in love with a woman so quickly won't be thrilled with waiting two years to marry her."

121

"You're probably right. So what should I do?" I asked.

"Only one thing you can do: Be honest with him and see what he says."

Of course she was right. I did need to call Jake, but knowing how very disappointed he would be when I asked to postpone the wedding planning, I decided to wait until I got home that night to call him. As we exchanged emails and texts throughout the day, I didn't mention anything to him about my exciting news, knowing it would be much better if we could talk directly because of the impact it would have on the wedding planning.

As it turned out, however, I never had the chance. Casey was able to arrange the first meeting of the Basilica project team for that afternoon and my first meeting with the clients was at the end of the day, and by the time that finished up I dove right into the project. When I finally took a breather, it was midnight already and way too late to call Jake.

Knowing the next day would be equally busy, I got up extra early to call Jake and fill him in on my big news.

"This just never happens, an associate being put in the lead position on a project this massive," I told him excitedly.

"I'm so happy for you, sweetheart," Jake said, and I could hear the smile in his face. "But I can tell there's a 'but' coming."

Could he really tell that from over the phone?

"Well, unfortunately there is."

"And?" he asked.

"And—please don't be disappointed—and as much as I want to move our plans ahead quickly, I just don't see how I can plan a wedding and do the church project at the same time."

"Oh."

"Jake, I know you're disappointed, but I want our wedding to be everything we have dreamed about."

"I won't lie, I am disappointed. You know I would marry you tomorrow if I could, but I do understand and I'm happy for you. I know it's a huge opportunity and you deserve it. But let me ask you one thing. You said the church will take two years to build. Are you saying we have to wait until it's complete before we can get married?"

"Not at all!" I assured him. "I'm not waiting that long to become Mrs. Jake Baxter! I'm just asking for six months or so before we start our plans. Six months will get the project underway and it won't be as crazy as it's going to be for the next few months."

"You know we can still do Vegas," he teased.

"I'll keep that in the back of my mind," I teased right back. Now that it was out in the open, I could fully enjoy the opportunity I had been handed. Still, I knew that six months was what I had promised Jake and I would need to stick to my word. With that difficult discussion out of the way, we talked about more mundane things before we each had to run off to work.

That was the pattern every day for the next few weeks. Phone calls, texts, emails flew between us, but we weren't able to get away for in person visits. Jake's business was also flourishing and he was working seven days a week trying to keep up. They had put on another crew to try and move things along, but the shortage of skilled construction workers meant he and Charlie were having to do more and more of the work themselves, leaving them little time for marketing of their completed houses and finding new projects to start. Delays in material deliveries caused even more disruptions, and weekend after weekend we had planned to spend together had to be cancelled at the last minute.

Finally having reached the breaking point of loneliness, we found time for a weekend together. With a whole team working with me, it was easier for me to get to Chicago and I told Jake I would be there by late Friday afternoon. As easy as I made it sound, it was anything but to get time off so early into the church project. Working into the early morning hours each evening, I was exhausted, but it would be worth it when I could hold Jake in my arms again. Still, as usual, it was a mad dash for me to get out of the office to make my flight.

"You can call if something comes up," I told Casey as I checked my plane ticket and turned off my computer, "but only if it's something that honestly can't wait. I owe it to Jake to put work behind me for this weekend, at least."

"You can count on me, Paige," she said as she trailed me to the elevators. "I am not planning on talking to you until Monday morning. Give Jake a hug for me, will you?"

"I will, and thanks for all the extra work you put in this week so I could make this trip. I really appreciate it," I told her. If she hadn't worked equally long hours, I knew I wouldn't be able to get away.

With one final smile, the elevator doors closed and my weekend had officially begun.

Chapter Eleven

"This wait to see you is killing me, Paige. How much longer till you're here?" Jake asked. The sound of power tools and hammering nearly drowned out his question, but I could hear how impatient he was. He had just recently undertaken his newest renovation project and for a moment I wondered if my presence would be enough to draw him away from his work.

I was equally anxious for our long-awaited reunion, and each of us had grown more frustrated with the delays that had kept us apart the past few weeks, but the day was finally here and I couldn't wait to feel his strong arms around me.

"I'm just a few blocks away, baby," I assured him, knowing I was doing all I could to get there quickly. A promise of an extra healthy tip for the cabbie had brought about a death-defying trip from the airport and I had to keep assuring myself all the near collisions we had experienced on the trip would be worth it when I finally saw Jake.

"Rats," I said into the phone. "We're still a few blocks away, but there's construction everywhere and we've almost come to a complete stop. It might take a little bit longer."

"Have the driver pull out onto a side street and maybe you can avoid it," Jake suggested, the frustration of yet another delay evident in his voice.

"Oh wait," I told him. "It's okay. Now we're moving again." The car began to pick up speed and a smile finally crossed my face. Just a few more blocks. I picked up the small suitcase from where it had been tucked near my feet in preparation for making a quick exit from the cab as I juggled the phone at my ear.

The sound of power tools on Jake's end of the call had been replaced by birds singing, and I knew he had exited the house to stand at the curb to greet me, most likely covered in drywall dust. The thought brought a smile to my face.

"Can you believe this day is finally—"

I never got a chance to finish my sentence.

"Paige? Paige, can you hear me?" Jake screamed into the phone. Something was definitely wrong and a feeling of dread overwhelmed him. This wasn't a simple case of a dropped call. Before the phone went dead, a horrible screeching sound had nearly blown out his eardrum and all of his subsequent pleas to Paige to pick up the phone again were going unanswered.

"What the hell was that? Did you feel that vibration? It was like something exploded nearby," Charlie said as he walked up to Jake, taking off his protective mask as he got closer. Both men were covered in a fine layer of dust and debris as the deconstruction of the house they were working on continued. Jake didn't seem to even notice he was talking to him. "I thought Paige would be here by now."

"What? Yeah, she should be, but I was just talking to her on the phone when it went dead," Jake said as he continued to try and reconnect with Paige. "She said she was just a few blocks away."

"Did you feel that explosion?" Charlie asked again, noting that Jake was still preoccupied with his phone. "Hey man, are you even listening to me?"

"I'm sorry," he said as he finally looked at Charlie. "What are you talking about?"

"Boy, you got it good for that girl," he teased. "I asked if you felt that explosion. It shook all the windows in the house. Should make it easier to knock them out when we get that far."

Jake still looked confused.

"Are you telling me you didn't feel that?"

"No, I did, but it happened right at the same time I was talking to Paige and the phone went dead...Oh Christ!" Suddenly a look of horror filled Jake's eyes and he didn't speak.

"You're not thinking that was Paige?" Charlie asked, hoping beyond hope that he was wrong as the shrill sound of emergency vehicles began to invade both of their thoughts.

Grabbing Charlie's arm, Jake hesitated to put into words what his mind was now telling him. "Do you hear those sirens? Are you sure it was an explosion? Could it have been an accident?"

Even as the words came out of his mouth, a Chicago Police Department squad screamed through the nearest intersection, followed closely behind by an ambulance rig.

"Oh my God! Paige!" Jake cried before taking off as fast as he could run in the direction of the now-slowly dying sirens, leaving Charlie standing opened mouth behind him before he realized what Jake was thinking.

"Jake, wait for me!" Charlie cried before hopping in his pickup to follow his friend. It had to be a mistake. Jake was just overreacting. While they were out ambulance chasing, Paige would pull up in a cab, safe and well, and wonder where they had disappeared to. At least, that was what he hoped. Deep down inside though he felt that his friend's life was about to be ripped apart.

Turning the corner, Jake could see the growing number of emergency vehicles converging on an intersection several blocks in front of him. A small thin, wisp of smoke wound its way above the crowd that had gathered at the accident scene. Even though the sun was shining high in the sky, the flashing red, white, and blue lights of the police and fire vehicles reflected off the windows in neighboring buildings adding an unreal backdrop to the unfolding rescue.

His heart beating so fast it threatened to jump out of his chest with each breath he took, Jake's steps slowed as he neared the scene, his lips moving in an unspoken prayer that Paige wasn't in the cab he saw pinned on its roof against a coffee shop building. As if in a trance, he slowly pushed his way past the growing crowd of gawkers intent on seeing for himself before being stopped by a police officer.

"That's far enough, sir," the officer told him as Jake moved by him. The officer quickly grabbed his arm to keep him from progressing into the scene. Jake, still in shock over what he was seeing, slowly looked down at the man's hand on his bare arm as if not comprehending what was happening.

"I think that's my fiancée in the cab," he said quietly. The steely look on Jake's face almost defied the officer to stop him. Without another word, the officer slowly removed his hand.

"I'm sorry, man, but you probably shouldn't go up and look. It's pretty bad, if you get what I'm saying."

Nothing the man said would stop him from going to Paige and, fearing the worst, Jake started once more to slowly approach the cab, seeing that the tires on the vehicle continued to spin and smelling the acrid odor of burnt rubber and gasoline. Coming around the back end of the cab, he almost stumbled over the body of a man—or at least half of his body. The other half was crushed under the weight of the cab. As an EMT placed a sheet over the dead man, Jake slowed his step and took a deep breath to steady himself before his eyes were temporarily blinded by the sun's reflection off a piece of metal. Looking in the direction of the light he realized he was looking at Paige's cell phone and his heart sank as he dropped to his knees next to the crumpled cab, terrified of what he would see. How could anyone survive that kind of impact? Tears welled in his eyes and his body began to shake in grief before a faint sound came from the wreckage. Suddenly he was on high alert as he peered closer into the vehicle.

"Paige!" he shouted. "Oh my God, Paige! Can you hear me? She's alive! I can hear her," he cried as a nearby police officer suddenly dropped to the ground next to him, shouting for the crowd to be quiet. They both strained to hear any sound coming from the car.

"Are you sure you heard something?" the officer asked after a minute of the only sound being something dripping from the vehicle.

"Yes, she's alive, I know it!" Jake stated emphatically. "You have to help her."

"I'm not so sure…Wait, you're right. It's faint, but I can hear something too." With proof that the emergency response was no longer just going to be a body recovery, the car was suddenly swarmed by police and fire responders trying to find a way to get the last victim out of the vehicle.

As Paige's faint moans continued, Jake wasn't about to wait for someone else to get to her, and before anyone noticed what he was doing, he had torn away the front windshield of the cab and crawled into the wreck, seemingly oblivious to the glass and sharp pieces of metal tearing at his skin. He felt no pain other than what was in his heart at the thought that Paige could be dying while everyone else tried to figure out what to do.

Maneuvering his body as far into the vehicle as he could, he finally looked up to see the woman he loved more than life itself wedged into a small area that somehow had miraculously not been crushed in the accident. Blood dripped down her face and she appeared to be unconscious, but she was definitely alive and he reached out to take her hand, the one part of her he could reach, as he begged her to wake up.

"Sweetheart, I'm here and we'll get you out as soon as we can," he said through tear-stained eyes. "Don't give up. Oh please, don't give up. I love you so much, Paige."

As Jake continued to talk to her, the police officer tried to get Jake out of the vehicle.

"Look, man, we need to let the EMTs get in there and see if they can help her. You need to get out so they can do their work."

"No, I'm not leaving her," Jake insisted. "Let them crawl in here with me, but I'm not leaving her. She needs to know I'm here for her."

None of their prodding, ordering, or cajoling could get him to leave Paige's side, and finally they just gave up trying and went to work. Getting an IV into her hand was about all they could do medically until she was freed from the wreckage, but at least it would keep her from going into shock and provide some relief for her battered body until she was freed.

By the time the jaws of life were ready to be implemented, protective gear was placed over Jake and the EMT at his side to keep them safe while the firefighters ripped the car apart. The shrill sound of the metal being torn piece by piece away from her body seemed to go on forever.

As the last of the vehicle was ripped back, Paige's body slumped toward the ground, held aloft only by the seat belt still strapped across her torso. A hard-sided suitcase had fallen to the ground as the metal was released.

"Look at that," one of the firefighter's said. "That suitcase might have just saved her life."

With the majority of the vehicle holding Paige captive now removed, the men worked quickly to cut her seat belt away before carefully placing her on a backboard and carrying her away from the vehicle. Paramedics immediately went to work as Jake attempted to reach Paige's side, but he was kept back once again as they worked to save her life. Since the work had begun to free her from the vehicle, she had made no further sounds and the dread that had wound its way around Jake's heart was beginning to build once again.

"She's still alive, man, so don't give up hope," the officer said. Jake finally looked away from Paige and into the eyes of the officer. "You probably saved her life, if you think about it. If you wouldn't have heard her, we might not have gotten to her in time, and that's the truth. Is she your wife?"

Looking back to where Paige lay still as death as the paramedics worked frantically to keep her alive, Jake hoped that they would still have that chance.

"She's my fiancée. She was on her way to meet me and we were on the phone when the accident happened. This is all my fault. I kept pushing for her to get here as soon as possible. She told me she offered the cabbie double fare if he could hurry."

"It's not your fault, man. From the looks of things, the cabbie did nothing wrong. Witnesses are saying that the car that hit them blew through the stoplight. Never even slowed down, is what we were told. Sucks that the driver of the car that hit them walked away with hardly a scratch. I know it looks bad, but I've seen people survive a lot worse accidents. I have a feeling about this one and I think she'll be all right. Just don't give up on her, man."

With a couple of strong pats on Jake's back, the officer moved on, leaving Jake standing there, too afraid to even dare hope that Paige would pull through.

Charlie had finally been allowed to make his way through the crowd to Jake's side just as the paramedics were loading Paige into the ambulance for transport to the hospital. She still hadn't regained consciousness.

"Sir, we're taking her to Mt. Sinai trauma center. Do you want to follow us?" the ambulance driver said hurriedly.

"Jake, let me take you," Charlie said, grabbing his arm to make sure he was listening.

"I want to go with Paige," Jake insisted.

"I understand that, sir, but I recommend you go with your friend. She's stable for now. Do you know where to go?" he asked again.

"Yes, I know where to go," Charlie assured him. Taking Jake by the shoulders, he steered him back toward the pickup.

"Come on, man. Let's get going. She's in good hands. I'll drop you off and then come back and close up the house and let the crew know what's going on."

Jake could barely pry his eyes away from Paige even as the doors of the ambulance shut. With a final slap on the door by a firefighter, the ambulance lights and sirens were activated and the vehicle began transport to the hospital as Jake and Charlie ran for the truck to follow them.

The ride to the hospital seemed to take forever and by the time they arrived Jake had almost convinced himself that Paige was gone. All he wanted was a chance to say good-bye and to tell her one more time how much he loved her. Every thought running through his brain was of the missed opportunities they had and how much time they had wasted being apart. And now, without warning, it appeared as if his world had come crumbling down.

As soon as the truck screeched to a stop in front of the hospital emergency entrance, Jake flew inside. It took a moment to find someone who could help and he raced to the reception desk. "Paige Cooper. Where is she?" he demanded.

"Are you family?" the receptionist asked.

"For God's sake, woman, answer my question!" he thundered. "Where is Paige?"

The look in his eyes was dark and angry and she quickly answered. "I'll get her doctor right away, sir," the receptionist told him before quickly picking up the phone, "Miss Cooper's family is here," she said before turning back to Jake. "The doctor will be with you as soon as he can."

Jake began pacing, desperate to see Paige or to at least have someone tell him she was still alive. Half an hour later, and just before he was about to once again unload on the receptionist, a doctor began walking his way.

"Are you Miss Cooper's husband?" he asked.

"Her fiancé. Is she alive? Can I see her?" Jake asked with barely controlled rage.

"Does she have any family here? I really need to talk to her family," the doctor said smugly, seemingly not at all concerned by the questions before him.

"I am her family. Just let me see her," he begged as the doctor seemed to reconsider.

"Miss Cooper is getting prepped to go up for surgery. She has a pretty severe pneumothorax of her left lung, broken ribs, and a broken wrist. She might also have internal injuries, but we don't know for sure. I'll come back down after surgery and let you know more when I know more."

"But she's not going to die, right? You're telling me she's not going to die? Can I see her before she goes to surgery?"

"We'll do the very best we can for her, but there are no guarantees." Laying his hand on Jake's shoulder, he saw the desperation of the man. "You can see her just for a moment, but we need to get going. Follow me. Be prepared, there are going to be a lot of people working around her and she's already attached to a lot of equipment, and there is a lot of blood, so it's not pretty."

The words of the doctor barely registered with Jake as he followed behind, holding his breath as he waited for his first glimpse of Paige. Turning the corner he suddenly saw her looking small and helpless in the midst of the chaos that was going on around her. The quiet voices of the hospital staff barely registered with him as he focused on the beautiful but now-battered face of his beloved, still covered in blood.

He hesitated a moment at the foot of the bed, unsure what to do until a nurse gently guided him around to the side of the bed. "You can go to her. Talk to her. She can't respond because of the tube down her throat, but hold her hand and let her know you're here. I am sure she's scared and you'll be a comfort to her."

The nurses and doctors parted to make way for him to come to Paige's side. Jake slowly reached out and grasped her small, lifeless hand in his own, realizing that her engagement ring was missing from her swollen fingers, but feeling the warmth that emanated from Paige's hand gave him hope. He leaned down and gently kissed her hand.

With tears in his eyes, Jake whispered, "I love you so very much. Please don't leave me." An unexpected slight squeeze from Paige's hand was the answer he was praying for and he never wanted to let go.

"I'm sorry, sir," the doctor finally said. "We need to take her up now. I'll come and find you when the surgery is over and give you an update."

Kissing her hand one more time, Jake whispered into Paige's ear. "I'll be right here when you get back." As they whisked her away, he closed his eyes and said yet another prayer.

Head hanging low, he slowly made his way out of the treatment area before being directed to a waiting room and collapsing into the first empty chair, oblivious to the stares directed his way from the other people in the room. As the time passed ever so slowly, the room began to empty until Jake was the only one left. Sitting in the same position for hours, head bowed, hands clasped together, he stared at the floor in front of him, worried that the lack of information meant something had gone wrong.

The stillness around him was shattered by the welcome sound of his mother's voice.

"Jake, we're here," she told him as she quickly wrapped her arms around him and his father and Holly took seats nearby. His father's comforting pat on Jake's arm did little to stem the tears falling silently down his cheeks. The hours of waiting had taken a toll on him.

"How did you know we were here?" Jake asked when he could talk.

"Charlie called and told us. She's going to be okay," his mother insisted. "God didn't bring her into our lives to take her from us so soon. I know that as sure as I know how much you love her, and you know I am always right, don't you?"

With a deep sigh and a nod of his head, Jake prayed that this time, of all times, his mother would be proven right, and they settled in to wait once again.

In the next hour, Charlie arrived along with members of their crew, all as equally taken by Paige as Jake was and all wanting to offer words of comfort in this trying time. As the hours passed, the room filled with Jake's family and friends, all hoping to lend their support. When the waiting room was full to bursting, Paige's doctor finally came in.

"Miss Cooper's family?" he asked as he looked around the packed room.

Standing and making his way to the doctor, Jake said, "Is Paige okay?" The fear throughout the room was palpable.

"Would you like to go somewhere more private and talk? There are a couple of things we should discuss," the doctor asked as he scanned the many faces in the room. If it was good news, wouldn't he have just said so?

"Just tell me she's okay first," Jake begged.

"She came through surgery pretty well." The room let out a collective sigh of relief, but the doctor continued, "Come with me and we can talk more."

The doctor held out his hand to encourage Jake to come with him, and with a worried look at his family, he finally followed the man to a small conference room.

"So what aren't you telling me?" Jake asked.

"As expected she had a pretty severe pneumothorax, five ribs are broken, the wrist is broken, and the right shoulder was separated. We stitched up a fairly large cut on her head and she does have a severe concussion."

At the doctor's words, all the tenseness in Jake's body released as a smile spread across his face. That didn't sound so bad. Paige was alive and that was the main thing, but then he remembered the doctor's words.

"You said there was two things. What else haven't you told me?" Jake asked.

"We can't say for sure, but with head injuries like she sustained, there are often lasting issues."

"Like what?" Jake stammered. Suddenly the fear was back.

"It's not always permanent, but oftentimes there will be some lasting memory issues. While it's rare, the issues can sometimes be quite severe."

"Are you telling me she's going to be a vegetable?"

"No, not at all. It's just sometimes patients who have sustained severe head trauma have trouble remembering things. It's usually only temporary for a few months after the injury, but you should be aware it's possible," the doctor told him.

"Are you saying like she won't remember where she put her keys, or she isn't going to remember who she is?"

"Honestly, it can be either end of the spectrum, or anything in between. We'll just have to wait until she wakes up to find out if there is a deficit or not. I just wanted you to be aware of the possibility."

Jake was silent as he attempted to come to grips with all that he had been told. Still, she was alive and that was the most important thing.

With the weight of his knowledge crushing him, Jake finally was guided into Paige's room. He couldn't help the gasp of shock that escaped from his lips. All the alarms and beeps and chirps of the equipment Paige had been connected to before surgery had been replaced by the near-silent drip of an IV affixed to her left arm. Paige's beautiful face was as white as the large dressing above her eye and marred by two black eyes. He quickly moved to her side to take her hand gently in his, hoping for that squeeze again that would let him know she was going to be okay.

With the breathing tube removed, he was able to gently kiss her lips and to feel her breathing. Totally fixated on watching her, he barely registered a nurse pulling a chair next to the bed and guiding him into it. He would have given anything to be able to crawl into the bed with her and hold her close, but she looked so fragile he was afraid to do more than stroke her hand.

Long after the sun had come up and night began once more, he sat there, not moving from her side and ever mindful of what the doctor had cautioned him about her memory.

Jake's family came in for a brief visit, with his mother echoing the words of all the nurses, who for hours had tried to get him to go home and get some sleep. But Jake refused to leave and eventually his family and friends left for the night with promises to return the next day.

The nurses coming and going from the room for vitals or changing IV bags became used to the sound of Jake's voice as he talked quietly to Paige until he finally succumbed to his own need for sleep, and with assurances from the nurses that Paige would not be disturbed, he climbed into bed next to her and held her gently before he drifted off.

Chapter Twelve

The pain I felt was like nothing I had experienced before. My head throbbed, my body felt like one giant bruise—even opening my eyes was a struggle. As my surroundings began to come into focus, I heard the sound of someone breathing next to me and wondered if David had stayed the night, even though I didn't remember him being in the apartment last night. Slowly opening my eyes, I turned to look at him.

A scream of pure terror erupted from me as I struggled in vain to get away from the stranger who lay next to me with his arm across my stomach. The terror became even more acute when I realized I wasn't even in my apartment.

My screams brought people running into the room from every direction as I tried frantically to get away from the man, who now was fully awake and trying to grab me as I pushed him away, noticing for the first time the cast on one wrist and the sling on the other arm. What in the world was happening to me?

"Paige, calm down, sweetheart. You're going to hurt yourself," the man kept telling me.

The world was spinning out of control around me and everyone was yelling at me at once.

"Paige, please calm down. You're going to be all right."

"Hold her down so she doesn't hurt herself."

"Get a sedative ready."

"Paige, please!"

Everyone around me was talking at once, with no one telling me what the hell had happened to me. Frantically looking from one face to the other in wild confusion, desperate to find one person I recognized who could tell me what was going on was futile. The faces looking back at me were those of complete strangers as I backed into a corner of the room, in massive pain, desperately seeking a way out of the room.

Finally a calmer voice broke through my confusion. The nurse standing to my left asked everyone to be quiet.

"Paige, I'm your nurse and my name is Holly. I know you're confused about what's going on, but please let me help you back to bed before you hurt yourself."

"Why am I here? Where the hell am I?" I demanded to know.

"You're at Mt. Sinai Hospital in Chicago. You were in an accident and you've been here for a couple of days."

"Paige, please honey, please let me help you," the man who had been in bed with me said.

"Don't call me honey! That man was sleeping on me. Get him out of my room," I shrieked as I shrank further into the corner, my arms wrapped tightly around my body in an unconscious protective reflex.

"Paige, what are you talking about? You know who I am," he said with a look of surprise and sadness on his face.

"I don't know you. I've never seen you before. Please, someone get him out of here," I pleaded.

"What's wrong with her? Why doesn't she recognize me?" the man asked the medical staff as I slumped to the floor of the room. My legs just couldn't hold me any longer and I was having trouble catching my breath.

"I....I can't breathe," I gasped in fear before the woman who claimed to be my nurse rushed to my side and with the aid of two orderlies helped put me back in the bed. My breath was coming in short gulps and it felt like an elephant was sitting on my chest.

Affixing an oxygen tube around my face and tightening it under my nose, the nurse instructed everyone to leave the room. The man I was so desperate to get away from didn't move.

"Jake, you need to leave too. Just give me some time to talk to Paige. I'll come find you when I'm done."

The man slowly left the room, his eyes never leaving my face, leaving just the nurse and a doctor alone with me.

"Good morning, Paige," he said calmly. "I'm Doctor Michaels and I've been caring for you since your accident. I hear you seem to be having trouble remembering, is that right?"

"What do you mean? I remember fine. Well, I might not remember that I had an accident, but I know who I am and where I live." I looked quickly at the nurse as she stood near my bed checking my blood pressure.

"But you have no memory of the accident?" he asked.

Struggling for a moment, I tried to remember before finally admitting defeat. "No, I guess not."

"Well, what is the last thing you do remember? Let's try something easy. What year is it?"

"2015," I told him, confident in that detail at least.

The doctor quickly scribbled something in his notes and looked at me with concern.

"Tell me about your life," he asked.

"I'm Paige Cooper and I'm an architect. I live in Minneapolis. My boyfriend's name is David Dawson and—" Suddenly I stopped in confusion and looked at the nurse. "Did you say I was in Chicago? Why would you say that? Why am I in Chicago? What's going on here? What happened to me?"

The fear I felt upon waking up to see a complete stranger laying nearly on top of me was nothing to what I was feeling now, and I looked at the doctor and nurse, desperate for answers.

"It's going to be okay, Paige," the doctor said. "It appears that along with your other injuries from the accident, you have a bit of memory loss."

"How can that be? I know who I am and where I'm from. How can that be?" I asked, desperate for something to make sense of this Twilight Zone I had woken up in.

"I know this is scary, but try and stay calm, Paige. Some cases of memory loss only impact a portion of our memories. You said that it was the year 2015. Actually it's 2018. Most likely it's only temporary and your memory will come back. Maybe not all at once, maybe not all together, but most likely you'll start to remember more and more."

Had I really lost three years of my life?

"And if I don't, then what?" I asked, not sure I wanted to hear his answer.

"Let's cross that bridge if we come to it," he said kindly as he scanned through his notes once more. "For now, let's talk about the things we can do something about. You don't remember the accident, which is probably a good thing at least for now. As you can see, you did suffer some injuries. Your left wrist is broken and we've put that in a cast for a few weeks. Your right shoulder was separated, but it doesn't look like any tears or breaks. You'll have to use the sling for a couple of weeks just until the muscles and ligaments tighten up again. There is always the possibility that you might need another surgery, but we'll keep an eye on that."

"Is that it, then?" I asked. Although it was painful, it didn't seem too bad.

"Sorry, but no," he said. "When they brought you in to our emergency department, you had a collapsed lung, a pneumothorax. Probably caused by the broken ribs you also suffered in the accident. Your case was severe enough that it required emergency surgery, which happened later that night. You've already noticed some difficulty breathing, right?"

I slowly nodded my head.

"Pneumothoraxes occur when air escapes outside of the lung and becomes trapped inside the space between your chest and the lung cavity. In your case, it was caused by the trauma of the accident."

"Will it always be this hard to breathe?" I asked. Suddenly I felt as if my world was spinning around me and I was grateful for the oxygen tube.

"Not at all, although it will be a slow road to recovery for your lungs. You'll stay in the hospital for a couple of weeks so we can control your pain and build up your lung strength. We'll get you started on breathing exercises and walking and when you're released you'll continue both of those at home for several weeks. Do you have a place to stay in Chicago?"

"Well, no. I still don't even know what I'm doing here. I don't know anyone in Chicago."

The nurse's quick glance at the doctor escaped my view as I tried to figure out what was going on.

"I'll just fly home when I'm released, I guess."

"That won't be possible," Dr. Michaels said. "The change in air pressure could collapse your lung again."

"Well, then, I'll rent a car and drive home."

"Sorry again, but until you're fully recovered you won't be allowed to drive either. Do you have family you can call to come and get you?"

"My sister lives in California and my folks are touring Europe. There's got to be some other way for me to get home without them coming here."

"Well, that's your choice, but you will need to stay in Chicago until I'm sure it's safe for you to travel."

"But what about my memory?" I asked, still not quite believing that I had lost three whole years.

"I know it's easy for me to say, but try not to dwell on it. Tomorrow one of my colleagues who has experience in memory loss will visit with you and he'll be able to give you more information about what happened and what you can expect in the future. But until then, please don't let it bother you too much."

"That's easy for you to say! You didn't just lose three years of your life!"

At least he had the good grace to look like he sympathized with my plight even if there was nothing he could do about it. With a squeeze of my foot through the blankets, he left the room.

A deep sigh escaped my lips as I closed my eyes to try and stop the tears that threatened to fall.

"Are you in pain, Paige?" the nurse asked. She had been watching me closely as the doctor told me what little I now knew.

"A little maybe, but its fine as long as I don't make any sudden movements. Did you say your name was Holly?" I asked, attempting a small smile.

"That's right. Holly Baxter. I've been with you since you got out of surgery and I'll take care of you while you're here."

The sweet smile on her face as she tucked the covers in around me was my undoing and I burst into tears. Holly pulled up a chair close to my bed and took my hand in hers before handing me a tissue. She let me cry until there are no more tears left.

"Feel better?" she asked kindly.

"Yes, thanks. I'm sorry for being such a baby, but this is all so confusing. To wake up in a hospital, in pain, and find a strange man touching me, and then to find out that I don't even remember my own life…Doesn't that only happen in the movies?"

"Actually you'd be surprised at how often it happens after a trauma. From what I heard, you were very, very lucky to survive the accident, especially with such few injuries."

"Do you know what happened?" Maybe her explaining what had happened to me would trigger my memory about it all.

"The way I heard it, you were in a cab and the cab got T-boned by a speeding driver. You were pinned in the car. They told me you had a hard-sided suitcase between you and the vehicle that hit you and it probably saved your life. I guess it created a space that you were wedged into. If you hadn't had it, or if you hadn't been so petite, you would probably have been crushed."

My mind reeled as I replayed her words over and over, trying to find something that I remembered, but it was just a blank slate.

"But where was I going? Why was I in a cab in Chicago in the first place?" I was desperate to have someone explain things to me, and while Holly's information was a start, it just left me with more questions.

"Let's just leave it at that today. You've had a big day for your first day and a lot of shocks. You just rest for a bit and later when Dr. Barrette comes in to talk to you about your memory issues, I'm sure you'll feel better."

"But—"

"No," she insisted. "Just rest for now and I'll be back later to check on you."

After apparently sleeping for the last two days, I doubted I would sleep much more, but Holly was barely out of the room before my eyes closed.

Holly didn't get far from Paige's room before Jake demanded answers. "What's going on? Why can't she remember me?"

"You need to hear it from her doctors. Follow me," she said before leading me to a small conference room at the other end of the hall.

Dr. Michaels had been joined by another doctor and they looked up when the pair entered.

142

"Mr. Baxter, this is Dr. Barrette. He's an expert in memory loss and can explain more."

Shaking hands, the two men finally sat down across from each other.

"So what's going on with Paige? Why can't she remember me?" Jake asked.

"It appears Ms. Cooper is suffering from retrograde amnesia. This is most often caused by damage to the frontal or anterior temporal regions of the brain. Retrograde amnesia means remote memories are more easily accessible than events occurring just prior to the trauma and the events nearest in time to the event that caused the memory loss may never be recovered. This is because the neural pathways of newer memories are not as strong as older ones that have been strengthened by years of retrieval and re-consolidation."

Noticing the look of confusion on Jake's face, the doctor tried again in layman's terms.

"Paige had a significant bump on the front of her head during the accident that's caused her memory loss. You already know that she suffered a concussion from that injury, but sometimes retrograde amnesia doesn't show up until several hours after the injury."

"So how long until she gets her memory back? This isn't permanent, is it?"

"It's hard to say. Some patients only have very brief periods of memory loss, while others take longer. It's hardly ever permanent, though."

"But why doesn't she remember me?"

"I haven't examined Ms. Cooper yet myself, but Dr. Michaels told me she believes it to be the year 2015. Did you know each other before that date?"

"Well, no," Jake admitted. "But even so how could she not recognize the man she loves and is engaged to marry?"

"That's it, then. She doesn't remember you because she didn't know you then."

"So, I'll show her pictures of us together. That will jog her memory," Jake suggested, suddenly hopeful that he could get Paige to remember him.

"That works in some cases but not all," Dr. Michaels said. "But I need to caution you against pushing her to remember. Judging from how she reacted to you this morning, I would hesitate to push the issue with her at this time. From a medical point of view she is still quite fragile and her lungs need time to heal or she could easily suffer another collapse. You saw how afraid she was of you and how hard it became for her to breathe."

"So what you're telling me is that the only thing modern medicine can come up with is I just sit around and hope she remembers me again?"

"Something like that, yes," Dr. Barrette said.

"For how long?" Jake asked as he slumped back in his chair and cast a sad glance at his sister.

"Unfortunately, for as long as it takes," Dr. Barrette admitted before both doctors stood up and exited the room.

Jake buried his face in his hands in frustration.

"It's going to be okay, Jake," Holly told him. "You have to look at the positives. No one thought she would make it out of that cab alive and yet she's still here and her injuries are healing."

"But she doesn't know me!" Jake said in anger. "She's the love of my life and she is terrified of me!"

"I know this is hard for you, but look at it from her point of view," Holly cautioned. "She wakes up in a strange place with a man she doesn't know touching her! Can you imagine how confusing and scary that was for her?"

"I understand, really I do, but if I can't do anything to jog her memory, am I just supposed to walk away from what we have together?"

"Of course not. Even if she never gets her memory back, she fell in love with you once and you can make it happen again. Every woman loves you, Jake. You just need to bide your time and I know it will work out."

Even as she said the words she hoped it was the truth. Paige could be the exception to the rule and never get her memories back. If that happened… well, she didn't want to think about what that would do to her brother.

"Can I see her?" Jake asked.

"As much as I know you want to, you saw how she reacted to you earlier. She thinks you're a stranger that crawled into her bed. I know this is going to hurt you, but I honestly don't think you should go anywhere near Paige until she gets her memory back."

"Come on, Holly," he said as he slammed his fist down on the table in front of him. "That's bullshit and you know it. How will she ever remember me if I can't even talk to her?"

"Just let Dr. Barrette examine her and maybe we'll know more after that. But until then, promise me you won't go anywhere near that room. I mean it, Jake. Promise me."

"Fine," he said angrily. "Until I hear more from Dr. Barrette I will stay away."

Chapter Thirteen

The hoped-for good news from Dr. Barrette's examination never materialized. Paige's amnesia diagnosis had been confirmed and it was now certain that she remembered nothing after the start of 2015. In addition, the phone number she had provided for her sister in California had gotten them nowhere, as the number was not currently assigned, leading to a dead end. Local law enforcement was brought in to help track down the sister, but no person by the name of Jennifer Cooper could be found in California.

More bad news came when Dr. Barrette seconded Holly's recommendation that Jake go nowhere near Paige, at least until Paige was stronger and the possibility of another collapsed lung had decreased a bit. Jake was none too pleased with the news, but there was nothing he could do. At least with Holly at the hospital caring for Paige, he would have updates on her condition.

"Morning, Paige," Holly said cheerfully as she walked into the room to take yet another round of vitals.

"Hi Holly," I said, much less cheerfully. "Hasn't anyone come looking for me yet?" I'd been in the hospital almost a week.

"No hun, sorry," Holly said as she adjusted the blood pressure cuff. "Most likely your friends and family back home weren't expecting to hear from you, so they don't know to be concerned."

"Did you hear Dr. Michaels tell me I have to stay in Chicago for a while after I get out of here? I don't know what I'm going to do. I don't have any money or credit cards. At least, I don't think so. What am I going to do?"

"Actually, I've been thinking about that," Holly said as she finished with her paperwork and directed her full attention back at me. "What would you think about staying with me for a bit?"

"You don't have to do that," I said, although a spark of hope popped up within me. "This is my problem, not yours."

"Paige, if you haven't realized it by now, I've grown quite fond of you. The house is pretty big with lots of extra room and it wouldn't be a problem at all. Please think about it."

"You're okay with a stranger staying in your house while you're at work?" I asked, not at all sure if it was a good idea.

"Well, that's the other good thing. You wouldn't be alone. Normally I work nights; I've just been filling in for a friend who was on vacation. She comes back the week you're scheduled to get out of the hospital, and then after a couple of days off I'll be back on the night shift. But you wouldn't be alone. My brother lives with me and he would be with you at night. He's a really nice guy and I think you would like him."

"I don't know, Holly. It's a really nice offer, but I don't know if I'm comfortable being around a strange man."

"Not even if I vouch that he's not strange at all?" Holly said with a smile. "Seriously Paige, he's the nicest man I know and he'll help me take good care of you. In fact..."

As her voice trailed off, I guessed there was something she wasn't telling me.

"What?" I asked when she didn't continue.

"Well, I know we're supposed to let you remember on your own time, but that guy who was here with you when you woke up, the one you were so scared of?"

The hairs on my arm stood up just thinking about the creep. "What about him? I hope you banned him from the hospital. Hanging around complete strangers' hospital rooms. How did he ever get in here in the first place?"

"Please don't be upset, Paige, but that was actually my brother."

148

"Are you kidding me?" I asked in a much louder voice than I knew was appropriate in a hospital. Suddenly my breath was coming yet again in quick little gasps and I tightened the oxygen tube beneath my nose before I could continue. "And you want me to live in the same house with him? I thought you were becoming my friend."

"Paige, please let me explain. Jake saved you." The look on her face seemed to beg me to listen to her.

"What do you mean he saved me?" I asked with a mixture of repulsion and fear and overall confusion. The nightmare that had become my life after the accident was just getting worse.

"After the accident. Jake was the one who saved your life," Holly told me.

"What? I don't understand."

"Let me start over. Jake was working nearby when the accident happened and he ran to the scene. The cab was upside down, pinned to a building, and the emergency people who were at the scene didn't think there was anything they could do."

"You mean they thought I was dead?" I asked in horror.

"I'm sorry to tell you this, Paige, but while the driver that hit you walked away relatively unhurt, the driver of the cab died. They didn't even know you were in the cab until Jake heard you. At first no one believed him, and I guess looking at how badly crushed the cab was, they couldn't believe that someone could be inside the wreckage and still survive, but he forced them to listen until they heard you too."

For a minute I thought about what she had told me, trying to remember myself, but still it was a completely blank slate. Someone had died in the accident and I couldn't even remember their face.

"Jake crawled into the wreckage and held your hand and talked to you the whole time, telling you it was going to be okay and that they were going to get you out. It took about an hour, I guess, before they could finally cut you out and get you to the hospital. Until you woke up and were so scared by him being there, he never left your side."

"But why? Why would he still be here?" I asked. "Why would he care so much for a complete stranger?"

Holly turned her face away as she busied herself with one thing or another before answering me.

"That's my brother. It's important to him to be there for people. In fact, he has asked to come and see you again, but since you were so upset that first time you saw him, Dr. Barrette and Dr. Michaels suggested he stay away from you. I know he would really like to see you again, but that's totally up to you."

Having it all explained to me it now made more sense, even if it still seemed strange to me that a complete stranger would spend so much time at my bedside.

"I'm still not sure, but maybe if you were here too?" I suggested. A part of me now felt beholden to the man, and maybe letting him visit would be enough to satisfy him.

"We can probably figure it out. Let me see if Jake and I can work out our schedules and I'll let you know. But for now I think it's time for you to get some exercise. How about a walk down the corridor?"

With just a bit of help to make sure I didn't end up tangled in the IV line, I set off for a walk while Holly went back to the nurses' station. As I walked aimlessly up and down the hallways of the hospital I thought about Holly's offer to stay with her and, more importantly for me at least, the story she had told me about her brother. Someone who was willing to risk their own life to help another couldn't be all bad, but the lingering fear from seeing him when I woke up wasn't easy to shake. Still, the way things were turning out it didn't appear I had any option but to accept her offer to convalesce at her house.

As my thoughts took a dark turn, I wondered yet again why no one from my life had come looking for me. Surely someone had missed me by now, but was it as Holly suggested that people back home weren't expecting to hear from me? But who takes vacations by themselves? I couldn't remember ever having done so before, so why would I this time—and why Chicago of all places? And if I was on a business trip, someone from the office would expect to hear from me, wouldn't they? Oh, why couldn't I remember even the simplest of things about what I was doing here?

Taking my last lap of the hallway, I passed the nurses' station yet again and saw Holly on her cell phone giving me a thumbs-up as I got closer. Not sure what she was trying to say, I stood nearby and waited for her to finish the call.

"That was Jake," she said as she walked over. "If you're still okay with it, he will drop by tonight at around six for a visit. That's when my shift is over so I can be there too."

"I guess that's okay," I offered with a nervous smile, surprised that it was happening so quickly after I had agreed to see him. "As long as you promise me you'll be there too."

"I promise," she said with a smile.

"But why is this so important to him?" I asked her yet again.

"That's just the way he is. And I suppose, since he kind of did rescue you, he feels responsible for you."

"That's just ridiculous, but if it means that much to him I guess I'll see him. And then when he finds out I'm not going to drop dead he can satisfy his curiosity and get back to his own life."

Something flashed briefly in Holly's eyes at my statement. It was as if she knew something I didn't. But as quickly as it appeared, it was gone, leaving me to think I imagined it before I headed back to my room.

"Charlie!" Jake yelled as he put the phone back into his pocket. The sound of saws and hammering and drills made it hard to hear inside the house and Jake tried once again to get his partner's attention. "Charlie!"

Standing on a ladder mudding the newly installed drywall, Charlie finally noticed Jake's agitation and he paused and looked down.

"For Pete's sake, what's the matter? Did someone get hurt again?" he asked. Injuries were relatively rare on their job sites where safety was a priority, but lately it seemed they were having more than their fair share of sprains and bruises.

"What? Wait, no. No one is hurt. That was Holly on the phone. Paige has agreed to let me visit!" The smile on Jake's face left no doubt that he was more than excited at the prospect.

"How did that come about? I thought the doctors said you couldn't visit her?"

"They did, but Holly told Paige that I had been the one to save her life after the accident and she agreed."

"Wait a minute. So she still doesn't know that you're engaged?"

"No."

"And she still doesn't know who you really are?"

"Well, no, but she knows Holly and I are brother and sister."

"And?"

"And what? She wants to see me and that's all that matters," Jake said excitedly.

"I'm happy for you, man, really I am, but you shouldn't get ahead of yourself," Charlie cautioned.

"What do you mean? She wants to see me and we'll talk, and then she'll remember she loves me and everything will be back to normal."

"Jake, didn't the doctors tell you not to push her to remember? And didn't they also say it could take months before her memory comes back, if it does at all?"

"Why are you being so negative about this?" Jake asked, frustrated that his friend wasn't as excited as he was.

"Have you given any thought to what you will say to Paige? You can't tell her who you really are and you can't even talk about the time you have spent together. You're a total stranger to her—a total stranger who scared the life out of her when she first woke up. She's not going to look at your face and suddenly remember you."

"It could happen," Jake said defensively, although he knew Charlie was right. If she was going to remember him just by looking at him, it would have happened already and Paige's doctor had specifically told him not to try and force her to remember, which would only make her more fearful. He needed to approach this as if Paige was as much a stranger to him as he now, unfortunately, was to her. He would have to make her fall in love with him all over again just in case her memory didn't come back.

It was easy for Charlie to see that what he had been trying to tell his friend was finally sinking in by the dejected look on Jake's face.

"Jake, you have to know I'm happy for you. I know how hard it has been for you to stay away from Paige these last few days, but if you do want her to come through this and remember you, I think you have to be careful what you say and do around her. Give her time, my friend. That woman loves you more than anything and she'll come back to you if you just give her a chance."

"I guess."

"Now, if you can stop day dreaming about Paige, can we get some work done?"

As the time for Holly's brother to arrive crept closer, Holly was nowhere to be seen. In fact, I hadn't seen much of her all afternoon and I prayed she would keep her word before her brother showed up. All afternoon I had been replaying that moment in time when I woke up and saw him draped across me and remembering the fear seeing him like that had evoked. Whether he had saved my life or not, I wasn't sure I could go through with seeing him again and I reached for the nurse call button to cancel the whole event just as a massive bouquet of calla lilies walked through the door. Had someone from my life actually found me?

As the bouquet lowered, my excitement left as quickly as it had arrived. This was no delivery person; it was Holly's brother. The smile he directed my way did nothing to diminish the nervousness I felt as he walked by me to place the flowers on the ledge by the window. It was the first hint of anything in my otherwise-sterile room that someone cared about me. Too bad they were from a stranger.

I had watched his entire entrance without saying a word and now clutched the bed clothes closer to my chest with a slight grimace of pain. As the man noticed, he took a step toward me, his smile now replaced by a look of concern, before he stopped himself well short of my bed.

"Hello Paige," he said softly. "Thank you for letting me visit you. My name is Jake. Jake Baxter. Well, I guess you already know that, don't you?"

Where was Holly? I watched him as carefully as a gazelle would watch a lion that was stalking it.

"Hello," I said timidly, unable to think of anything else to say at the moment before Holly finally breezed into the room.

"Hi Jake," she said to her brother before coming to my bedside. "I'm so sorry, Paige. It's been one of those days and I couldn't get away as soon as I had hoped. Oh my, what beautiful flowers!" she exclaimed as she noticed the new addition to the room and walked over to smell the flowers. "Who are those from?"

"Me," Jake said. "Calla lilies are her favorite."

The look of surprise at that statement was evident on all three of our faces before Holly quickly said, "That's true, Jake; they are my favorite. What kind of flowers do you like, Paige?"

With Holly in the room, I forgot for a moment to be scared. "I love calla lilies too. Thank you for bringing them," I told Jake. He still stood by the window watching me carefully, but being careful not to approach me. From across the room he didn't appear as scary as he had the first time we met.

"From what Holly tells me, I have more than just flowers to thank you for," I said with a slight smile. "It sounds like you might have saved my life. I don't know if Holly has told you, but the accident caused me to lose some of my memory and I can't remember what happened. Maybe you can help fill in some of the blanks for me?"

Jake quickly glanced at his sister with a raised eyebrow as if asking if he should talk about the accident. Since Holly had already told me what she knew, I found that odd behavior, but she nodded at him before looking back at me.

"I'm happy to help where I can, although I don't know that there's much more I can tell you. Do you mind if I sit?" At my own nod he pulled a chair closer to my bed. For the briefest of moments I clutched the sheets a bit tighter, but then relaxed when he kept the chair a respectable distance away from me.

"My partner Charlie and I were working a few blocks from the accident scene. We heard the crash and I ran to see if I could help. Police and other emergency responders were there pretty quickly and it looked like there wasn't much anyone could do to help."

"What do you mean?"

"Well..." he looked at Holly before continuing. "I'm really sorry to tell you this, Paige, but the cab driver died. He had been pinned under the cab and didn't make it."

"And?" I prompted.

"There wasn't anything I could do, but as I was walking by the wreckage, something shiny caught my attention and I stopped for a moment. When I looked down to see a broken cell phone lying in the street I bent down to pick it up. That's when I heard it—just a faint moan of someone in pain. With all the sirens and everyone talking at once, I thought at first I imagined it, but then I heard it again. It sounded like it was coming from the wreck, but the cab was crushed from more than one angle and it was hard to imagine someone could actually be inside and still be alive. I dropped to my belly and crawled closer to the car and heard it again. A cop told me to get away from the vehicle, but I told him what I had heard and when we finally got everyone to be quiet, he heard it too. That sound was you."

Tears came to my eyes as he talked, but not because I was remembering. It was because of the tears in his eyes as he relived the experience.

"As soon as the cops realized you were still in there, they immediately started working to save you. It took a while, but they finally got you out and got you to the hospital."

"What Jake's not telling you, Paige, is that he actually crawled into the wreck to hold your hand while they were trying to extricate you. He put his own life in danger to make sure you weren't left alone. As many times as they told him to get out, he wouldn't leave your side. I know he's my brother and all, but he's a hero in my book. If it wasn't for him, you probably wouldn't be alive today."

The way Jake continued to stare at me was unnerving, and even though I didn't remember a minute of the whole ordeal, Holly was right. Jake was my hero and I now felt badly for how I treated him that first day.

"Thank you, Jake," I finally said. "I don't know if I'm ever going to remember any of it, but right now it's enough to know what happened and I'll always be grateful for what you did for me. I guess I owe you an apology for how I behaved that morning when I woke up and I'm sorry. It's kind of hard to explain how terrifying it is to wake up in a strange place and see a man you don't know right next to me, but you certainly didn't deserve my screaming at you and I'm sorry. If I'm going to be Holly's houseguest for a while, it might be a good thing if we're friends."

Offering his hand to me, I couldn't control the flinch of fear his action caused, but I knew he had seen it and he looked sad. I had to get past the unsettling feeling the man caused in me and I slowly offered my own, albeit fully casted, hand in return.

"I would like that very much," he said as the smile that had been on his face since he entered the room widened even more.

Not knowing what to expect from the visit, I didn't know what else to say. Jake didn't look like he was going anywhere and Holly also seemed to have settled in as she claimed a spot in the recliner tucked in the corner of the room. What seemed to me to be an uncomfortable silence took over the room before I finally spoke.

"Do you work at the hospital too, Jake?" I finally asked.

"No," he said. "Blood isn't my thing. I leave that to Holly."

Since I had been told I had been covered in blood when they got me out of the cab I found that hard to believe, but I let him continue.

"I'm an architectural designer. Do you know what that is? Well, of course you do. I mean, Holly told me you're an architect."

I wondered for a moment what else Holly had told him about me, but at least we had something to talk about.

"I am and I love it. I've only had my license for a few years, but I couldn't imagine doing anything else," I told him with the first bit of excitement I had shown since the accident. As I said it, I wondered again why my firm hadn't tried to find me. Maybe I really was in Chicago for a vacation.

"What types of projects are you designing?"

"Actually, even though I'm licensed as a designer, at heart I'm really just a contractor. I own a business with my friend Charlie Simmonds and we buy up old historic homes on the south side of Chicago and renovate them. We're trying to bring the area back to life, even if it is one or two houses at a time."

It was the last thing I wanted to hear and my excitement quickly waned. Although my work at the moment mostly consisted of new buildings, my passion in life was restoration of historic properties to their original design. It was heartbreaking to me to think of someone coming into a historic property and modernizing it as Jake seemed to be doing.

"Oh, I see," I told him, surprised by how disappointed I felt. Unsure where to take the conversation next, I was spared the decision when an orderly walked in with my dinner tray.

"Jake, I thinks that's our cue to leave," Holly said as she put her phone away and stood up. She had hardly said a word the whole time she was there.

156

Jake looked like a child whose favorite toy had been taken away from him, but he begrudgingly stood up to leave.

"I hope you'll let me come back and visit tomorrow," he asked as he stood near my bed.

"I appreciate it, but you don't have to do that," I said, still not sure why it was so important to him to keep checking up on me.

"I know I don't have to, but humor me, will you? Since I saved your life and all, I just want to make sure you're okay."

"Well, I guess if you want it's okay with me," I told him. As nice as everyone in the hospital had been, I was bored to tears most of the day with no one to talk to, and having someone new to visit with wouldn't be a bad thing. He reached once more for my hand and gave my fingers a soft squeeze before walking away.

"Jake, I'll meet you outside in a minute. I just want a word with Paige before I go."

His eyes never left mine as he finally walked out of the room and I wondered at the strange familiarity in the way he looked at me. Clearly he was a man who felt comfortable around strangers—something I never would have the ability to do.

"So, what did you think?" Holly asked.

"What do you mean?"

"Well, he's nice, right? You're not scared of him anymore, are you?"

"No, I guess not. You're right. He's very nice. It just still seems weird that he wants to keep coming back. He must have better things to do with his time than babysit me. I got the sense that he...no, never mind."

"What? He what?" she asked.

"It was like he wanted to ask me out, like on a date. The way he stared at me...I don't have a lot of experience in dating, but he looked like he was interested in me. I know that sounds stupid."

"It's not stupid at all. You're a beautiful woman, Paige, and you're just his type. I can see the two of you together."

"Don't be silly, Holly. I'm sure it is just him feeling like now that he's saved my life he's responsible for me. I'm just reading him wrong is all. You have a good evening and I'll see you tomorrow."

"Right you will, hun. Now, eat your dinner before it gets cold," she said with a pat of my arm and a smile before she left the room.

Pushing the food around on my plate but not really eating anything, I thought about Jake. He was definitely good looking—something I hadn't noticed the first time I saw him—but it was hard to miss the striking hazel of his eyes. Framed by dark eyebrows, his eyes stood out and seemed to look right through me when he spoke. He had short dark hair styled in a preppy kind of spike style, and he moved like a man totally at ease and confident in himself. The button-down shirt and jeans he had worn barely concealed the muscular build underneath, and with a shock I found myself wondering what it might be like to be held in his arms.

Talk about a 180-degree turn from thinking the man was a pervert! But having gotten to know him just a bit, it seemed my earlier assessment was unkind and undeserved. The man obviously cared about me because he had saved my life. He'd get over that soon enough and even if I never regained my memory, at some point in the near future I would be going back to Minneapolis and most likely would never see him again. Until then, he would be nice to visit with.

"So what did you think, sis?" Jake asked when Holly finally joined him at the elevators. "That went well, right?" The smile on his face said more than words could.

"Yeah, I think it was okay. Paige doesn't seem frightened by you anymore at least. But I do think you need to be more careful and remember what her doctors told you."

"Oh, you mean about the flowers," he said as he remembered that slip up.

"Jake, you can't try and force her to remember you. If she's going to stay with us, you're going to have to try and forget everything you know about her and let her remember on her own."

"I know. Don't you think I haven't thought endlessly about that very thing? All I want to do is take her in my arms and protect her. Did you see how she flinched when I tried to shake her hand? It's heartbreaking for me not to be able to help her."

"Maybe she shouldn't stay at your house," Holly suggested. Although she had told Paige it was her house, that wasn't exactly true. Holly actually lived in a small one-bedroom apartment near the hospital with no room for a houseguest. The house belonged to Jake and Holly would be moving in just while Paige was staying there. At some point they would have to come clean to Paige with that information, but that time wasn't now.

"That's not an option and you know it," Jake said in frustration. Even if Paige didn't remember him, he wasn't letting her out of his sight until she did.

"Fine, but you're going to have to do a lot more to make sure she doesn't suspect who you really are until she remembers on her own."

At the look of defeat on her brother's face, her tone softened. "Look, little bro, I know this is really hard on you. More than anyone I know how much you love Paige and how long you waited to find her, but she will come back to you if you just give her a chance to remember. The pain you're going through now will all be worth it the moment she does remember what you share. She loves you, and you two deserve a lifetime of happiness together."

Chapter Fourteen

Jake must have taken my acceptance of his visit to my room as approval to come whenever he felt like it. After the first visit the flood gates seemed to open and each day, sometimes twice a day, he would appear at my doorway armed with non-hospital food, more flowers, a card, or some other small gift. My favorite gift of all, though, was my battered suitcase and purse.

"I thought you might need these," he said as he placed the beat up items on my bed.

"Are they mine?" I asked, not recognizing the items.

"I sure hope so," Jake said with a laugh before realizing that I wouldn't remember them. "They were taken from the accident site and I just got them back from the tow yard where they took the wreck."

"You did that for me?" I asked in surprise.

"I figured you'd need something to wear when they spring you from this place, so I checked it out to see if they still had your things and this is what they gave me. Sorry to tell you though your purse has been cleaned out, but it looks like whatever's in the suitcase is untouched."

"You went through my purse?" I asked, feeling slightly violated.

"No, but they told me at the tow yard that any money and credit cards you might have had were long gone."

"It's okay, I guess," I said finally. At least I had some clothes to wear now.

Before I could open the damaged suitcase, I noticed what appeared to be dried blood on the top.

"Is that blood?"

"Sorry, I should have washed that off before giving it to you. Please don't be upset," Jake asked.

Unlike Jake, the sight of blood didn't bother me, but seeing the blood, most likely my blood, made me stop for a moment as I tried yet again to remember. Brief flashes of disjointed memories flew through my mind and I closed my eyes to concentrate on what I was seeing.

"Paige, are you okay?"

Opening my eyes to Jake staring at me in worry, I didn't know how to answer him.

"Yeah, I guess so. Seeing my things, I hoped it would bring back some memory of the accident, but there's still nothing." The disappointment was written all over my face.

"Paige, please believe me. You will remember. You have a wonderful life and eventually you'll remember everyone you love."

What an odd way to phrase it. I already remembered my family and friends. But his comment left me wondering about something else I had noticed the night before. There was a slight tan line visible on my left-hand ring finger. Could that mean I was married? Although I always wore jewelry and tan lines were evident on my other fingers, why would there be a tan line on that finger?

"You're probably right. At least, I hope you are. It's just so frustrating to not be able to remember three whole years," I said before getting out of the bed I was more than tired of and pacing around the room.

"So you still don't remember anything?" he asked, watching me closely.

"No. Every night I lay in bed and close my eyes, going back through things I do remember and hoping that one of them will have been after 2015, but there's nothing. Dr. Barrette said it could happen soon or months from now or maybe even never." Stopping my pacing for a moment I looked directly at him. "Jake, what happens to me if I never remember?"

Even though I was the one going through it, he looked at me as if the thought of never remembering was crushing him, and I thought I saw tears welling up in his eyes before he turned and looked out the window.

"I guess then you'll have to make new memories," was all he said. Easy for him to say. He wasn't the one who couldn't remember.

162

The difference between Jake's first visit to my room and those that followed was Holly was nowhere to be found. At first that made me a bit uncomfortable, but Jake never said or did anything to make me fearful and eventually I began to forget that he had ever seemed scary to me. As it turned out, the man was extremely easy to talk to and before long it seemed as if I had known him forever. While I wouldn't define us as friends, I did feel comfortable around him and actually began to look forward to his visits, if only to break up the monotony of the long days spent with nothing to do.

It didn't hurt that the man was extremely good looking. He was a man's man—well-muscled yet lean in stature, with a deep voice and an easy smile that was intoxicating to me. His dark brown hair was longer than I was used to in a man, but it was an attractive feature, especially as it offset his light hazel eyes. Most every time he came to visit he was dressed in well-worn jeans, T-shirt, and a button-down shirt, and he looked like the working man he was. A man in a suit was handsome, but I quickly discovered that being around someone who worked with his hands for a living had its own attraction for me.

At night, alone in my hospital room with the many sounds of the hospital an ongoing symphony that did nothing to help me sleep, his voice was in my head and thoughts of the man invaded my dreams. Jake was now visiting twice a day and I wondered how he got any work done after spending so much time with me each day.

Waking from a cat nap one such day, I saw him standing near the window, arms crossed, watching intently as I slept. For a moment I flashed back to the first time I had seen him.

"How long have you been standing there watching me?" I asked, rubbing the sleep from my eyes while trying not to be unnerved by him.

"Not long," he said quietly. "I didn't want to wake you."

There was something familiar and comforting about the way he looked at me that I couldn't quite put my finger on at first, but then I figured it out. Jake had a way of slowly blinking his eyes as he watched people that to me suggested he was carefully listening to what the person was saying to him and that he was entirely comfortable with the conversation. It's like the slow blink of a cat laying in the sun, eyes partly closed, and each time it slowly blinks, the cat acknowledges there's no danger and he can relax as he surveys the world around him. It sounds silly, but when Jake looked at me that way I felt safe and secure knowing that he was on guard.

"Tell me more about yourself," I prompted as I sat up in bed and crossed my legs in front of me. "Tell me about your business." Usually I was the one doing all the talking.

As the question left my mouth, I could see the excitement build in him.

"I'm sure it's nothing like the firm you work for, but we're growing and Charlie and I are pretty proud of the work we do."

"What exactly is that?" I asked.

"You already know we buy up old houses on the south side of Chicago and renovate and sell them. We don't make a lot, but it's enough to keep us going and keeping our prices low allows families to buy the properties. The south side has a big disparity in income and demographics from low income to upper-middle class, but a large portion of it has become run down and really forgotten as the crime rates have increased in the area and people are moving away."

"But why there? Why focus on rehabbing houses there and not, for instance, on the west side?" I asked.

"Because the need is greater on the south side...and because it's where I live. I ended up buying the first house Charlie and I worked on, so it's important to me to see the area thrive."

"I see," I said without much enthusiasm.

"You don't seem very interested," he said as he looked at me questioningly.

"It's not that. It's just, well, although I design a lot of new buildings, my passion is saving historic properties. Taking an older home and ripping all the character away so that it feels modern to a family is not my idea of preservation. Although what you are doing certainly has its place, to me it's just a tragedy that the craftsmanship and detail of the old homes is being destroyed."

"How can you say that? You know that's not what we're doing!" he exclaimed emphatically.

"How would I know that?"

"I mean, it's just that...well, of course you wouldn't know because I didn't explain," he said hurriedly. "Let me start again. We do add in modern

164

conveniences, but we also make every effort to save and restore the historical features of the house. Old fixtures are reused, millwork is reused, wood floors are refinished, and the heavy old doors are restored and rehung. And if we can't reuse the originals, we work with artisans to craft replicas so that the original historic look of the property is not lost. I'm as passionate about restoration as you are, and that's one reason we met in the first place."

As soon as the words were out of his mouth, he knew from the confusion on Paige's face he had made a huge mistake.

"What are you talking about? What does that have to do with how we met?"

"No, I mean Charlie. It's one of the reasons Charlie and I met and why we went into business together," he said hastily.

"Oh," I said.

"When you get out of here, I would love to show you one of the houses we're working on," he said as I tried to process how weird the last part of our conversation had been.

"I'd like that very much, but that's assuming they ever let me out. I'm beginning to have my doubts." Although I had only been in the hospital for a couple of weeks, it seemed like forever, especially in light of the fact that not one single person from my life had even tried to find out what was going on with me.

"Holly said she thought you were getting out in a day or two," he offered to my surprise.

"That would be great, but no one has said boo to me about it," I told him. "Every morning the doctors come in, look me over, ask a few questions about what I do and don't remember, and that's it. There's lots of breathing exercises and going for walks, but no one tells me anything. And no one from home has even tried to find me! Don't you think that's strange? Maybe I don't have any friends."

"How could that be? You're charming and funny and smart, not to mention gorgeous! I'm sure everyone back home just doesn't realize something's wrong. As your memory starts to come back, you'll realize how wrong you are."

"You seem awfully sure about it for someone I barely know," I suggested.

"Let's just say I'm a good judge of character," he said with a sly smile.

"Well, even if I do have friends, it's a pretty sad state of affairs that not one single person in my life has shown up or even called."

Tears formed in my eyes as I thought about it. Maybe I was truly alone in the world. Were my parents and my sister even still alive? Maybe no one was looking for me because there was no one to look!

"Paige, are you okay?" Jake asked with a worried look on his face as my tears fell.

Angrily brushing the tears away, I didn't know what to tell him. "It's nothing."

He didn't believe me and came to the side of the bed and took my hand in his. For the first time I didn't flinch at his touch.

"Come on, Paige. Aren't we friends by now? You can tell me what's wrong."

"What has happened in my life in the last three years?" I asked him through the tears. "Maybe my parents and my sister are dead and that's why they haven't come looking for me! What if I'm all alone in the world?"

"Oh Paige, you're breaking my heart. I wish I could convince you that everything is fine, that everything is going to be fine. You have so many people in this world who love you and everything is going to be okay. Please believe me," he pleaded with me.

There was true sadness in his eyes and I wanted so much to believe him, but there was no reason to. He just didn't have the answers I was looking for.

"Even if I can't remember, don't you think I would feel it if my mom and dad had died?" I asked.

Jake looked back at me with extreme sadness.

"I'm sure you have a family who loves you, Paige. But try not to worry. I'm sure you'll start to remember soon."

"I wish that were true," I sad sadly as the tears began to dry up. "In three years a lot of stuff could have changed. Maybe they moved somewhere else and I just can't remember. Same thing with my sister. Maybe she doesn't live there anymore."

"There you go," Jake said. "There could be lots of things that have changed in the time you can't remember and that would explain why no one has come looking for you."

Suddenly feeling awkward that he continued to hold my hand, I slowly withdrew it from his while noticing the look of disappointment on his face as I did so, and I hurried to change the subject.

The rest of the night passed by in quiet companionship as we enjoyed watching a movie on TV before Holly appeared in my doorway, trailed by Dr. Michaels making his late rounds.

"Well Paige, I think we've done all we can for you here at the hospital. I think tomorrow I'll sign your discharge papers and you can get out of here. I understand you'll be staying with Nurse Holly?" Dr. Michaels looked at Holly for confirmation.

"That's right, and we're happy to have her," Holly said.

"You'll get formal discharge papers tomorrow with instructions for continuing care, but basically you should rest, but make sure you stay active. Rest while sitting up, and do very light, low-impact activities, such as walking. It will be a few more weeks before you're fully recovered, so don't push yourself to resume regular activities too quickly, as that could trigger another lung collapse."

"I'm not exactly sure what my regular activities were," I said with a chuckle. After two weeks I could finally see a little bit of levity in my situation.

"Make sure your breathing is normal and pain has passed before you engage in household chores, high-impact exercise, and other physically strenuous activities. You might want to sleep in a recliner for the first few days. Sleeping in a recliner or with lots of pillows to prop you up in bed will cause less downward pressure on your chest cavity and lungs and you'll breathe easier."

"You can also put a pillow on your side, Paige, to make it more comfortable while sleeping, but I can help you with that when you get to the house," Holly said.

"And when can I go home to Minneapolis?" I asked.

"I'll want to see you one more time before giving you clearance to travel. My office will contact you through Holly's number and we'll get that scheduled in a couple of weeks. Until then, do you have any other questions for me?"

"No, but I did want to thank you. I know that I have been a pain since I first woke up and I'm sorry that I created such a scene. You all have been nicer than I deserved and I can't thank you enough."

"Don't give it another thought," Dr. Michaels said. "You're a wonderful young woman and I expect you to make a full recovery—memory included!"

"From your mouth to God's ears," I said with a wink as he walked out of the room.

"You have a big day tomorrow, Paige, so Jake and I will say goodnight, but I'll be in to do my usual rounds later tonight," Holly told me. She had just begun her shift.

Jake seemed surprised that Holly was urging him to leave, but he grudgingly got up from the very uncomfortable sofa he had been sitting on and gathered his things.

"Thanks for the company, Jake," I told him. "I guess I'll see you tomorrow."

"Call me when you know what time you'll be released and I'll come and pick you up," he said.

"Don't you have to work?" I questioned. Most of his visits had been restricted to his lunch hour and after work. "I don't want you to get in trouble."

"You forget, I'm the boss," he said with a smile. "Just give me a call and I'll be here to take you home."

"Thanks, I appreciate that," I told him.

Taking my hand in his, he stood and watched me without saying a word, and for a moment it looked like he wanted to kiss me before the moment was gone and he walked toward the door. "Sleep well," he told me softly.

A slight nod of my head was my only response before I realized just how tired I was and hit the button to turn off the lights in the room before settling back into my bed with a smile on my face. Not only was I finally being released, but I was going to be able to spend even more time with a man who was quickly becoming a friend, and maybe even more.

"Holly, wait up," Jake said as he sprinted down the corridor to catch his sister.

"Make it fast, Jake, I have a lot of patients to see." Even as she said it, she was making her way quickly to the nurses' station.

"Paige asked about her parents tonight," he said.

"So?"

"So, they died a couple of years ago and she doesn't remember it. Does that mean she is going to go through the grieving process all over again when she does remember?"

Holly stopped what she was doing to look at him. "Wow. That would be a heck of a thing to go through twice, wouldn't it?" Holly said. "I don't know the answer to that, but I'll check with Dr. Barrette and see what he has to say. You know, the more I think about that, there could be a lot more bad things she might have to re-live. You know, Jake," she said as she turned to look at her brother, "we are really going to have to be careful what we do and say around Paige. Maybe it wouldn't be a bad thing to broach the subject of 'what if" with her."

"You mean like what if her parents did pass away in the time she can't remember?"

"Yeah."

Chapter Fifteen

*A*s promised, after a long day of waiting for the discharge papers to come through, Jake arrived to take me home. As nice as everyone at the hospital had been, it was a relief to be discharged. As the orderly wheeled me to the patient pick-up area, I saw Jake standing next to a pickup truck that had clearly seen better days. The battered and aged truck seemed to match what I knew of Jake, though. Hard working, not overly concerned about appearances as much as getting the job done. It suited him.

It was the first time Jake had seen me out of a hospital gown and I nervously smoothed back a wayward strand of hair as I stood up from the wheelchair. Dressed in jeans and a T-shirt, I finally felt like a normal person again.

When I had opened my little suitcase after Jake brought it to me, I wasn't sure what I would find inside. To my surprise, it was mostly casual clothes, a couple pairs of jeans, a few shirts and a sweatshirt, and one very nice dress—clothing that I might have packed for a weekend getaway. The discovery answered the question as to why no one from work had come looking for me, but raised even more questions about my friends and family not missing me, and if I really was on vacation, why Chicago of all places?

"Now this is a much better look for you," he said with a smile as he gave me the once over before offering his hand to help me into the truck. "Let's get you home."

Staring out the window at the passing scenery, I could see Jake casting furtive glances my way as he kept up a steady stream of one-sided conversation.

Even though we had just seen each other the night before, he chatted nonstop while I tried in vain to find one thing out my window that seemed familiar to me. Eventually we pulled up to a wonderfully restored craftsman house and suddenly my attention was piqued.

"Is this Holly's house?" I asked excitedly. "It's gorgeous! Looks like early 1900s architecture."

"Actually, Paige, it's my house. Holly is staying with me."

"Oh, I thought Holly said it was hers."

"She likes to claim it for hers since she found it for Charlie and me," he said with a chuckle. "But it's mine and it was the first rehab project Charlie and I did. I liked it so much I bought it. How do you think we did with the restoration?"

I wandered around the first floor without saying much until I turned back to look at him. "It's beautiful. You do wonderful work and I'm sorry I doubted you." The home was wonderfully restored and something I would love to live in myself.

"You're forgiven. Would you like something to eat? Holly left for work already so it's just you and I tonight, I'm afraid."

"You don't have to go to any trouble for me. I'm just grateful I have a place to stay until I can get back home, and I don't want to be a bother. Just go about your night as if I'm not even here. I can read in my room."

"Nonsense," he said. "Aren't we becoming friends? I was rather looking forward to having some company. After a long day at work it's going to be nice to come home to a friend. But first, let me show you your room."

By the time Jake had shown me the room and I put away my few meager belongings, I came back downstairs to the wonderful aroma of non-hospital food. Making my way back to the kitchen, I expected to find him there, but it was empty.

"I'm out here at the grill," he shouted when he noticed me through the kitchen window.

Making my way out to the deck on the back of the house, Jake stood at the grill nursing a beer while tending to a single steak and a single chicken breast and a few other foil-wrapped items.

"You might not be hungry, but I was so I hope you'll join me," he said. "There's a bottle of wine already open, or I can get you a beer if you prefer. Your chicken will be done in just a minute."

"How did you know I like chicken?" I asked. Although I ate red meat, I did so sparingly.

"You told me," he replied, although I certainly didn't remember doing so. "I mean, that's what you usually had in the hospital, so I assumed you prefer chicken."

Pouring myself a small glass of wine, I stood nearby as he expertly worked the grill.

"Looks like you've done that a time or two," I told him.

"I've had a lot of microwave dinners in the past and had to learn how to grill out of self-preservation."

"Didn't your mother teach you to cook?"

"Mom can barely make cereal in the morning. Our housekeeper did all the cooking when I was growing up. Once Ian, Holly, and I all moved out, we had to learn on our own," he said with a laugh.

"You had a housekeeper?" Growing up I didn't know anyone who had staff in their house.

"Well, now you know my deep secret—my family has money," he said. "But don't hold it against me, because I should have said my parents have money. As you can see, all three of us kids work and we work hard for our money. None of us live off the family fortune."

As Jake filled each of the dinner plates I handed him with our respective meals, I asked about his brother as we sat down to eat.

"Ian? We don't see much of him these days. He lives on the west coast with his family. I know Mom and Dad would love to see more of him, but Holly and I talk to him often."

On my initial inspection of the house I had noticed a treasure trove of family photos spread throughout the house. His was obviously a very close family, but while there were plenty of family photos, there wasn't a single one of Jake with a girl. I hadn't had the nerve to ask Holly if he was in a relationship, but someone so good looking would certainly be.

"So Ian's married?" I said as casually as I could hoping for more information. "But you and Holly are not?"

"Nope. Holly was engaged once, but then changed her mind well before the wedding day. It was devastating to Mom, who would love to have a house full of grandchildren, but Holly hasn't come close since then."

"And you?" I asked, surprising myself with my directness.

He waited a beat before answering.

"I'm not married, but I am in love with a beautiful and talented young woman. In fact, we're engaged to be married." The look on his face as he talked about his fiancée was of a man totally in love.

Having no right to feel as I did, I felt my heart plummet, knowing how much I was starting to care for Jake. I had no claim on him, but the news hit me harder than I expected and I tried hard to keep the disappointment off my face.

"Oh. Does she live in Chicago?"

"No, actually she lives out of state." Jake's eyes were locked on mine and I couldn't tear my gaze away.

"Oh, long distance. That must be difficult. So when are you getting married?"

"We haven't set the date yet. Actually, a couple of weeks ago I thought we were going to pick a date, but something came up and now it's on hold."

"That's too bad," I told him. "Hopefully you can work it out. You're lucky. Some people never find the person they were meant to be with."

"Do you have a boyfriend?" Jake asked. The way he was staring at me was making me uncomfortable, but I didn't know why. Talking to the man about my love life just seemed wrong in so many different ways.

"Yes," I started to say as a look of anger flashed across Jake's eyes before he finally looked away from me. "Well, at least I think I do." With the memory loss who knew? "His name is David Dawson and he's also an architect at SNK."

Then it dawned on me. Why hadn't David come looking for me? I needed to call David! As all this was flashing through my mind, Jake's demeanor had quite suddenly changed. He stood up and began to clear his place setting before walking back into the house with no explanation.

My meal only half-eaten, I didn't know how to respond. Was the meal over? What had I said that upset Jake so? Up until that point we had been having a nice dinner and I actually was feeling comfortable in his home. Obviously I had said or done something to ruin it. My appetite now gone, I picked up my own plate and began cleaning up the kitchen.

Jake was moving around somewhere upstairs, his heavy footsteps leaving no doubt he was angry, but I didn't know what to do to make whatever I had done better. It looked like I would be spending the rest of the evening on my own.

Finding the cordless phone and grabbing a book to read, I walked out back to the hammock to call David with growing excitement about connecting with my life again.

"Hello," said a female voice I didn't recognize.

"Uh, sorry, I think I have the wrong number," I said before hanging up and dialing again.

"Hello," said the same, albeit now a little angry, voice.

"I'm sorry. I was looking for David Dawson, but I must have the wrong number." I had dialed very carefully the second time and knew I didn't misdial.

"This is David's number, but he's not here. Can I take a message?"

Finally it dawned on me. It was David's housekeeper. Although he had what I would consider a small apartment, one that was half the size of my own, he insisted on having a housekeeper to cook and clean for him.

"Please. Tell him Paige called and I'm in Chicago. I had an accident and can't drive myself home and I need him to come and get me. I'm staying with Holly and Jake Baxter and here's how he can reach me." I quickly rattled off the phone number I was calling from and Jake's address, both of which were on a note Holly had given me earlier. "Please ask him to give me a call back as soon as he can," I asked before throwing the note in the trash.

Even though I hadn't reached David directly, at least the wheels were in motion to get me home, and I settled back into the hammock with a smile on my face. It wasn't long before the book lay unopened on my chest and I drifted off to sleep.

"Paige?" Having been sound asleep, it took a moment before I became fully alert. "Why don't you come inside and sleep in bed, or at least the recliner like the doctor recommended?" Jake was standing above me with his hand out to help me out of the hammock. It was dark out already and the temperatures had grown substantially cooler since our meal.

"I'm sorry," I told him. "I guess I shouldn't have had that wine. It made me sleepy."

He helped me to my feet and wrapped a blanket around my shoulders as if I were an invalid being brought in from the cold, which I guess I was in some respects. All signs of his previous unhappiness seemed to have disappeared as he walked up the stairs with me before stopping in front of my bedroom door.

"Jake, I'm sorry," I told him as we stood there. I had the strangest sense of déjà vu as if he and I had been through this situation before.

"For what?" he asked.

"For whatever I did or said at supper that upset you. I didn't mean to make you angry."

"You didn't do anything," he told me as he looked down at his shoes. His failure to look me in the eye implied he wasn't being totally honest with me. How I knew that, though, I didn't know.

"I think you're being too nice. Obviously I did something and whatever it was, I'm sorry. Can we still be friends?" My time in Chicago was limited, but there was something about being near him that made me smile and I didn't want to lose that.

"Of course we can be friends," he assured me as he once again looked at me. "And honestly, you didn't do anything wrong. It's just something I have to work through on my own. But I'll set the world straight again and soon. Good night, Paige," he told me before placing a soft kiss on my forehead and walking away.

Closing the door softly behind me, I leaned against it and touched my fingers to where his lips had left a lingering warmth as the realization hit me. It was more than friendship that I wanted from the man. The desire for him that was building within me might be understandable—he was, after all, exceedingly handsome—but I needed to force myself to remember David. My parents didn't raise Jen and me to be cheaters, and as much as I might want Jake, I had to remember that.

Choosing to pile pillows on the bed rather than sleep in the recliner, I changed into the now well-worn concert T-shirt I had slept in for years and settled into bed. My lung recovery was going well and the ribs were healing nicely, but sleeping continued to be a bit of a challenge. Most any sleeping position I normally favored had become uncomfortable, and with Holly's advice in mind, I tucked one last pillow at my side and tried to sleep.

It didn't help. Hours later I was still wide awake. At first I tried to blame my inability to sleep on my medical issues, but finally had to admit that it was Jake. Each time I closed my eyes, a pair of hazel eyes drifted through my mind keeping me from sleeping. Reading would probably have helped me get to sleep, but my book had been left in the hammock and I didn't want to wake Jake by stumbling around an unfamiliar house trying to find it. Unable to sleep and knowing the sun would be up soon, I sat near the window as the neighborhood started to wake and lights came on in a few houses. A small car making its way slowly down the street slowed to pull into Jake's driveway and I realized it was Holly coming home from work.

The creak of a door further down the hall, followed by the sound of water running in the bathroom, told me Jake was also up. A quick glance at the bedside clock showed it was not quite 5:30—a full hour before I would normally be getting up for work myself—and I was just finally getting tired. Crawling back into bed and forcing myself to close my eyes after a long sleepless night, I finally drifted off.

Hours later I woke up to a now-silent house. Jake had already left for work and I assumed Holly was sound asleep. Trying to make as little noise as possible, I showered and dressed before making my way downstairs, unsure what to do with myself until I found a note from Jake on the kitchen table. He had left a pile of books and a few DVDs of some recent movies he thought I might like, and knowing he had been thinking of me gave me a warm feeling.

Grabbing a glass of orange juice from the fridge, I wandered around the house once again, noticing more details of the home's restoration. Jake had done an outstanding job on the house and it would be a great place to raise a family.

The thought should have made me happy for him, but instead I felt sad and a bit lonely. He was a great guy and if he had found the woman he loved I should be happy for him because that's what friends do. Trouble was, that's not how I was beginning to think of Jake. Each time we were together, I discovered something else about him that made him just that much more attractive to me. The way he walked. The way he threw his head back when he laughed. The fluidity in his every movement that exuded confidence in his own abilities and manhood. The way his eyes crinkled at the corner when he smiled. The way he gestured with his hands when he spoke. The well-worn boots and jeans he wore most every day. His dry sense of humor that appeared when I least expected it. Everything about him was endearing to me and I knew he was the type of man I could spend my life with. My attraction to him was becoming overwhelming.

In need of a concrete reminder that I shouldn't be feeling that way about the man, I searched the house again looking for a photo of Jake and his fiancée, and once again found none. How odd! In a house full of family photos, there should be at least one of the couple.

My search for photos complete, I headed for the back yard and picked up the book I had left on the hammock and was well into the murder mystery before being startled by the phone. It took me a few rings to actually find the phone, leaving me slightly out of breath when I answered.

"Baxter residence," I said breathlessly.

"Paige, are you okay?" Jake asked. "You sound like you've been running."

"I'm fine. Just took me a while to find the phone. I promise I've done nothing more exciting than read a book all morning," I assured him with a laugh.

"I'm glad to hear it. Would you like me to bring you some lunch?"

I was beginning to feel a bit hungry, but hadn't really thought about it and didn't want to interrupt his day.

"That's nice, but I'm sure you have better things to do than wait on me."

"It's not a problem. The house we're working on today is only about a mile away. I'll pick something up on the way."

"Or I could make something and have it ready when you get here," I suggested.

"That would be great!" he said, and I wondered if that had been his plan all along. Still, making him lunch was the least I could do after he had opened up his home to me.

It was almost 1:30 by the time Jake's truck pulled into the driveway and I hurried to get things ready for him as he walked into the kitchen and made a beeline toward where I was standing at the stove before suddenly stopping in his tracks and backing away. Just for a moment I had the feeling he was going to kiss me, and I wouldn't have objected if he did. For whatever reason it seemed so natural to me to be standing there in his kitchen, welcoming him home with a kiss.

"Hi. Lunch will be ready in just a minute," I told him as I felt my cheeks began to flush with a mixture of desire and embarrassment, and I turned back to what I had been doing.

He quickly changed direction and washed up at the kitchen sink before sitting down at the table as I placed a plate of sandwiches in front of him and ladled soup into his bowl.

There was an odd sort of tension in the air between us, leaving me unsure of myself and I hesitated to open my mouth. The normally steady flow of conversation from Jake was also absent and we ate with only a few comments. Where had the easy conversation we previously shared gone? As he ate, I studied him under lowered lids, overwhelmed yet again by how handsome he was, until I noticed a small piece of insulation that had attached itself to the collar of his shirt. Barely realizing I was doing so, my hand reached up to remove the debris just as he turned to see what I was doing and my hand brushed his cheek. For a moment neither of us moved.

Holly walked in just before I pulled my hand back and stared at both of us in surprise.

"I see you two are getting along well," she said with a grin before pouring herself a cup of coffee. "Jake, what are you doing home?"

From her question, I gathered coming home for lunch was unusual for Jake and I felt a little thrill that he had done so for me.

"Forgot my lunch," he told his sister as he looked back at his bowl. Funny he hadn't mentioned it to me. "We're working nearby and Paige volunteered to make me lunch."

It wasn't a lie exactly, but he was acting as he had been caught doing something wrong. Did Holly think I was hitting on her newly engaged brother? Getting to my feet, I offered Holly a sandwich and quickly placed it in front of her.

"Thanks for lunch, Paige. I better be getting back to work," Jake said as he deposited his plate in the dishwasher. "I'll see you guys later."

Holly seemed to be studying me as Jake left the house and it was making me uncomfortable.

"It's not what you think," I said, deciding to address the issue head on.

"What exactly do you assume I'm thinking?" she asked with a smile.

"I was only trying to remove some drywall that was stuck to Jake's shirt."

"Hmm," she said as she sipped her coffee. "To me it looked like the two of you were about to kiss."

"Not funny," I said. Now I was more than a little uncomfortable. If Holly hadn't walked in, that's exactly what I had thought was going to happen. "It was completely innocent."

"You don't have to convince me, Paige. You're two consenting adults and it's easy to see that you and Jake have an attraction to each other."

Oh my God! Was it that obvious?

"I assure you nothing is going on. I don't know what you think you're seeing, but I have a boyfriend and I know Jake has a fiancée. There's nothing going on between us. We're just friends."

"Paige, it's okay. Don't get worked up. I'm just teasing," she assured me with a laugh. "Does Jake know you have a boyfriend?"

"Yes."

"And what did he say when you told him?"

"We didn't really talk much about David before Jake changed the subject."

"I'll bet," Holly said.

"What does that mean?" I asked.

"What? Oh nothing. I guess I better take a shower before I have to go to work. Thanks for lunch, Paige. Do you need anything?"

"No, I'm fine, thanks. I think I'll take a walk later this afternoon."

"Why don't you wait for Jake and the two of you can go together tonight? As nice as this block is, this area's not really safe to be walking alone. Or you can come back to the hospital with me and I'll sneak you into our gym. Jake can pick you up on his way home."

"Thanks, but I don't want to get you in trouble. I'll just wait for Jake. But can I ask a favor?"

"Sure, anything."

"Can I use your computer? I thought it might help me with my memory if I could google myself and see what comes up. Maybe I have a social media page with pictures."

"That's a good idea, but unfortunately my laptop is being repaired right now. I dropped it down the stairs last week and Jake takes his computer to work with him. I hate to eat and run, but I better get going or I'll be late for work. Thanks for lunch."

"Jake, it's me," Holly said into her phone when she got back upstairs to her room.

"What's wrong?" he asked.

"Paige just asked me to use my computer so she could find pictures of her life."

"Damn," he said. "I never thought of that. What did you tell her?"

"What could I say? I lied. I told her my computer was in the shop and you take yours to work with you. She's probably going to ask tonight to use yours, so don't come home with it."

"That's all we need is for her to get on my laptop and see all the pictures of the two of us together. Thanks for the heads up. I'll have Charlie take it home with him tonight."

"Good idea. Now why don't you tell me what I walked in on at lunch? The two of you looked a bit cozy. Is Paige starting to remember you?"

"Not that I can tell, but I know her well enough to know she's starting to have feelings for me again, even if she doesn't remember us."

"She told me that she has a boyfriend. What's that about?"

"He's a guy that she dated before we met. A real piece of work, apparently. After she dumped him, he started causing problems for her at work and he was fired a few weeks before her accident."

"I'm sorry, Jake."

"What do you mean?" he asked.

"It's got to be hard for you to hear Paige talk about a boyfriend when there's nothing you can do about it."

"It's harder than you know. Last night when she was telling me about him, I lost my cool and stormed out of the room."

"Oh Jake, you have to be careful. I know it's hard, but you can't get mad at her because she doesn't remember you."

"I know, and I wasn't angry at Paige. I'm just incredibly frustrated by the whole situation. She even tried to apologize to me even though she had no idea what she had done to make me behave that way. You're right. I have to be more patient, but something has to trigger her memory again and soon, because I don't know how much more of this I can take. I just love her so much, Hol, and this is tearing me up inside. It takes all my willpower not to pull her into my arms every time I see her."

The agony in her brother's voice as he talked about Paige was heart-breaking for Holly.

"Just remember that for Paige's long-term health, you can't slip up. I know it's hard for you, but think about how happy you'll be when she finally remembers."

After Holly left for work, the house was quiet and once again I wandered the house. It felt like I was looking for something, but I didn't know what as I walked from room to room, occasionally stopping to look at a photo or something sitting on a shelf, but not really knowing why I was doing it. Walking into Jake's office, taking in all the built-in shelves loaded with books, I spotted a well-worn hat hanging from a doorknob. It was an old Cubs baseball cap, and as soon as I held the hat in my hands my mind was filled with images of Jake in the cap, smiling as he drank a beer at a game and cheering on his team. If I closed my eyes I could feel the sunshine on my face and hear the sound of the crowd as I looked at Jake. Just as Jake turned to look at me, the vision disappeared and my eyes snapped open. The moment had been as real to me as if I had been there with him and it startled me so much I dropped the hat as a sudden chill went through me.

Wrapping my arms around my body, I tried to conjure up the scene once again, but it turned out to be as elusive as my memories had become. Whatever the cap triggered for me had to have been a daydream, and I carefully put it back where I had found it.

What I needed to shake off the weird feeling was fresh air. The backyard maple trees were beginning to shed their leaves and for a minute I thought about grabbing a rake and doing some yard work until remembering Dr. Michaels' caution to avoid strenuous activities for a couple more weeks. Maybe a nice nap in the fresh air was called for instead.

Heading to the hammock, a sudden motion under the fence at the far end of the yard caught my attention. Walking closer I watched in amusement as a little brown paw reached under the fence. Just as I reached the spot, a furry body erupted from under the fence and a small dog of undetermined heritage landed at my feet startling us both.

"Hello there," I said as the dog righted itself and sat nicely at my feet, looking up at me with a tennis ball firmly locked in its mouth. "Where did you come from?"

"Rufus," came a woman's cry from the other side of the fence. "You mangy dog, where are you?"

"If you're looking for a little brown dog he's over here," I told the woman behind the fence as I continued to pet the dog.

"I'm sorry, he does that all the time. I'll come around the front and get him."

A few minutes later, a harried-looking older woman with a leash in her hand joined us in the backyard. She limped and walked slowly as if she was in pain.

"I'm so sorry he's bothering you," she said as she clipped the leash to the dog's collar. "He's got so much energy and I just can't seem to wear him out."

"Hi, I'm Paige," I told her as I extended my hand. "I'm staying with Jake for a bit."

"I know," she told me. "I've seen you here before. My name is Mary. You and Jake make a nice-looking couple."

"Oh, we're not a couple," I assured her.

"But I thought you were engaged?" she asked in confusion.

"Well, Jake is engaged, but it's not to me. I just met him a couple of weeks ago actually. I was in an accident and ended up in the hospital, and Jake and Holly were nice enough to let me stay with them while I recuperate."

"I know I'm getting up there in age, but I could have sworn you were the woman I've seen here. Jake told me you were engaged and you always look so happy together."

"I haven't met his fiancée myself, but we must look a lot alike."

She looked like she thought I was lying to her and I didn't know what else to say. Trying to break the tension, I asked her about her dog who was now tugging at the leash as he tried to catch a falling leaf.

"Your dog sure is cute."

"Thank you. I guess that makes up for all the torment he puts me through. Can't tell you how many times the little guy has dug under Jake's fence. It seems pretty easy for him to get over here, but he never seems to find his way back the other way," she said with a laugh. "But I'd be lost without him. My husband died last year and now Rufus is the only company I have."

"I'm sure he's lots of fun, though. He seems so well behaved…well, except for when he's digging under the fence!" We both chuckled as we watched Rufus dig in yet another spot near the fence.

"He's actually a good dog, but I have a hard time wearing him out. I have a few medical issues and can't really walk far enough to take him out. He loves to play fetch with his ball, but with my bad shoulder I can't throw the ball either."

Watching the dog, a memory of playing with my own dog as a child came to me. My life these days didn't allow for pets because I worked such crazy hours and I kind of missed having one.

"Mary, what would you think if Rufus came over to play with me for a couple hours each day while I'm here?"

"Oh, I couldn't ask you to do that," she said, although her face lit up at my suggestion.

"I know I'm only here for a week or so, but there isn't much for me to do while Jake and Holly are at work so you'd actually be doing me a favor."

"If you're sure?" she said hopefully.

"I am," I assured her. "In fact, since he's already over here, why don't I start right now? If you're good with it, I'll bring him back to your house when Jake gets home."

"Thank you, Paige. I knew from the first moment I saw you that I'd like having you as a neighbor. Rufus, you be a good boy now." Apparently she still didn't believe that I wasn't Jake's intended.

With a last scratch behind Rufus' ears, Mary handed me the leash and started her slow walk home.

By the time I finally heard Jake's truck pull up, I estimated I had thrown the ball a couple hundred times. Mary was right. Rufus was like the Energizer

Bunny. He never stopped, but it was great for me and what otherwise might have been a long afternoon had passed quickly.

"Paige?" I could hear Jake calling for me in the house.

"Out back," I shouted as I clipped the leash back on Rufus.

"I see you've met our neighborhood digging machine," he said as he came out of the house and bent down to give Rufus a good scratch behind the ears.

"Not only have we met, but we've spent the last two hours playing fetch after he appeared under the fence. Thank goodness the shoulder I hurt in the accident wasn't my throwing arm."

"He lives next door. I'll bet Mary is frantic looking for him."

"All sorted. In fact, I've been playing with him to try and help her out. She said she can't get him enough exercise so I volunteered."

"That was nice of you, and I'm sure she really appreciated it," Jake told me.

"She seemed to, but she said something a little curious."

"What was that?"

"She thought I was your fiancée. Said she had seen me several times before. When I assured her I had just met you, she was really confused."

"Well, she's older…" he started to say without looking at me.

"I suppose that's it. I told her that I must look a lot like your fiancée."

"You do," he said as he tossed the ball once again for Rufus.

"Actually I was meaning to ask you about that," I told him.

"What do you mean?"

"You have pictures all over the house of your family and friends, but I didn't see even one of you with your fiancée."

"And?"

"And it just seemed kind of strange to me is all. Doesn't she like having her picture taken?"

"Something like that," he said evasively. "How about I take Rufus back to his mom?"

"That would be great," I said. "And while you're doing that, I'll start supper."

Taking the leash from my hand, he wandered around the side of the house as I went into the kitchen.

Standing at the kitchen window, I watched as Jake stood at the back door of Mary's house and she came outside to collect her dog. I expected the exchange to be a short one, but they stood there for a very long time talking and occasionally looking back my way before Mary, with a look of profound sadness on her face, gave Jake a hug and he finally turned for home.

Joining me in the kitchen, he quickly washed his hands before helping me.

"So did you have a nice day?" he asked casually.

"It was okay," I said. "You and Mary seem close."

"She's a good neighbor. Since her husband died, I've been helping around her house."

"I was watching you out the window. You were having quite the conversation and she seemed upset."

"She was a bit, I suppose."

"Now I feel badly," I told him. "She seemed fine—well, a little confused, but fine—when I was talking to her earlier. I hope it wasn't something I did." The fact that they had spent so much time looking my direction made me suspect I was involved somehow in her sadness.

"Well, in a way it is. I hope you don't mind, but I was explaining to her why you're here. I told her about your memory loss and she feels badly for you."

"I don't mind, but it's not like she can do anything about it anyway," I told him, feeling my own bit of sadness.

"Nevertheless, it was important for her to know," he said before stopping what he was doing to lean against the counter and stare at me. "Paige, I wish I could help you get your memory back. In fact, I'd do anything to take away the pain you're in from all of this. I want you to be happy, and seeing the sadness on your face every day is tearing me apart."

Tears sprang to my eyes at the distress I saw on his face. It was as if he felt personally responsible for what I was going through and I didn't understand it.

"You're gonna make me cry," I told him. The words were barely out of my mouth when he crossed the room and took me into his arms.

For a moment all I could do was melt against him as he held me close and slowly rubbed my back before kissing me softly on the lips. For weeks

I had felt completely alone and suddenly this man I barely knew was offering me physical comfort, and for a moment at least, everything felt right again....until I remembered his fiancée and pushed him away.

Wiping the tears from my eyes with the back of my hand, I turned my back to him while trying to compose myself. What was it about the man that drew me to him? Feeling his arms around me, I had felt safe and happy and I had no right to those feelings with him at least.

"I'm sorry, Paige. I shouldn't have done that," Jake said angrily before stomping out of the room, leaving me confused, concerned, and most of all desiring him.

Not sure if Jake was coming back or not, I continued to prepare the meal and when he still hadn't come back downstairs, I ate, left a plate of food warming for him in the oven, and went upstairs intending to spend the night cocooned in my room. Passing by his bedroom, I could hear him on the telephone, but couldn't make out what he was saying.

Faced with a lonely evening alone in my bedroom, I needed a change of scenery, especially when so much desire for the man was coursing through my body. A walk would expel some of that energy. Still light out, it should be safe enough no matter Holly's thoughts on the subject, and I quietly let myself out the front door.

As confused as I was becoming about my feelings for Jake, one thing I was now sure of was that I should leave the house as quickly as I could. I wasn't the only one with feelings or he wouldn't have kissed me. That didn't change the fact that for all intents and purposes, it seemed I was stuck living with him. Knowing that we had feelings for each other would certainly make my time in the house difficult, but I had limited options. I had no money and no credit cards, David still hadn't called me back, and I had no one else. Only Jake and Holly's kindness in taking me in was putting a roof over my head, so it appeared I would just have to find a way to deal with what I was feeling for Jake while keeping him at arm's length to prevent a repeat of our earlier kiss.

Concentrating so hard on solving the dilemma I found myself in, I hadn't been paying attention to where I was walking and before I knew it, I was lost. It was starting to get dark and I was in an area of the city that felt unsafe, even if I couldn't say why. With no cell phone and no money to make a call on a pay phone, if such a thing even existed anymore, I couldn't even flag down a cab because I didn't know Jake's address. Not expecting to need it again, I had thrown away Holly's note with the address and phone number.

With no rhyme or reason to do so, I started walking in a different direction, hoping to at least find someone who might be able to help me. The faster I walked, the more I struggled to take deep breaths. Logically I knew that most of the fear I was feeling was in my mind, but Holly's warning and just simply being lost were contributing to what I was experiencing, and logic didn't come into it. Finally I saw the lights of a gas station a few blocks away and I made a beeline for the establishment, hoping to find someone who could help. The clerk, locked securely behind a glass partition, wouldn't let me use the phone, and I walked back outside and sank to the curb, unsure what else to do.

"You okay, lady?" A group of young men who looked like every gang member I had ever seen on TV stood nearby. Dressed in white tank tops and baggy jeans, with blue kerchiefs on their heads, I wasn't sure which of the men had spoken to me.

With tears in my eyes, I admitted I was anything but. "Actually I'm not. I'm not from around here and I don't know how to get back to my friend's house."

"Why don't you just call your friend to come and get you?" one man asked as the whole group moved closer to me. If I would have had a purse with me, I would have held it a bit closer. The group was pretty intimidating, although as they got closer I realized they were only teenagers.

"I don't have a phone," I admitted. "I asked the clerk in the store to let me make a call, but she just laughed at me."

The whole group started to laugh. "Yeah, she can be a bitch," the boy who had been asking the questions said.

"Do you want to use my phone?" he offered, holding out a cell phone to me. In that particular moment, it was the nicest thing anyone had done for me and I gratefully accepted.

Holding it in my hand for a moment, I realized how fruitless it was. I had no clue what Jake's phone number was.

"You do know how to use a cell phone, right?" my new friend said to the amusement of the group before he hushed them.

"Of course I do, but I don't know the number to call," I admitted. "I was in an accident a few weeks ago and something happened to my memory."

"No lie?" he said in surprise. "Same thing happened to my uncle. He couldn't remember anything for more than ten minutes after his accident. So who are you staying with? Maybe we can hook you up."

"His name is Jake. He renovates houses not too far from here," I told him, even though I suspected the name would mean nothing to these teens.

"Mr. Baxter?" the youth said with a big smile. "Hell, we know Jake. If you want we can give you a ride home. J Kool here lives just a few doors down from Jake."

"Really?" I asked hopefully before the thought occurred to me that it would be a mistake to get in a car with a bunch of young men that were strangers to me. Every child knew not to do that, but what choice did I have? "I'd really appreciate the ride. Thank you."

As we walked toward the car, the young man introduced himself and his friends. "I'm Marcus, this is J Kool, and this is James." Marcus even opened the car door for me and as I got in, I hoped the clerk was making note of us leaving just in case my body ended up behind a dumpster somewhere.

"My name is Paige Cooper and I don't know what I would do without you guys tonight. So how do you know Jake?" I asked as we started to drive off.

"My brother and my cousin both work for him," Marcus said. "Kept both of them off the streets and out of prison. I'm hoping when I'm done with school I can get hired on. Mr. Baxter only hires if you've finished high school."

After a few minutes, the view from the car window was indeed starting to look familiar to me and soon we pulled in front of Jake's house to see him pacing from side to side on the porch, cell phone in his hand as he gestured angrily with the other. He gave just a passing glance toward the car as Marcus came around to help me out and I began to walk toward the house.

"Jesus Christ, Paige! Where the hell have you been?" Jake shouted as he finally realized it was me and vaulted off the porch to gather me in this arms. "I was so worried about you."

"I went for a walk…"

"You went for a walk? Are you crazy, woman? Didn't Holly tell you not to go walking in this neighborhood alone?" he said even though he still hadn't released me.

"We found her up at the Shell station on First Avenue, Mr. Baxter, and she looked like she was lost so we offered her a ride home." Marcus and his friends stood nearby and, rightly so, they seemed quite proud of their role in my safe return home.

Jake finally realized what they had said and let me go before shaking each of their hands and thanking them for helping me.

"I'd like to thank each of you also. You might not have been able to tell, but I was pretty scared when you found me and I appreciate the ride home more than you know." Quickly providing Marcus with my office phone number, I asked them to look me up if they were ever in Minneapolis after graduating. "It's not as flashy as working for Jake, but I'm sure I could help find you a job with our firm doing something!"

As Jake escorted them back to their car, I couldn't help but overhear parts of their conversation as I waited for Jake to come back.

"Lucky we found her..."

"...pretty woman, wasn't safe for her..."

"Is she your girl?"

That last question in particular brought a smile to my face, even though it would never be the case.

As the boys drove away, Jake turned slowly back to me. I got the distinct impression he was trying to regain his composure before he spoke and I didn't blame him. The way he flew off the porch when he saw me get out of the car left no doubt he was angry.

But he said nothing. Instead, he put his arm around me and as one we turned to go back into the house. Turning to go upstairs, I was surprised when he pulled me back to him and once again enveloped me in his arms. We stood that way for a very long time, neither one of us speaking, and all manner of thoughts went through my head. As scared as I had been just a little while earlier, I felt safe and secure in his arms and I never wanted him to let go.

Jake finally spoke. "Don't ever do that to me again. I was so scared for you, Paige," he whispered into my ear as he slowly rubbed his hand up and down my back. His simple declaration washed over me in a flood of emotion.

"I'm sorry," I whispered back as we pulled back and stared into each other's eyes. No one had to tell me that the desire I saw in his eyes was mirrored in my own. "Jake, I…"

"Yes?"

"I…would you make love to me?" All the fear I had felt for the last several hours just made me want to be held in his arms. Without another word, he swept me up into his arms and carried me up to my bedroom. Carefully closing the door behind us, he set me down in front of him. For a moment I thought he was having second thoughts.

"Are you sure about this?" he asked. Were thoughts of his fiancée going through his mind as he asked the question? Was he looking for me to save him from himself?

"I know you're engaged and I know this is wrong for so many reasons, but I can't deny what I'm feeling for you any longer," I told him before pulling him down to my lips for a kiss that left both of us desperate for more.

With deliberate slowness, Jake removed our clothing, allowing me to see the well-defined muscles I had always known were hidden by his clothing. The sight of his naked body further fueled the desire I felt for him and as he gently touched me in the most intimate of places I could barely control what I was feeling for him.

"Please Jake, I want you so much," I whispered into his ear, hoping to feel him even closer.

"I don't want to hurt you, Paige," he whispered back. "You're still not fully healed from the accident."

"I'm fine," I assured him.

That single assurance seemed to release the floodgates and we spent the next several hours exploring each other's bodies and fulfilling our desire for each other. More than any other man I had ever been with, Jake seemed to know intuitively where to touch and what to do to bring me to the highest level of satisfaction. I gave myself fully to him, knowing that I was safe in his arms, and each time we made love that night, it was as if we were made for each other. We just fit perfectly together and I couldn't ever remember anything as satisfying in my life.

"So what really happened to you today?" Jake finally asked as we cuddled together in the dark. It was almost daybreak and Jake had to be exhausted after getting no sleep all night.

"I just needed to get out of the house so I started walking."

"Even though you knew how unsafe it was in this area?" he asked as he pulled me just a bit closer even though the danger was long gone.

"Honestly? I didn't think about it until I realized I was lost and remembered I no longer had a cell phone and no money for a cab...even if I did know your address. So I just kept walking thinking that at some point I would find someone who would help me."

"You're lucky it was Marcus and his friends you ran into," he said as he traced the line of my chin with his finger. "I don't want to think what could have happened to you if they hadn't."

The thought had also occurred to me and I realized just how stupid it had been to leave the house without him. So many of my decisions since the accident had been wrong. I just hoped that sleeping with Jake wasn't one of them.

"I'm sorry I worried you," I told him as I turned to face him again. "Ever since I met you there's been something pulling me toward you and I don't know what to do with those feelings. It's like I've known you forever, and I know you're engaged and I'm with David and that makes wanting you wrong, but every time I try to convince myself of it, you do something else wonderful and I'm right back feeling that same attraction."

"Is it really that wrong?" Jake asked. Knowing him the way I did, I was surprised he was being so cavalier about our sleeping together.

"Of course it is. Neither one of us is free to give in to our attraction to each other and yet look where we are. At the end of next week, when I am cleared to go home, I'm sure what I feel for you will go away in time, but I want you to know that I will always be grateful to you for saving my life and even if my memory eventually comes back, I'm never going to forget you."

It may have been my imagination, but it seemed as if Jake's body tensed when I brought up going home.

"Paige, I need to tell you…" Whatever he was going to say was forgotten as the sound of Holly's car pulling into the driveway brought us back to reality. We had been up all night.

Giving me a gentle kiss, Jake quickly gathered his clothes and slipped out the door without another sound. The creak of his hallway door told me he was safely in his room before the front door opened. Pulling his pillow to me, I breathed in deeply for the faint hint of cologne that I had come to associate with him as a single tear wet the pillow before I fell fast asleep.

Chapter Sixteen

After that evening we tried to keep the change in our relationship from Holly, but more likely than not she figured it out anyway. If the look on Jake's face when he looked my way was anything like the look on mine when I glanced at him, she couldn't help but notice. Nevertheless, she never commented on what she may have suspected, but more than once I caught her looking at us with a look of satisfaction, even as I was beginning to develop feelings of shame over my now-intimate relationship with Jake. For whatever reason, the guilt I was now feeling was more for Jake's fiancée than what I was doing to David.

He still hadn't called back and I was beginning to wonder if he ever would. Our relationship had its ups and downs over the years, but until the days since my call started to add up, I never doubted he would come to my rescue. Now I had to face the fact that he might never call me back and I might have to find my own way back to Minneapolis.

Being in the hospital for so long and then cooped up at the house was making me stir crazy. Although Jake and I had settled into a nice variety of activities each evening and spending each night in the same bed, the days while Holly slept upstairs were long and boring. When Jake suggested I accompany him to a job site, I leapt at the chance and was up early that morning.

"Maybe I can even help with some of the work," I suggested as we drove to the project house.

"You're supposed to be taking it easy, remember?" Jake said as he gave my hand a squeeze with one hand while keeping a steady grip on the steering wheel with the other.

"Like it's hard to move a paint brush up and down," I teased.

"If I remember, you're pretty good at it," Jake told me.

"I am, but how did you know that?"

"Uh, I'm sure you told me that somewhere along the line," he said quickly, although like so many things he was reminding me of lately, I didn't remember doing so.

We had already had numerous conversations about the unexpected things Jake knew about me: how I liked my coffee black with just a splash of tap water, how I cut my sandwiches into four triangles like my mother had, how I always tucked my feet up under me when sitting on the sofa, and how I always sang Barry Manilow tunes in the shower. Every time I questioned how he knew about those things, he said I must have told him, but honestly, I was quite sure I never had. Either the man was a mind reader or something else was going on.

It was the same with the paint conversation as we pulled up to the house and made our way inside. After so much peace and quiet at Jake's house, the noise was jarring as drills, hammers, saws, tile cutters, and the group of workers talking or yelling back and forth all contributed to the clamor. I put my hands over my ears and looked at Jake with a smile as he put his hardhat on and adjusted his tool belt. Seeing him at work, in his natural element as it were, sent a tingle of desire through my body and I knew my face was flushed.

Handing me my own hardhat, I started to object, but Jake was having none of my complaints.

"It's not optional, Paige. Everyone wears one on site. Besides, don't you think you've had enough hits to the head lately?"

"You might have a point there," I said sheepishly as I accepted the hard hat and he showed me how to adjust the size and place it on my head.

"Paige, is that you?" an older man said as he walked toward me with a smile on his face. As with everyone else in Chicago he was a stranger to me and I steeled myself for the conversation that was to come. I didn't notice

Jake gesturing wildly at the man as he stood behind me, and before I could say anything to the man, Jake spoke.

"Charlie, this is Paige Cooper. She's the woman I was telling you about from the accident. The one who can't remember," he said very pointedly.

At first Charlie looked at Jake like he was a lunatic before something changed. "Oh! Yeah. Right. Pleased to meet you for the first time, Paige," he said as he shook my hand and I looked at Jake in bewilderment.

"Please to meet you too, Charlie. You must be Jake's partner."

"Yes, yes I am," Charlie said as he continued to pump my hand before realizing what he was doing and releasing me.

"So, you've come to watch us work?" he asked.

"I'd like to do more than watch," I told him. "I'm a pretty good painter if you need some help."

"But you don't have your paint shirt on," Charlie said as he looked at the pristine white T-shirt I was wearing underneath the plaid work shirt Jake had borrowed to me.

"That's funny you said that because I have a painting shirt back home that is more paint than shirt."

Charlie just looked at Jake in confusion.

"Don't worry, Charlie. I might get a lot of paint on me, but honestly, I'm a good painter and I'd like to help today if I can."

"We'll take free help wherever we can get it, Paige. Charlie, why don't you show Paige where we keep the painting supplies and get her set up in the master bedroom? Paige, I'll check in on you later, but if you need anything let me know."

Charlie didn't appear to be much of a conversationalist, as that was pretty much all he said to me the rest of the morning. It wasn't as if I didn't try to engage him in conversation, because I did. We were working in the same room and it seemed only polite to chat while we worked.

"So how long have you and Jake worked together?" I asked.

"A while."

That's how it went all morning. I'd ask a question and he would look at me with a confused look on his face before giving me a one- or two-word answer until I got to the one question it seemed was too much for him.

"So Charlie, tell me about Jake's fiancée. I haven't met her yet and everyone says we look a lot alike. Do you see a resemblance?"

Charlie was so startled by the question that he immediately backed away from me and tripped over a tray of paint, sending it flying across the room. Thank goodness they had thought to put paper down before we started painting or the wood floors would have been ruined.

"Uh, I think you need to talk to Jake about that," he said hurriedly as he tried to clean up the mess he made.

"But you've met her, right?"

"Yeah, uh, yeah I have, but you really need to talk to Jake."

"Why? Can you tell me why everyone I've met thinks I'm her? And another thing, why doesn't he have any pictures of her around his house? He has pictures of everyone else in his life, so why not her? He is engaged, right?"

"Please, Paige, talk to Jake. I can't talk to you about this," he stammered.

"Why not?" His behavior was really becoming odd. "Is he engaged or not?"

Finally he stopped what he was doing and looked at me. "Truthfully… I don't know what's going on anymore. But please, talk to Jake. It's not for me to talk about this, especially with you."

"What's that supposed to mean? Especially with me?"

"Jake, you better get up here," Charlie shouted downstairs. He and I just looked at each other in a Mexican standoff until Jake appeared in the room.

"What do you need?" he said as he entered the room. Neither one of us was saying a thing, and he looked at Charlie, then me, and back again at Charlie. "Come on, guys, what's up?"

"I don't know what to say around her," Charlie said, nodding his head in my direction as if I wasn't even in the room. "I'm afraid I'll say something I shouldn't. She was asking about your *fiancée*, for Pete's sake!"

The change was so slight I might have missed it if I hadn't been looking directly at Jake, but I could see his body tense and his eyes narrow at Charlie's comment. Something was definitely going on and I began to wonder if Jake even had a fiancée. But why would he lie about something like that?

"It's okay, Charlie," Jake told him. "Why don't you go down and finish up the trim in the guest bathroom? I'll finish up here with Paige."

Shaking his head as if we were the crazy ones, Charlie mumbled to himself all the way down the stairs.

"What was that all about?" I asked. "What was Charlie so afraid he might tell me?" Now that we were alone, I wanted Jake to take me in his arms, but at the moment it seemed more important to get some answers.

"It's nothing, really," Jake said as he busied himself finishing the paint spill cleanup. "Charlie knows I am a little closed mouth about my love life and I guess he didn't want to speak out of turn. It's no big deal."

"Sure seemed like a big deal for him to get so worked up. I couldn't get more than a one-word answer out of him all morning until I asked about your fiancée, and suddenly he was in a panic. You are engaged, right?"

"I already told you I was."

"Maybe I can meet your fiancée before I go home?" I suggested. Suddenly it was very important for me to have some proof the woman even existed.

"That's not going to happen," he said, the tone of his voice suggesting he was saddened by the thought.

Like me, he was probably too ashamed of cheating on his fiancée.

"I'm sorry. I didn't mean to pry. Your relationship is none of my business and I have no right to stick my nose in where it doesn't belong, especially after what we've done." In reality I felt I had every right to ask because I was smack dab in the middle of the whole sordid mess.

"You have every right. You're part of this too," he said as he crossed the room and gathered me into his arms.

So I was right. It was guilt. But that still didn't explain Charlie's comments. Nevertheless, I let myself revel in the feel of Jake's strong arms around me and melted into his embrace, knowing full well that any of the crew could walk in at any moment. But I didn't care. In a few days I would be back home in Minneapolis and all of this would become a distant memory. Jake would eventually get married and my life would go on with or without my memory of the three missing years.

Jake had started to rub my back as we stood together and suddenly I had the most intense sense of déjà vu that sent a shiver through my body as he continued to run his fingers up and down my back in a slow, almost sensual motion.

"What's wrong?" Jake asked as my body tensed. "Did you just remember something?"

"No, at least I don't think so. But I just had this strong sense of déjà vu. Have you ever had that? Where you're doing something and it just seems like you did the exact same thing before?"

"Paige, that's a memory!" he insisted with excitement.

"It's not though. Because I've never been in this house before and I never knew you before and unless this exact same situation occurred with someone else in my life, it's not a memory. But it felt so weird! I think it was when you started to rub my back that triggered it."

"Have you remembered anything at all?" he asked as we finally pulled apart.

"Not really, but I have started to have flashes of memories—disjointed, and fast and confusing flashes—but I'm not sure what they mean. It's almost like the synapses in my brain started working again and these bursts of images fly through my head when I least expect it. It's starting to occur pretty regularly."

"So you are remembering," he said with even more excitement. The Jake I had come to know would certainly be happy for me when I got my memory back, but even for him, his reaction seemed over the top.

"You sound like you're trying to get rid of me," I teased, hoping that wasn't the case.

"What? Hell no! It's just I know how much it means to you to remember and I was happy for you, that's all."

Deep down I suppose I had been hoping Jake would say he didn't want me to go, but ultimately he was just being a nice guy.

"I better get back to work," I told him before picking up my paint brush again. "I don't want to cause any more problems for Charlie."

Turning my back to Jake I went back to work, not because I was worried about Charlie, but to hide the tears that had unexpectedly developed as I was overcome with emotions. Sadness, frustration, anger, loneliness, and fear were all in the mix and my mind was a mess. While anxious to get back to my real life, the thought of leaving Jake behind was causing me no end of sadness. I also knew that once I was gone, for Jake at least, the thought of me would quickly be forgotten. I was a just a single blip in his life, an unexpected inconvenience from the moment he happened upon the accident until I go home.

The fact that I had let myself develop feelings for the man was all on me and now I was in too deep. Having slept together, everything had changed for me. Making love meant something to me. There were no one-night stands in my background and sleeping with Jake had, in effect, changed that for me.

Suddenly I felt Jake's hands on my shoulders and I stiffened.

"Hey, what's really going on in the beautiful head of yours?" Jake asked as he turned me to face him. When he saw the tears, he reached up to gently wipe them away. "What's wrong? Why are you crying?"

"It's nothing," I told him.

"Don't do that, Paige," he said with just a hint of frustration. "Don't tell me it's nothing when I can see you're crying. By now don't you think we owe it to each other to be honest?"

Of course I did. But if I was going to be completely honest, it was time for the same from Jake.

"Okay then, if you want the truth, I'm frustrated that you won't talk to me about your fiancée. Do you think it would be disloyal if you told me about her? Probably not as disloyal as it is for us to have shared the same bed every night for a week, though, right?"

The angry words just slipped out of my mouth, startling even me. Jake stared at me and I could see the muscles in his jaw clenching, even though he didn't say a word. Releasing his hold on me, he took several steps back as if he couldn't stand to be in the same room as me.

"Someday you'll know how unfair that statement was and that I'm anything but disloyal to the woman I love, unlike your beloved David who can't even be bothered to call you back. I'll have one of the crew give you a ride back to the house."

Before I could even comprehend what he had said, he stormed out of the house, squealing the tires on his truck as he pulled away.

What had just happened?

"Hello?"

"Holly, I'm sorry I woke you up, but I really need to talk. Can you meet me for lunch?"

"Why can't we talk here?" she said as she rubbed the sleep out of her eyes.

"I need to talk about Paige."

"Oh. What did you do now?"

"Can you stop with the questions and just meet me?"

"I'm not even out of bed yet," Holly said. She knew full well that Jake wouldn't be asking if he didn't really need something, but it was still the middle of the night for her.

"How about in an hour, then? I'll go to the lumber yard and pick some stuff up and meet you at Baker's Square. I'll buy you a piece of pie," he said as an added incentive.

"You might have to buy me a whole pie for this, little brother! Fine, I'll meet you there. But what should I tell Paige? Won't she be expecting you home for lunch?" Holly hadn't missed the change in Jake's routine and knew he was now coming home for lunch every day.

"She's not there. I brought her to work with me today and it didn't go so well. That's what I need to talk to you about."

"You didn't just leave her there, did you?" Holly asked in surprise.

"Kind of, but I asked one of the crew to drive her home. She should get there before you leave."

"Jake Baxter, what have you done?" Holly said as she finally sat up in bed, all senses now on alert.

"Nothing, and that's the problem. I'll tell you about it when we have lunch. Just don't tell Paige where you're going."

"Fine. See you in an hour."

By the time Holly joined him for lunch, Jake knew he would have to come clean to her about how he and Paige were spending their nights.

"Oh Jake, what were you thinking," Holly said in frustration. Still, knowing how much in love Jake and Paige were, it seemed only natural that Jake would want physical intimacy with her again. "So now she thinks both of you are cheaters?"

"I'm afraid so," he said as he pushed his food around on his plate. "And today she accused me of being disloyal to my fiancée. I should have just told her the whole truth. Lying to her has to be worse than coming clean, right?"

"Jake, it's not a question of what's worse. You know what her doctors said. Pushing her to remember can actually cause more problems for her. You know that," she told him. "Look at me please," she asked gently.

Slowly he raised his head to look at her and the anguish she saw in his face brought tears to her eyes.

"What am I going to do if she never remembers me?" he said quietly. "She's my entire world and in just a few days she's going to walk out the door and I might never see her again, thanks to you." He knew that Holly had already purchased a plane ticket for Paige to fly back home. While he couldn't fault her for her generosity, it still grated on him that she did so behind his back.

Choosing to ignore his dig about the plane ticket, Holly tried to reassure him.

"You can't think like that. We know her. You know her. Paige wouldn't have slept with you if she didn't have feelings for you, and that means her love for you is still in there somewhere. Don't give up on her just because she said something she doesn't even realize is hurtful. I know she's going to remember."

"I wish I could believe that," Jake told her. "I always thought falling in love with Paige was a dream come true, but maybe it really was a nightmare that neither one of us can come out of. At least Paige might never remember what we've lost. Guess she's luckier than I am."

"There's still time," Holly told me. "But we're not going to solve it here. Come on. Let's go. I have to be at work early today and you should get back to work too."

"I didn't get you your pie," he remembered.

"That's okay. I'm not really in the mood anymore."

After Jake stormed out on me, I wasn't really expecting him to join me for lunch, but I was surprised when Holly also rushed out of the house as soon as I was dropped off, leaving me alone for the afternoon. Rufus turned out to be my only companion, and after another couple hundred throws, the poor pooch finally was worn out enough to lay under the shade of a tree and take a nap. I swung in the hammock for a while, thinking about Jake and his pseudo-fiancée. She may indeed be real, but as I had yet to see any proof she existed, that's how I had taken to thinking of her.

In the past month or so, I thought I had learned most everything about Jake. Nothing I had asked him had been off-limits until I started to ask about his fiancée, so what was the man hiding, and maybe more importantly, why? The man seemed to be an open book, at least where I was concerned, so what made talking about the love of his life so different? Was it because he had feelings for me? I could think of no other reason.

But what kept me up at night, even now, was knowing that whatever feelings he might have for me, I had some of my own and they were scary to me. Never in my wildest dreams would I have expected to fall for the man who terrified me so when I woke up in the hospital, but somewhere along the line it happened. I had fallen in love with Jake. I loved everything about the man and I wanted to shout it to the world, but instead, because he was engaged to someone else, I had no choice but to keep those feelings deep inside me and try and not let my face give it away. Knowing that he would never love me back was torture.

What would happen when I left for home in just a few days? Would my feelings for him go away? Being honest with myself, I knew they wouldn't. The strength of what I was feeling for Jake was overwhelming and even though I had never been in love before, this felt like it would last a lifetime.

When Jake got home that night, it was as if nothing had happened between us. He didn't mention our fight and neither did I. A supper spent with barely a word exchanged between us was as uncomfortable and strained as anything else we had shared together until Jake quietly mentioned that there was a special reception at a Frank Lloyd Wright house in Chicago that evening and he had purchased tickets for the two of us. He barely looked at me as he said it.

Forgetting the strain between us, I erupted in excitement. "That's fantastic! When is it?"

"In an hour. Can you make it?" he asked, still not looking at me.

"To see a Wright house, I can definitely make it," I assured him. "But what should I wear?" My meager belongings only included one dress, although it was a nice one.

"It's a private event, so a dress should work. If you don't have one, I'm sure Holly has one that you can borrow."

"No, that's okay. I had a dress in my suitcase. I better get going," I said as I quickly started to clear the table before Jake said he'd do it and I rushed up stairs for a quick shower and change before joining him back downstairs.

Descending the stairs, my first glimpse of him took my breath away. He was dressed in a suit coat and dress shirt, open at the collar, and I had a flash of déjà vu as if I had seen him that way before. He looked so dashing my heart did a flip-flop as he stood at the bottom of the stairs looking up at me.

My dress wasn't anything super fancy and while I didn't remember buying it, it fit my body perfectly, accenting all the womanly parts that men seemed to find so attractive. Jake was no exception and I saw his eyes look me up and down more than once before he exhaled a slow breath.

"My God, Paige, you look beautiful!" he told me as I blushed at his compliment.

"Thank you, and I have to say, you clean up quite nicely." It was the first time I'd seen him in anything other than casual clothes and I didn't know which look turned me on more.

"Shall we go?" he said as he offered me his arm, and we got into the truck before I started asking question after question about the Frank Lloyd Wright house we were going to see.

"You know all this already," Jake said to my surprise.

"What do you mean?"

"Well, I mean, didn't you study Wright's architecture when you were in school?"

"Of course we did, but I don't remember the Robie house. My favorite of his designs is the Fallingwaters home in Pennsylvania."

As we chatted, the miles flew by and before I knew it, we were in front of the house on the University of Chicago campus. Emblazoned with warm welcoming lighting, we could hear soft music emanating from the house as a crowd of well-dressed people joined us for the event. Without even realizing

I was doing so, I had slipped my hand into Jake's and we looked every bit the couple as we wandered through the house.

Everywhere I looked was something marvelous. Tour guides were stationed around the house providing information on the design, and as one explained how Wright had designed everything on the inside of the home also, I realized I knew that.

"Welcome back," a tour guide said to us as we entered the kitchen.

I looked at Jake, surprised that the woman knew him.

"We don't often get return visitors, but I'm happy you both could join us tonight," she said.

"I'm sorry," I told her. "You must have us confused with someone else. This is the first time we've been to the house."

The woman looked back at me in total confusion before she apologized for her error and moved on.

"That was weird," I said to Jake as we moved on to another room. "Oh, wait. I'll bet she thought I was your fiancée. Have you been here before with her?"

Bringing up his fiancée was the last thing I wanted to do since our evening was going so well, but I couldn't help myself. It was yet another complete stranger who thought I was Jake's soon to be bride.

"As a matter of fact, I have," he said, this time without any hint of sadness or anger.

Maybe he no longer cared if I mentioned her. The man was so confounding to me, at least when discussing his fiancée. If I was engaged, I would talk about my fiancée to anyone and everyone who would listen. But in this one very important part of his life, he was just a mystery to me. It had to be guilt about our sleeping together. There was no other explanation for it.

Whatever was going on in that handsome head, the rest of the evening was as pleasant as could be and when the evening ended neither one of us wanted to go home. Instead Jake drove us to one of the beaches surrounding Lake Michigan where we walked hand in hand along the shore as if nothing unpleasant had happened that day.

"So tomorrow's your follow-up appointment with Dr. Michaels," he said.

"It is, and I hope he's going to clear me to go home," I replied, even as I realized the mixed emotions that possibility brought forth within me.

"Holly seems to think that it's a done deal since she bought me the plane ticket already."

"Good for her," he said with more than a touch of unhappiness. Was it my imagination or was he sad to see me go home?

Jake and I had already discussed my phone call to David and my surprise that he hadn't contacted me back. It if weren't for Holly's kindness, I would literally have no ability to get back to Minneapolis.

"I thought it was really kind of her to do that, especially since that appears to be the only way I would get home. Bet you'll be glad to see the end of me when I'm gone."

Suddenly Jake stopped walking and looked down at me. "Don't say that. Don't ever say that," he told me angrily as he grasped my arm in a painful grip that made me pull away from him.

"Damn it, Jake, I don't know what to say to you anymore," I cried as I rubbed where his hand had been, knowing that his grip was sure to leave a bruise. "We have a lovely evening and once again I say something perfectly innocent and you get angry. What do you want me to say? Once I'm gone everything in your life can get back to the way it was before you rescued me from the accident. You and your fiancée can get married and have a house full of kids and have a wonderful picket-fence life. What else do you want?"

"I want you. I've always wanted you," he said before crushing me in his arms and kissing me passionately.

Responding as fervently as ever to his kisses, my thoughts were a whirlwind in my mind. I wanted him more than anything too, but even with his declaration of how much he wanted me, he said nothing about ending things with his fiancée and I pushed him away.

"We can't do this anymore," I told him, trying to catch my breath through the desire his kiss had fueled. "I can't do this anymore. Think about your fiancée!"

"You're all I can think about and I can't stop. You have no idea of how hard this is for me!" he cried.

"It's hard for me also, but I'll be gone in two days. I'd like to leave being friends and at this rate, I just don't know if that will be possible."

"If you only knew…" he said sadly as he stared at me. The muscles in his jaw were clenching and unclenching and I knew he wanted to say something, but nothing came out of that beautiful mouth.

"What?" I demanded. "If I only knew what?" Why was everything that came out of his mouth the last few days so cryptic?

"Nothing. It's late, I'm tired, and I'm sorry I ruined our evening. Let's go home."

"Jake, please talk to me," I begged. "What's going on and what aren't you telling me?"

For a moment it looked like he was going to say something, but he just shook his head and started to walk away from me. "Let's get you home."

With no choice but to follow him, we went home.

Chapter Seventeen

*M*y doctor's appointment the next day confirmed what Holly already seemed to know and I was cleared to travel once again.

"Dr. Barrette believes that once you're back in familiar surroundings, the memories should start to come back pretty quickly," Dr. Michaels told me.

"And if that doesn't happen?"

"It's always a small possibility, but I don't want you to focus on that, Paige," he said. "Before you leave we'll have you fill out a form and get authorization to transfer all of your records to your personal physician so they can continue to monitor you, but if anything comes up, please don't hesitate to let me know."

"Thank you, Doctor. As kind as you've been, I have to say I hope this is the last time I see you," I told him with a smile before leaving to join Jake in the waiting room.

After our discussion the previous evening, I knew any excitement I showed about the result would be met with anger or whatever he had been feeling, so I didn't say much about the news until he asked.

"Dr. Barrette says my lungs are fully healed as are the broken bones. See? No cast," I said as I waved my now uncasted wrist at him.

"And your memory?" he asked.

"No change, I'm afraid, but he insists the odds are in my favor for it to be fully restored."

"So that's it, then? You're going home?" The only emotion I could detect in that statement was resignation.

"I guess so."

Neither one of us said anything else on the ride home before Jake dropped me off at the house and went back to work. Holly was just getting ready to go to work when I got home.

"Hi Paige," she said with a smile as she packed her bag. "How'd the doctor appointment go?"

"I guess I'll live," I told her with my own smile. "Got the cast off, ribs are healed, lungs are in pretty good shape, and he cleared me for travel."

"That's great," she told me. "But we're going to miss you."

"You might, but I'm sure Jake will be happy to see me go."

"Why would you say that?" she said. "He likes you very much."

"Sometimes I think you're right, but…well, I don't know. A lot of the time he seems less than pleased with me and the things I say. But after tomorrow you two can get back to your own lives and won't have to worry about me anymore."

"Paige, sit down with me for a minute," she asked as she pulled out a chair at the kitchen table and sat down before I joined her. "Someday, soon I hope, you'll get your memory back and everything you've gone through in the last month will make sense to you again. I know it's hard for you to believe, but Jake wants nothing but the very best of you. He's my brother and I love him dearly, but sometimes he doesn't always handle things as well as he should…especially when he's in love."

"So you're saying that he's acting this way toward me because of his fiancée?" I asked.

"That's exactly what I'm saying," she assured me with a chuckle. "He's not giving up on her and I don't think you should give up on yourself. When your memory comes back…"

"If it comes back," I interjected.

"*When* your memory comes back, this will all seem irrelevant. Let's just hold on to that thought, okay?"

Giving my hand a quick squeeze, Holly realized she was going to be late for work. "Gotta run, but I'll see you before you leave tomorrow morning, right?"

"Definitely."

After playing with Rufus for a couple of hours and saying my final good-bye to Mary, I needed something to do. With a clean bill of health from Dr. Michaels, I decided to clean the house as kind of a thank-you for Jake's hospitality the last couple of weeks.

Saving Jake's office for last and not wanting to see things I shouldn't have, I intended to simply dust, vacuum, and empty the trash can when something sticking out from a pile of papers on his desk caught my eye. It was the AIA logo. Even though I shouldn't be snooping, I couldn't help myself and I carefully pulled the pamphlet out and turned it over. It appeared to be a brochure for the association's annual conference. Surprised that Jake would have attended, I was just about to page through the brochure when the phone rang and I hurried to put it back where I found it before running to the phone.

"Baxter residence."

"Paige, dear, is that you?" asked an unfamiliar woman's voice.

"This is Paige," I said hesitantly. "I'm sorry, do I know you?"

"It's Karen. Jake's mom."

"Oh, Mrs. Baxter. How are you?" I said. Obviously I knew Jake's parents lived in Chicago, but she was addressing me almost as if she knew me. Jake and Holly must have told her about me.

"I'm sorry, Mrs. Baxter, but Jake and Holly are both out."

"Mrs. Baxter? Paige, I've asked you to call me Karen. It's not like we're strangers after all."

"Um...okay." What was it with this family? Now Jake's mom was telling me things I didn't remember too?

"The reason I'm calling is to let you know that Luke has finally had the blueprints hung in his office and we can't thank you enough."

What was the woman talking about? Just as I was about to ask what she meant I could hear a muffled masculine voice in the background before she came back on the phone.

"I am so sorry, my dear. I shouldn't have called. Jake is going to be very unhappy with me. Please forgive me. Good-bye."

Next thing I knew she had ended the call, leaving me wondering what in the world had just happened. Was all of Chicago crazy? Neither Holly nor Jake had mentioned that their mother was a little off, but then again, if that had been my mom, I probably wouldn't have mentioned it either. In the grand scheme of things I would chalk it up to just another weird thing that happened to me in Chicago. I couldn't get out of town fast enough.

By the time Jake got home, I had worked myself up into quite a state after his mother's phone call. The woman didn't sound crazy and in fact had seemed very nice. But who was Luke and what blueprints was she talking about? I confronted him as soon as he walked in the door.

"Is your mother of sound mind?" I said as I stood with my hands on my hips, barring his way further into the house.

"What's that supposed to mean?" he asked in surprise as he put his things down on the bench by the door.

Without hesitation I relayed our entire conversation to him.

"Exactly who did she think she was talking to, and don't tell me your fiancée!" I said, louder than necessary. All my frustration at the cryptic comments, people believing I was someone else, and being stuck in Chicago had finally boiled over.

"Calm down," he told me, making me even angrier.

"Don't tell me to calm down. I'm sick and tired of everyone here lying to me and I want the truth for once."

"Paige, stop it. I'm not going to have this discussion over and over again. I've told you everything you should know and that's it. End of discussion."

"What are you so afraid of?" I taunted him. "Are you afraid to face your own feelings? Are you afraid to admit that you feel something for me?"

"Paige, I'm begging you, please stop asking me. I can't have this conversation with you again."

I could see the anger brewing in him and still couldn't stop the angry words spilling from my mouth.

"Well, we are," I said as he tried to move me out of his way so he would get by me.

"No, we're not, and if you won't move, then I'm going to leave before I say something I'll regret." There was true anger in his voice.

He turned around to leave, but I reached out to grab his arm as he reached for the door knob.

"Jake, stop," I said just as angrily. "What in heck is going on here?"

"I can't," he said without even turning around to look at me. "I can't explain it."

"Why the hell not? I tried to give you all the benefit of the doubt, but what aren't you telling me? Why does everyone, including your own mother, keep thinking they've met me before or that I'm your fiancée? And why won't you even talk about your fiancée to me? Do you know you've never even told me her name? This is starting to feel like an episode from the *Twilight Zone*. Please…just tell me the truth. What is really going on here?"

Slowly he released his grip on the door knob and turned around to face me. For a moment neither of us spoke, both trying to figure out what to say and how to get past our anger.

"It's you," he finally said softly.

"What's me?"

"You're my fiancée. It's you, Paige."

"Stop playing with me. What's really going on?" I said with barely contained fury.

"Paige, I'm not lying to you and I know I'm supposed to let you remember on your own, but you're my fiancée. It's you and it's always been you. There never was another woman. The reason why everyone thinks you are her is because you *are*. I've been in love with you since the day we met and we're getting married."

The intensity of his words scared me more than if he had yelled at me. His gaze never wavered from my eyes as I struggled to look at him.

"If that was true, how come you don't have a single picture of me or the two of us together?"

"You know your doctor told us we can't force you to remember. He told us to take all of the pictures from our life together out of the house. I even took them off my phone so you wouldn't accidentally see any of them," Jake said as he tried to convince me what he was saying was true.

"So if we're engaged, how come I don't have a ring?" I asked as I waved my empty hand at him.

"You do…well, you did. At least, before the accident. They must have cut it off your finger when you were brought to the hospital. Paige, please,

I'm begging you. Everything I'm saying is the truth. You have to remember how much I love you."

"Stop it. Stop lying to me! What is wrong with you? Why would you lie about it?" My lungs, which until that moment had felt fine, suddenly started to feel compressed and my breath was coming in short little gasps that had nothing to do with my accident and everything to do with the unbelievable story he was trying to make me believe.

"Please listen to me," Jake said as he closed the distance between us. For the first time since we met I was afraid of him and I flinched as he came closer. If he could tell such outlandish lies, what else might he be capable of? Before I could stop him, he took my face in his hands and kissed me.

I could feel the tears rolling down his cheeks as he did so and suddenly my mind was filled with a snippets of thoughts, each flashing in and out so quickly I could make no sense of it. The memories so vivid and yet so distant, as if I was just on the verge of understanding what I was seeing before it was gone again. The feel of his lips on mine, the sensation of his beard stubble scratching my cheek, and the smell of his cologne overwhelmed me and I slumped into his arms. Without any further encouragement, I found myself kissing him back before suddenly pushing him away from me.

"Paige, please…"

"No, don't take another step. I need to get out of here." My head was spinning with everything that had happened and I was struggling to breathe again. I needed to leave. There was no way I could stay in this house one more night.

Pushing my way past Jake, I raced upstairs and slammed the bedroom door behind me as I tried to catch my breath. Grabbing my battered suitcase, I started to throw my meager belongings in as the doorbell rang downstairs. The sound barely penetrated my mind until I heard a man's voice and Jake yelling.

"She's not going anywhere with you, Dawson!" Jake yelled.

Dawson? Had David finally come for me? Hurrying to the top of the staircase with my suitcase, I could only see two sets of legs, but I recognized the voice.

"I know she's here, Baxter, and I'm not leaving without her. Paige honey, where are you?" he shouted through the house.

"David? Is that you?" I said as I quickly came down the stairs to see David and Jake standing toe to toe as Jake glared furiously at him. "Oh my God, it's you. Please get me out of here," I begged as I ran to his side and held on to his arm.

"Paige, you're not leaving with this ass. Think about what he did to you. He's nothing to you anymore," Jake begged.

"No. You're wrong, Jake. You're nothing to me and you never were. I don't know what you were trying to pull here, but it didn't work. It was a mistake for me to ever have had anything to do with you and your family and it's over. I'm going home where I belong and I never want to see you again."

"Paige, please. Please, you have to remember what we mean to each other. Please don't leave with him. Please, just try to remember. I know you felt it when we kissed. I could see it in your eyes. You remember me. I know you do. I love you."

"How can I remember something that's a lie?" I told him. "I don't know why you did all this. I thought you were my friend, but you're nothing to me and never will be. Please…just leave me alone."

Tears were falling freely down my face as I stared back at him, wondering how I could have been so very wrong about him. Whatever feelings I thought I might be having for him had evaporated the moment he lied to me.

"Come on, honey," David said. "Let's get you home."

As we hurried out to the car, I knew without a doubt that Jake's eyes never left me and when he slammed the front door behind me, I felt it in my soul as we drove away.

The drive back to Minneapolis will full of revelations. David told me he had gotten a new job while I was in Chicago and was now working for one of SNK's main rivals. He had never really been happy at SNK so I guess I wasn't surprised, although the timing of the change, while I was missing, seemed a little odd to me. For the first couple of hours I listened to David talk and tried to put the horrible scene with Jake behind me. Then I realized that not once had he explained why it took him so long to come and get me.

"David?"

"Yes, dear?"

"Why did it take you a whole week to come and get me?"

"What do you mean?" he asked, never taking his eyes off the road.

"I called you over a week ago, so why did it take so long for you to come here?"

"Paige, you couldn't expect me to just walk away from my new job now, could you?" he asked.

"But you could have driven down last weekend, or at the very least you could have called. Why did you wait so long?"

If I had called Jake, he would have come to me in a matter of hours. Now why did that thought pop into my head?

"It doesn't really matter because we're on our way home now, right?"

Giving me a pat on the leg as one might have to pacify a child, he went back to his soliloquy about his new job and how wonderful they thought he was. Losing interest in his self-promotion, my thoughts drifted back to the look on Jake's face when he realized I was leaving with David. If the dictionary contained a picture defining the word *crushed*, Jake's face would have been it.

Maybe he had come to believe his own lies and convinced himself we really were engaged! Whatever was going through his head, it was obvious he felt hurt, but no more so than me. My heart was breaking. David droned on and on as the miles slipped by leaving me to stare out the window, longing for my life back.

It was hours later when we finally got close to my apartment building and I was relieved to find I still lived in the same place.

"You can just let me off out front," I told David when it looked like he was turning toward the underground parking entrance.

"What do you mean?" he said. "I'm coming up."

"I'd rather you didn't," I told him. "I just want to take a hot bath and go to bed."

"Don't be ridiculous, Paige," he said angrily. "I didn't drive all the way to Chicago just to be sent home. It's been a long time since you left and I was looking forward to spending some alone time."

Maybe it was the phrasing that he used or the lustful way he looked at me, but my skin began to crawl at the thought of spending the night with him. There was no way I was letting him come up. As we pulled to a stop in front of the building, I quickly grabbed my suitcase from the back seat and got out of the car.

"Paige, stop messing around. I'll park the car and be up in a minute," he shouted through the now-open window. His raised voice was attracting the attention of people coming out of the building and I walked back to the car and leaned in for more privacy.

"David, no. Not tonight," I said assertively. "I'll call you tomorrow." Ignoring the anger on his face, I walked inside to the building manager's office looking for a spare key to my apartment. After explaining about the accident, I collected the key and headed upstairs.

Closing my apartment door behind me, I slumped against it, relieved to finally be home. Everything seemed just as I had left it, although I could tell my maid service had moved some things around.

The mail that had arrived while I was in Chicago was piled neatly on my desk and with only a quick glance through the stack, I set it aside to deal with later. Opening the fridge for a bottle of water, the picture of Jen and me from our last get-together caught my eye and I immediately called her.

"We're sorry, the number you have dialed is no longer in service…" The recorded message was a dagger in my heart until I checked my computer and discovered her number had changed. The address in my contacts list was for Arizona. When had she moved to Arizona? With shaking hands, I called the new number I found for her.

"Paige, is that you?" said the voice I loved so much.

"Oh my God, Jen! Finally!" I said with unabashed happiness. Tears started to fall down my cheeks.

"Where have you been?" she asked. "I've been trying to call you for a month. I thought you were mad at me about something."

As quickly as I could, I filled her in on everything that had happened to me in the last month, the unsuccessful attempts by the Chicago police to find her in California, and the doctor's prognosis about my memory loss.

"He said the people around me weren't supposed to prompt me to remember for some reason. Something to do with my health being too fragile and possibly suffering a setback. But I'm so tired of not knowing what's going on in my own life. No one understands how hard this is!"

"Oh Paige, I'm so sorry I wasn't there for you. When I got married we moved to Arizona."

"You got married?" I said in surprise. "And you didn't tell me?" How could my only sister have married without me?

"Of course I told you. For Pete's sake, you were in the wedding!"

"I don't remember," I admitted sadly.

"Oh honey, I'm sorry. That was really mean and I didn't mean to be. Oh my God!"

"What's wrong?"

"Paige, I just thought of something else you don't remember and it's going to be hard. Maybe I shouldn't tell you. That's what your doctor said, right?"

"Well, now you have to. You can't just leave me knowing something bad is out there."

"It's Mom and Dad."

"They're dead, right?"

"You remember that?"

"No, but when Mom didn't call out the National Guard when I went missing, I was afraid that might be the case." Tears continued to roll down my face having had my worst fears confirmed. "What happened?"

Sadly my sister told me everything that had happened, from Dad getting sick and passing and Mom's steady decline without him until she, too, passed away. "They're buried together in Fort Snelling cemetery. You know Dad always wanted that military honor and there was no way we could separate them for eternity."

Overwhelmed with grief knowing my parents had both died, I started to sob in earnest while Jen waited patiently for me to calm myself.

"Paige, I'm so sorry you have to go through this again. It was hard enough on you the first time. Why don't you fly down here and we can spend some time together? We can look through some old photo albums and maybe it will help you remember. I don't care what the doctor said. What if you never remember?"

"That's what keeps me up at night," I told her, even though that was far from the only thing that kept me up these days. "But I can't. I have to get back to work. At least I can still remember how to do my job!"

"I understand, but if you change your mind, you know where to find me," Jen said. "Paige?"

"Yes?"

"I'm sorry I wasn't there for you. I love you so much."

"It's okay, and I love you too."

Even though the call with Jen didn't fix everything that was wrong in my life, I finally felt like someone cared about me again and it meant the world to me. All the emotions of the call, combined with the long drive home, had left me exhausted. A good night's sleep in my own bed was what I needed. After all, tomorrow would be a work day and I was looking forward to it.

Chapter Eighteen

*W*alking into my office the next morning was strange. People welcomed me back, but no one really asked any questions about my extended absence. Expecting to be bombarded by questions from Casey, I was disappointed to find she was away from her desk, so I put my things down, grabbed a cup of coffee, and settled in to work. Having momentarily forgotten about my memory loss, I was startled to discover the password for my computer didn't work. Trying it over and over, I finally realized I didn't remember it. Until Casey arrived, I wouldn't be able to do much of anything, so I unrolled the plans sitting on my drafting table and looked them over.

The project seemed to be for a church and it was a magnificent design. Still in the early stages and unsure who the architect of this beautiful building was, I studied the plans with a smile on my face.

"Oh Paige, I didn't expect you in so early. Welcome back!" Casey as she walked in and handed me a stack of messages. "How was the trip?"

"Is that all you have to say?" I asked in surprise. "Aren't you going to ask me where I've been for the last month? How come no one is surprised to see me this morning?"

Casey had a guilty look on her face and I knew she was withholding information from me. "What's going on?" I asked.

"We knew you were coming back today and we knew that you were in an accident."

"You knew and no one contacted me to find out how I was?" The hurt knowing that people who were supposed to be my friends knew about the accident and hadn't even sent flowers was overwhelming to me.

"We didn't know what to do. A nurse from Mt. Sinai in Chicago called Mr. Nolan shortly after the accident and explained what had happened and about your injuries and the memory loss. She said we weren't supposed to try and make you remember, and none of us knew if we were supposed to call or come visit. Paige, I'm so sorry. We worried about you the whole time and then we found out you were coming back today, and I guess we thought that meant everything was okay. You *are* okay, right?"

The look of concern on her face told me she was telling the truth and I couldn't be angry. It certainly explained why everyone had greeted me as if I had just been gone for the weekend.

"I guess I'm okay. A few aches and pains still, but I'll live," I told her as she sat down across from me.

"The nurse said you couldn't remember anything in the last three years. But you can now, right?"

"Nope. Three years of my life just completely wiped away. I guess it's a good thing that I still live and work in the same place." It still wasn't easy to joke about the memory loss, but if I didn't I might go crazy.

"Oh no! I'm so sorry, Paige. So what do you remember?"

"Literally everything except for anything that happened during those three years. Obviously I remember you and I suppose most of the people here. I remember my family and friends, and David, of course."

"David? You mean David Dawson?" she asked in surprise.

"Yeah, silly. Of course I remember David. Why did you say it that way? He drove all the way to Chicago to bring me home."

"It's nothing. Paige, did you know he doesn't work here anymore?" Casey asked. "Oh dang, we're not supposed to prompt you with memories. I'm sorry."

"It's okay. David told me already and it's probably a good thing. I never really felt comfortable dating someone I work with anyway. So what else have I missed? Was someone using my office while I was gone? The plans on my table are fantastic!"

"Don't be silly. Those are your designs for the Basilica project," Casey told me with a smile. "It's funny that you don't recognize your own work. Well, not funny, but you know what I mean."

Apparently I had a lot more to catch up on then I was expecting. The church was a massive design. How did it end up on my work table?

"Yeah, I know. You know something? I'm just beginning to realize what recreating three years of my life is going to be like. Think how embarrassing it's going to be when I run into people I met during that time and don't recognize them."

Casey stared back at me in horror as if something truly awful had just occurred to her.

"Geez, don't look at me like that. Did I already do that?"

"Uh, no, at least, I don't think so," she said hurriedly. "I'll do my best to give you a heads up when someone is coming in that I think you should know so you won't be embarrassed or have to explain what's going on with your memory."

"I appreciate that, Casey, more than you know. But I do have one really important problem now and maybe you can help me out with it."

"What's that?" she asked in all seriousness.

"What's my computer password?" I asked with a laugh.

The password turned out to be the least of my problems through the day as I got back into the swing of things. Although on the surface it appeared not much had changed at work, the reality of it was completely different. Not only had people come and gone in the last three years, but my client list was substantially different. The only saving grace was it appeared the vast majority of my time recently had been spent on the church designs that I had so admired.

Mr. Nolan made his way to my office just before lunch and I was surprised that a senior partner would be coming to see me.

"So, Miss Cooper, you're back," he said as he sauntered into my office. "We've missed you."

"I'm sorry for my absence, sir, but I had a bit of an accident." The man made me extremely nervous, especially since I knew he rarely tolerated associates and had even less time for the female variety.

"I know all about it," he said to my surprise before I realized how silly I was being. It was his firm. If everyone else knew what had happened to me, he certainly did also. "So, I hear you are having some memory problems."

"That's right, but it shouldn't impact my work. This afternoon I'm meeting with the church project team and hope to be caught up on the project by the end of the day." I still don't know what had happened to land such a prestigious project in my lap, but I wasn't about to question it either.

"I'm not worried. One thing I know for sure, you walked in the door with great talent and I know that you didn't forget that. I hear through the grapevine that you spent some recovery time with the Baxters. Lovely kids, Jake and Holly."

"You know them?" I asked in surprise.

"Of course. Oh, that's right. You probably don't remember we already had this conversation. Their father is a close friend of mine. Well, hell's bells, I already forgot we've been told not to try and force you to remember things. Sorry about that, Paige."

Did the senior partner just address me by my first name? What in heck happened in the last three years?

"Anyway, I know you have a lot to catch up on, but I wanted to welcome you back. If you need anything, you know where to find me."

And with that statement he left my office as I walked to the door, expecting to see everyone else on the floor watching him, but no one except me seemed the least bit surprised that he had come to see me.

After a lengthy meeting with the project team, during which the group had no option but to fill in my missing memories about the project we were working on, I was beginning to get my bearings once more and the rest of the day passed without further problems.

"Paige, David Dawson's on the phone," Casey said sharply as the day was drawing to a close. She had never been a fan of David's, but even so, she didn't even try to hide her disdain for having to talk to him.

"Thanks," I said before reaching for the phone. "Hi David," I said pleasantly.

"Well, at least you're over whatever your problem was last night," he said by way of greeting.

"I don't know what you mean," I snapped back. "I was tired is all."

"Okay, I forgive you," he said, even though I hadn't asked for his forgiveness. "So tonight I thought you could cook something for us and then we can watch a movie at your place. I'll come over after work."

His tone was so patronizing it caught me off guard for a moment. Knowing I should be grateful he had driven all the way to Chicago, I almost agreed until I remembered just how much work I needed to catch up on. The excitement over the church project was intoxicating and I couldn't wait to get back to the designs.

"I'm sorry, David, but I'm swamped here and I don't think I'll be able to make it tonight. Maybe something this weekend when I've had a chance to catch up?"

"That's okay. I'll just have the doorman let me in with the spare key. Don't wake me up when you come in."

For the second time in as many days, my skin began to crawl as I thought about coming home to David in my bed. What was wrong with me? The man was my boyfriend after all, and it's not like we had never slept together. But I couldn't shake the feeling.

"The doorman won't have a spare key anymore. I had to use it myself after losing my keys in the accident. Let's just plan on getting together this weekend, okay?"

"Paige, I'm not going to wait for you forever," he said. Was he threatening me? Suddenly the little flashes of memory that had recently begun to appear started spinning through my mind again. Something about this situation was familiar to me, but I just couldn't pinpoint it.

"I'm sorry, David. I'm not asking you to. Let's plan on something this weekend, just the two of us. We can have a romantic dinner somewhere and spend the whole weekend together."

The promise of a weekend seemed to pacify him, at least for now, and I quickly ended the call as Casey came in to say goodnight.

"Is there anything else I can do for you, Paige?" she asked as she put her coat on.

"Thanks, but I'm fine. I really appreciate all the help you've given me today, Casey. At least I know one thing hasn't changed in my life in the last three years. You're still the best!"

"Don't work too late," she cautioned. "You're still recovering, you know."

"Hey, I just got away from all the doctors. Don't you go to the dark side too, my friend!"

"Somebody has to remind you," she said, before realizing what she had said as we shared a laugh at her comment.

"Say hi to Bruce for me and I'll see you tomorrow."

It wasn't long before I was once again the only person working on the floor. In that respect, at least, nothing had changed, and I spent the next several hours working on the church project. It was midnight before I had enough and headed home. Digging for my keys, I discovered the replacement cell phone Casey had purchased for me that morning. The phone had been buried at the bottom of my purse and I pulled it out to check for messages.

The same unfamiliar number had called almost a dozen times without leaving a message. Probably a wrong number, but if not, they'd probably call back tomorrow. Either way, I was too tired to worry about it and I finally made my way home.

My sleep that night was interrupted over and over again by flashes of memory, and when I finally woke up, I tried to remember what I had seen. It was starting to happen more frequently and I prayed that it meant the beginning of the end of my memory loss. Each time a face I didn't recognize approached me at work, I was beginning to freeze, wondering if it was someone I should know. Trying to hide that I simply didn't remember wasn't working and people had started to talk behind my back. Even something as simple as my surprise at a new coffee maker in the break room elicited laughter from my colleagues, but they weren't the ones living through it. At least in Chicago I didn't have to pretend to know people I had no memory of.

My first few days back at work had been busy, leaving me no time to think about Jake, but each morning, lying in bed as I waited for the sunrise to come through the large windows, he was all I could think about. As angry as I was at him for lying to me, I missed everything about him desperately. But he had lied to me. I might never know why he did or how in the world he thought he could convince me that we were engaged, but he lied and as much as I wanted him, I knew I won't be able to forgive him for that.

My only real regret about leaving the way I had was not saying good-bye to Holly. She had been nothing but kind to me and I felt like a heel for leaving without saying good-bye. But at least I could try and make amends. Quickly getting out of bed and as difficult as it was to leave Jake out of it, I found some stationery and penned her a quick note of thanks for all her kindness while I had been in Chicago. Ending the note, I had one last thought and jotted a quick P.S., asking if she knew what had happened to my personal items, mostly the jewelry that I always wore, when the ambulance brought me in. It seemed strange that I hadn't received it back. I asked if she could find out for me.

With more work than I could handle most nights, I didn't make it home until well after midnight, leaving no time to think about Jake, Holly, or even David. It wasn't until Friday afternoon when I realized that I had promised David a romantic weekend with just the two of us and had done nothing about it. Deep down I had been hoping that he would arrange it, especially after I had been missing for so long, but then I did remember something: David never initiated anything like this himself. That was something that had always irked me about him.

If I had my druthers after such a busy week, I would have loved to have done nothing more all weekend than read a book or go for a walk, but David was having none of it and he was angry when he found out I hadn't made arrangements for a getaway.

"Guess it's just like old times," he said peevishly.

"I don't think that's fair, David, especially after the hours I put in this week. Besides, it's not like you couldn't have made plans yourself."

"Maybe that's just what I should have done. Made plans for myself and not us!" he sniped.

Ignoring his comment, I tried to pacify him.

"We can still spend the weekend together. Why don't you come over and we can have a nice dinner at my place and watch a romantic movie? Then tomorrow we can go out for a walk and enjoy the start of fall." It wasn't much, but it was the best I could come up with.

"That's it? Those are your big plans?"

"I'm sorry it's not what you're expecting, but let's make the best of it," I asked.

"Fine," he said grudgingly. "I'll be over after work."

As we hung up, I knew I didn't really want to spend the weekend with him. Maybe it was my feelings for Jake interfering, but I found myself hard pressed to drum up any real feelings for David at the moment. It was going to be very long weekend and it didn't start off well. It was a mad dash trying to get off work early enough to shop for groceries and get home before David arrived, and it didn't put me in the best of moods when he finally rang the doorbell. That should have been my first clue that the weekend wasn't going to turn out well, but I was committed now and saw no way out of it.

Dinner went well enough, mostly because I cooked David's favorite meal, and we said little as we ate. The silence between us was anything but relaxed from my point of view, and I couldn't help but compare it to the times Jake and I spent together in comfortable silence. Making the comparison between the two of them wasn't fair to David, but I couldn't help but do so as I watched every move David made, even as I tried to remember what had attracted me to him in the first place.

He was intelligent, obviously, but I was beginning to remember that he wasn't kind. He treated those around him as if they were somehow less than he, even in cases when it was clearly the other way around. Continuing to compare him to Jake in my head, I also realized he didn't make me laugh. When Jake and I were together I always had a smile on my face and laughter came easy. Being around David it was difficult to find the kind of happiness that I felt with Jake and there was little to smile about

After dinner, as I cleaned up the kitchen, David picked up the paper and began reading. The thought occurred to me that if Jake was in his place, he would have been right at my side helping with cleanup. But I needed to forget about Jake. David was the man in my life and even though I wasn't feeling as close to him as I should, I had three years of our relationship to catch up on and I tried to push thoughts of Jake out of my mind before joining David on the sofa.

"What movie would you like to watch?" I asked as he finally put the paper down. "Netflix has some of the new rom-coms."

"How many times do I have to tell you I don't like those chick flicks?" David said before grabbing the remote from my hand and flipping through the hundreds of channels before settling on *Ocean's 11* without even asking my opinion. His only consideration toward me was putting his arm around my shoulder as the movie began.

Long before the movie ended, my mind had drifted from the screen back to Chicago as I wondered what Jake was doing. As angry as I was at him for trying to convince me his lies were the truth, my eyes welled up at how much I missed him. The feelings that I had developed for him hadn't gone away and I didn't know if they ever would. When I looked back at the TV, the movie was almost over.

Watching the characters gather in front of the fountains at the Bellagio at the end of the movie, I heard the familiar strains of "Claire de Lune" before being hit with a blinding image of Jake, dressed in a suit, with twinkle lights shining in the background, the sound of waves crashing on a shore, as he and I danced to the same soft music coming from my television. Grabbing my head in both hands, I squeezed my eyes shut trying to make sense of the image in my brain. It was all in vivid color and I could feel a breeze blowing on my skin and the warmth of Jake's hand on my back as he rubbed his hand up and down just as he had done in Chicago. My head felt like it was going to explode with the details of everything I was seeing.

"What's wrong?"

I heard the words, but couldn't answer him, too afraid that if I stopped concentrating on the image I would lose it.

"Paige, what's wrong?" David asked more forcefully.

The moment was gone. David was looking at me like I had gone crazy. "Why are you holding your head like that?"

"I don't know. I just had the most vivid image and I don't know what to make of it."

"Did you remember something?" David asked. There was a look of apprehension on his face for some reason.

"No. What I was seeing couldn't be a memory because it had someone in it that I didn't know before."

"Who?"

"It doesn't matter," I told him, shaking my head.

"Who was it?" he asked more forcefully. "And don't say Baxter."

"What does Jake have to do with this?" I asked in surprise.

"Don't think I don't know that something was going on with him while you lived in that house," David told me.

"I don't think I like what you're implying," I told him, even though he was spot on. But how did he know?

"I'm not implying anything. I'm flat-out accusing you."

"David, you're being childish."

"Well, at least I didn't cheat on you!"

How could I argue that? But more so, why did I want to? David wasn't who I wanted, and even if I couldn't have Jake, the realization that I didn't want to be with David anymore washed over me.

"I don't think we should see each other anymore," I said softly.

"Now, Paige, I was just angry," he said. Was it me or did he look frightened? "Don't make a decision you're going to regret just because we had a fight."

"It's not just because we had a fight. I just realized you're not a very nice person and I don't know what I've been doing with you all these years. I deserve to be treated like I matter and I don't think I really matter to you, at least not in the ways I should." That was it in a nutshell. "It's time for you to go."

"You better think twice about this, Paige," he said. His tone had gone from being scared to angry in the blink of an eye. "If I walk out that door, I'm not coming back and I'm going to make sure you regret it."

"Are you seriously threatening me?" I asked him.

"It's not a threat, it's a promise," he told me angrily before grabbing his bag from the bedroom and slamming the door behind him as he left my apartment.

There it was again—that sense of déjà vu—only this time, I knew deep down that I had been through this situation before. Why would he threaten me? Was he that small of a person that he couldn't take rejection? Of course he was, and I sensed that I already knew that.

Thinking once again about the music from the movie and the image it conjured in my head, I hurried to my phone, searching for the song in the hopes the image would come to me again, but it didn't work and I had to admit to myself that as much as I wanted it to be real, it was only a daydream.

Having spent the rest of the weekend going over everything that I had been feeling since arriving back in Minneapolis, my head was spinning and I spent most of Monday in a fog. I waited until the end of the day to share my breakup news with Casey.

"Paige, you weren't meant to be with David, so don't feel bad," she said.

"Maybe I'm not meant to be with anyone. I don't know why I didn't see how self-centered and priggish David is before now. Can I tell you something? The whole time I was gone, I felt deep in my soul there was a man who loved me and was just waiting for me to come back. Obviously I thought that was David, but I couldn't have been more wrong. Say, do you want to go out for drinks after work?" I asked her. "Maybe I can meet someone new to make me forget about David."

"I don't think that's such a good idea, Paige," she said to my surprise. She, along with my sister, had worked hard to make me go out more in their never-ending quest to see me settled down with the perfect man so her negativity was unexpected.

"Why not? I thought you'd be dragging me out whether I wanted to or not."

"Uh...well, usually...but not anymore," she stammered as her face turned a brilliant shade of red.

"What's wrong with you today?" I asked.

"It's just that I think you should take it easy. Maybe wait until your memory comes back or something."

"Why? What difference would that make?" I asked.

"Well, what if you run into some guy you already dated and you don't remember him? Think how embarrassing that would be. And you don't want to hook up with just any guy. I'm absolutely certain your Mr. Right is just waiting for you to come back to him."

"Okay, I guess that could happen. But what do you mean, come back to him?"

"I just, well, maybe you've already met him and now, with David out of the picture, you'll see him with new eyes. That's what I meant."

"Well then, maybe this weekend we can see a movie or something. Have a girl's night out, if Bruce doesn't mind," I suggested. The relief on her face was apparent.

"That sounds like a plan. Well, I better get finished with that report if I want to get out of here on time tonight. Do you need anything else, boss?"

"No, I'm good. Since we're not going out, I think I'll work a bit later. I had a great idea for the church project and I want to get it down before I forget. If I don't see you before you go, have a nice evening. Will you close the door behind you, please?"

As Casey went back to her desk I took a seat at my drafting table and started work on the church project again. It was progressing nicely, which would make the Diocese happy after being stalled for a month after my accident. Mr. Nolan had reported the only thing that kept them from pulling the job from SNK was how happy they were with the design, and I didn't want to jeopardize anything else with them.

The ringing of my cell phone was the only thing that interrupted my work. Grabbing it off my desk I glanced at the caller ID. Yet another call from the same unidentified number that had been calling several times a day since I got back to Minneapolis. Even though it was a new phone, all of my friends and family had already been added to my contacts and their calls would have come up on caller ID. I don't know how the caller got my number, but as they never left a message, it was obviously a wrong number. My time was too busy to answer every spam call that came through, so I ignored the call like I had the dozens of others and went back to work.

"Working late again, Paige?"

Looking up from my work I was surprised to see Mr. Nolan in the doorway. I hadn't heard him open the door.

"Afraid so," I admitted as I put down my tools and faced him. "But then I've got a huge project on my drawing table and a lot to catch up on."

Thinking he was just noting my work hours, I was surprised when he walked in and sat down in one of the matching chairs in front of my desk.

"How's the memory coming?" he asked in that gravelly voice of his while motioning for me to sit in the chair next to him.

"Not much change," I admitted, wondering where this conversation was going as I sat down.

"Sorry to hear that," he said, giving me a fatherly pat on the arm.

Was he worried I wasn't doing a good job at work? Senior partners just didn't get involved in the lives of their associates.

"I can assure you, sir, my memory loss isn't impacting my work. I've been staying late every night trying to get caught up. There should be no impact on my work quality either."

"Did you think that's why I was asking?" he said in surprise. "That's not it at all. From all reports you're doing a spectacular job and worth every penny I'm paying you."

"Well then, if I may, why did you ask, sir?"

"Luke asked me to check in on you."

"Excuse me? Luke who?" I had no idea what he was talking about.

"Jake's dad, Luke Baxter."

"Jake's dad?" I asked in total confusion.

"Yes. We played golf over the weekend in Chicago and he asked me how you were doing."

"But why would he care? I've never even met the man," I told him.

To my further surprise, the normally unflappable Jerry Nolan turned a lovely shade of crimson and he started to stammer in embarrassment.

"Oh, that's right," he said when he could finally talk. "I'm sure Jake and Holly told him about you and since we're long-time friends he was just curious is all. Well, I better let you get back to work. Don't be here too late. And Paige?"

"Yes, sir?"

"Don't give up on the memory. There are an awful lot of people who love you depending on your remembering."

With that, he was out the door, leaving me with my jaw hanging down, wondering what had just happened. Who was he talking about? I was so tired of everyone around me talking in circles. It was as if they all shared a secret and I was the punchline.

Unwilling to spend more time dwelling on all the strange goings on around me, I went back to work.

Chapter Nineteen

$\mathcal{I}$t had already been a month since I was back in Minneapolis, and my life had settled into a routine. Most of the weird comments being made to me had long since stopped, and even though I hadn't regained my memory, it didn't seem to matter much to me anymore. The only person in my life that was still acting strange was Casey. Several times I had come out of my office to find her on the phone, with her hand over the receiver, whispering to whomever was on the other end. Each time I caught her, she would tell the person "I gotta go," and hang up quickly. At first I questioned her about it, but then just gave up when she refused to answer any of my questions. We might be friends, but that didn't mean she wasn't entitled to her own secrets. I just hoped that whatever she was up to didn't involve me.

Mr. Nolan still came by, supposedly for updates on my work, but each time he wanted to know what I was, or more specifically, wasn't remembering. He never said so, but I suspected he was there at Jake's request and he may have been sending back updates on my lack of progress. The thought made me happy, even though I wasn't sure Jake was at the root of Mr. Nolan's questions.

David's threats of retaliation never occurred and I heard through the industry grapevine that he had been let go from his new firm soon after we broke up. Rumor had it that in an effort to impress his new bosses with how much money he could bring to the firm, he had been poaching other architects clients. It sounded just like something he would do and made me glad I had ended things with him.

The unidentified calls to my cell phone had also tapered off until who-mever it was stopped completely. Obviously the person had finally figured out they were calling the wrong number. It was the last of the strange things that had been happening since I got back and I was grateful my life was get-ting back to normal.

"Good evening, Ms. Cooper," my doorman said as he opened the door for me. It was a wonderfully crisp fall day and the walk home had been a chilly one.

"Hello Joseph," I said with a smile. "How was your day?"

Joseph had been a doorman in my building for decades. In his seventies, he was the perfect man for the job. He loved to talk to everyone and knew ev-erything about the area. He was beloved by all of the tenants, myself included.

"About the same as every other day," he told me as I walked by him on the way to the elevator. "Oh Ms. Cooper, I almost forgot. A package came for you." Running ahead of me, he went to his desk and pulled out a me-dium-sized, heavily padded, manila envelope. "Whatever's inside must be pretty important. It came certified."

Accepting the envelope from him, I gave it a cursory glance before tuck-ing it into my satchel.

"Thank you. I'm sorry I can't stay and chat, but my sister is supposed to call in a few minutes and I don't want to miss her. Have a good evening and say hi to your wife for me."

"Good evening to you too, young miss."

The phone was ringing as I walked into the apartment and for the next hour or so, Jen and I filled each other in on our week. Her disappointment that I hadn't remembered much mirrored my own. Still, it was nice to be able to talk to her again.

Turning on the TV after we talked, I thought I would try and catch the late news before my eye caught sight of the manila envelope, still laying where I had tossed it with my other mail. Turning it over in my hand, I noticed a re-turn address from Chicago, but it was a street name I didn't recognize.

Carefully ripping the padded envelope open, I pulled out the single sheet of Mt. Sinai Hospital letterhead and unfolded it, surprised to see it was from Holly. It had been several weeks since I had sent her the thank-you note.

236

Dear Paige, Sorry this has taken me so long to respond, but I've had a heck of a time trying to track down your personal belongings at the hospital. Turns out it was all misfiled. Trust me, there are some unhappy staff in patient relations after all my yelling about it.

Dad says, via Jerry's reports, that you haven't regained your memory yet. I'm so very sorry...more than you know, actually. Jake, of course, does nothing but worry about you, and I think that's what made your leaving the way you did so awful. He spends all of his time working and I hardly ever talk to him anymore, except when he is asking about you.

Maybe we should have found ways to help you remember. I know, I know—the doctors said not to do that, but since their way didn't work it might have at least been worth a chance. The thought of you not remembering the wonderful life you had breaks my heart and I thought we would have a lifetime of friendship together. You are always going to have a special place in all of our hearts and I hope that someday...real soon....those very special memories of yours will be right back in that wonderful mind.

Until then, please know that Jake and I will keep you in our prayers. We love you...more than you know."

Her words about Jake brought back every single feeling I had for the man and tears filled my eyes. Even after all the lies and the horrible fight when I left, I was in love with him and there was no denying it. Yeah, he might worry about me, but for all I knew, he was married already and we would never be together. Whatever higher being brought him into my life must have done it as the cruelest of jokes.

I read Holly's note one more time before realizing there was something else in the envelope. Dumping it on the kitchen table, a small plastic bag filled with jewelry fell out. I always knew that I would have been wearing jewelry at the time of the accident and I was happy to have it back. Without opening it, I deposited the bag in my jewelry box and got ready for bed.

My dreams that night were punctuated by images of the accident and each time it woke me, I wasn't sure if it was an actual memory or just my imagination using the information I had been told. The strong feeling of being confined in a small space was prevalent and I could smell the sweet, stale odor of blood and the acrid smell of burning rubber even as I felt the blood running down my face. My ears rang with the sound of emergency sirens and the shrill sound of the equipment being used to cut me out of the cab. Then the images went dark until the dream replayed over and over again throughout the night.

Finally jolted out of my sleep, I sat up in bed, shaking, covered in sweat, trying to breathe normally again and convince myself it was just a dream. But the more I thought about it, the more I realized the dream was too detailed to not be an actual memory of the accident. Laying down once more, I closed my eyes as another flash came to me: I had been on the phone when the car hit us and in my head I saw my cell phone flying out of my hand as the cab crumpled around me.

The doctors had said I was unconscious throughout the entire ordeal in the cab, but I no longer believed it. With horrifying clarity, every painful, agonizing sensation washed over me until I began to sob uncontrollably.

My doctors had also said that not being able to remember a traumatic event was one of the body's coping mechanisms: protecting itself from the shock and fear and pain. Going through it now, alone in my apartment, I had to agree. Even knowing that I survived and that the pain was well behind me didn't dilute the feelings that washed over me now that I had remembered. More than anything I wanted someone to hold me and tell me that I would be okay, but the only person that would understand what the accident was like for me, the only person who had witnessed what I went through, was back in Chicago.

By the time I finally got my crying under control, the sun had come up and I could think about it a bit more logically. I didn't doubt for a minute that I was unconscious for most of the attempts to free me, but in the back of my mind I heard voices talking to me, felt someone holding my hand and comforting me, and it all made sense to me.

Suddenly it was important for me to see the jewelry in the bag, to have some tangible proof that I had survived the accident. Dumping the contents on my dresser, it was hard to miss the dried blood that was still caked on the earrings and the necklace I had been wearing. An unfamiliar ring buried beneath the other pieces caught my eye and I pulled it out for a closer look.

It was a diamond engagement ring.

My hands began to shake. Was Jake telling the truth all along? He had insisted that we were engaged and that I had been wearing an engagement ring in the crash. I had seen the telltale tan line on my ring finger where an engagement ring would have been and still I didn't believe him. My heart skipped a beat at the thought that he had been telling me the truth the entire time. Could it really be true? But why hadn't anyone told me right away? Why put me through weeks of believing that no one in my life cared enough to come and find me when the one man my life should have revolved around had been there with me the entire time?

If it was true, if I had been in Chicago because of Jake, he must be devastated that I didn't recognize him and what we meant to each other.

Carefully, with a mixture of hope and fear, I slipped the ring on my finger. It was a perfect fit, but I still needed more proof and I slipped the ring back off, not yet sure I had the right to be wearing it.

Starting to pace my apartment I thought back to the time Jake brought my favorite flowers to the hospital, how he knew how I took my coffee, and what made me laugh and what made me cry. He knew exactly how I liked my back rubbed when I needed physical comfort. Remembering all the people I met in Chicago who said I was his fiancée, I realized either my life had become the world's biggest conspiracy, or he had been telling me the truth!

But the most damning evidence was how easily I had fallen in love with the man even when I didn't remember him. From almost the first moment we met after the accident, I had felt an overwhelming attraction to him. I felt comfortable around him, as if I had known him for years. Was that because I did? How had we met? How long have we been together? Did everyone in my life know we're engaged, including Casey and my own sister?

Then something else hit me. David! If I was really engaged to Jake, why had David let me think I was in a relationship with him? A shiver ran up my spine at the thought that I might have slept with David. What was his role in this charade? Was there no one in my life I could trust with the truth?

Like a mad woman, I scoured my apartment looking for some proof that what I now suspected was the truth. Every file on my computer was opened as I looked for an email, a photo, an appointment, a receipt—anything that would prove Jake was my fiancée—but I found nothing. There were no unexplained mementos laying around, no photos of us together even though, like Jake, my apartment was filled with photos of family and friends. Logging in remotely to my work computer I searched for any evidence there and again found nothing.

Frustrated and confused by everything I was now coming to believe might be the truth, I just needed to get out and walk to clear my head. Maybe some sunshine and fresh air before going to work would help clear the cobwebs away and I would finally remember something concrete.

I only made it to the lobby before Joseph stopped me.

"Ms. Cooper, I know you're on your way out, but I really need to ask you what we should be doing with the box. My boss is on me to get it out from behind the desk."

"What?"

"Are you okay? You don't look so good," he said with concern.

"No, I'm fine," I assured him, even though I was anything but. The hours of crying had definitely left their mark. "I'm sorry, what box are you talking about?"

"The pictures. The ones Mr. Dawson took out of your apartment. He said he'd pick them up in a couple of days and it's been several weeks. Do you want to keep them or should we dispose of them?"

"David took pictures out of my apartment?" I asked in surprise. "When?"

Suddenly Joseph realized I had no idea what had been going on.

"I'm sorry, Ms. Cooper. Mr. Dawson said he was helping you out by cleaning out some stuff you didn't want before you came back. I remember telling Pat that it was odd we were seeing him again because we all thought you had broken up with him, but Mr. Dawson insisted that he was your boyfriend so Pat let him in your apartment. We thought it was okay," he said sheepishly.

"I don't care about that," I told him. "Joseph, where's the box? I need to see it."

Joseph went behind the reception desk and placed a large sealed box on the counter. "It's pretty heavy, miss. Do you want me to take it up to your apartment for you?"

Desperately wanting to see what was inside, I also didn't want to open it in full view of all my neighbors, so I asked him to take it up to my apartment.

When he had placed it on the kitchen table and slowly closed the door behind him, I peeled the tape off the box and glanced inside. The first photo I saw was of Jake and me at a Cubs game…just like the vision I had when I saw the Cubs cap in his house. Looking more carefully, I could see my ring finger was bare.

Digging further into the box I found pictures of me in the middle of a house under construction wearing my paint shirt with a paint brush in my hand and a goofy smile on my face; Jake and I with arms around each other at an outdoor party in a place I didn't recognize; Jake and Holly together; and many, many selfies of Jake and I together taken in even more places I didn't recognize.

In each of the photos my left hand either wasn't visible or there was no ring on my finger until I got to the bottom of the box, where a large framed print lay face down. Slowly turning it over as I took it out of the box, I gasped in surprise.

The photo was the image I remembered after hearing "Claire de Lune." A large full moon hovered in the upper right corner of the photo and twinkle lights hung from the trees. Jake was dressed in a dark suit and I was in a beautiful black dress. But what wasn't in the vision in my mind, but captured for eternity in the photo I was looking at, was Jake on one knee in front of me, apparently proposing. Startled beyond belief, I nearly dropped the picture as tears fell freely from my face and I tried to remember Jake proposing to me. This was no staged photograph. It had to be real. Why couldn't I remember?

The more I studied the photo, the more the surroundings looked familiar to me and then it hit me. Glensheen! This was taken at the mansion in Duluth. But when? Carefully I removed the photo from the frame and peeled the backing away. It was just a few months ago, but it might have been a lifetime for all I could remember.

Jake Baxter had proposed to me! I wanted to stand on my balcony and share my news with the world, but first I needed someone to confirm that it was really true. There was only one person that knew everything about my life. Casey. If it was real, she would know. Grabbing the picture, I carefully slipped it into an envelope and headed to the office, calling her while I walked and asking her to meet me in my office as soon as she got in.

Casey beat me to the office and as I walked up to her, my face giving away nothing of the turmoil I was feeling, I nodded toward my office, indicating she should follow me. Closing the door behind her, I took off my coat and sat down before handing her the envelope.

"What's this? Paige, what's going on? You're scaring me," she said nervously.

"Open that envelope and tell me if that's real or something someone made up as a cruel joke."

My tone left no doubt she should do as I asked and, watching me carefully, Casey slowly removed the photo as a smile came over her face.

"Thank God!" she said. "You finally remember."

"You mean it's real?" I asked in a mixture of relief and excitement. "I'm engaged to Jake Baxter?"

"I wanted to tell you so badly, especially when I found out you thought you were with David, but they warned us over and over not to prompt you."

A long, slow breath escaped my lips and tears came to my eyes.

"Did he propose to me at Glensheen?" I asked.

"Yes, and you said it was the most romantic thing a man had ever done for you," she told me.

"And did we have a horse-drawn carriage?" That part hadn't been in the image in my head, but I just suddenly knew.

"Yes, did you just remember that?" she asked excitedly.

"I think I did," I told her equally excited. "Tell me something else I don't remember. How did Jake and I meet?"

Just as Casey started to explain, I remembered myself and I held up my hand to stop what she was going to say. It was at an AIA conference in Chicago, just like the brochure I had found in Jake's office. Quickly I opened the calendar on my computer to see when I had been there and realized it was also just a few short months ago.

"Casey, did I meet him at the AIA conference in Chicago and was I the keynote speaker?"

"Oh my goodness! Paige, you're remembering! What else do you remember?" she asked excitedly.

"It's all just bits and pieces, really, but I am remembering things. How long after I met Jake was this picture taken?" I asked.

"Literally just weeks. Jake said it was love at first sight for him, but it took you a whole month to admit you were in love with him. Paige, you have to tell him you remember! He's been in agony over this."

"I know and I want to, but I needed to be sure before I contacted him. Wait a minute…how do you know what's he's been going through?" I asked.

"He calls here every day asking about you. In fact, you've walked in when I've been on the phone with him several times. You weren't answering your cell phone when he called so he called me."

So that explained all the secretive phone calls she had been making, as well as the unidentified calls on my own cell phone. Thank goodness. For a minute I thought maybe she was having an affair!

"Casey, I don't care what the doctors say. I want to know everything I missed."

"Well, if you're sure…"

For the next hour or more Casey filled me in on everything she could remember that had happened to me in the months leading up to the accident, including my original breakup with David, his threats and how it impacted my work, his eventual firing from SNK, my getting the church project after the AIA conference, and everyone at work knowing that Mr. Nolan referred to me as his "star player." But the part I was most interested in involved Jake and she quickly gave me the cliff notes version of our love affair.

"Paige, you have to call Jake. He's going to be over the moon."

"I will, but I want to do more than that. Casey, I have to see him. I don't care if it costs me my job or the church project, but I have to tell him in person. Please get me on the first flight to Chicago. I'm going to tell Mr. Nolan I need a couple of weeks off or I'm quitting. I hope he'll give me the time, but if not, you'll be looking for a new boss because either way I'm going to Jake. And if Jake calls, don't tell him a thing. I want this to be a surprise. But before I do all that, I need to do something I should have a very long time ago."

"What's that?"

"I'm going to confront David Dawson."

Leaving work behind me, I borrowed Casey's car for the short drive to David's apartment, hoping to find him at home. My angry knock on his door probably woke the neighbors, but at that point I didn't care. David had let me believe we were a couple and I needed to know why.

"Keep your shirt on," came David's angry voice from behind the door. The surprise on his face when he opened it to find me standing in front of him would have been priceless had I been in the mood. "Paige, what in hell are you doing here? Decided to come crawling back for a little of this?" he said as he gestured towards his body. He made my stomach turn.

"David, I need to talk to you," I said as I brushed by him into the apartment.

"Well sweetheart, now's not exactly the best time, if you catch my drift. I'm not alone."

Even as he said the words, a scantily clad, very young woman stood in the hallway outside his bedroom. She looked all of twenty.

"David, honey, what's going on? Who's this?" she said.

As soon as I heard her voice I recognized it. It was the syrupy sweet voice of the woman who had answered the phone when I called David after the accident.

"Go back to bed, Sheila," he told her. "This won't take long." Turning his attention back to me, he asked again what I wanted.

"She's a little young, even for you," I pointed out.

"What do you want, Paige?" he asked again.

"Why?"

"Why what?"

"Why did you pretend we were a couple? Why did you let me think that?

"So you remember now, do you?"

"David, please…I want to believe there is some sense of decency within you, but obviously I was wrong if you could lie to me so easily. My God, I almost slept with you!"

"I told you you'd be sorry. Honestly? I never expected the opportunity to just fall into my lap like that. Being able to make a fool of the great Paige Cooper? Priceless. Let's face it, pretending we were still together was even better payback for getting me fired than I could have imagined. When Sheila told me about your call, it took about a week for me to figure out how to pay you back."

"You mean you planned it?" I asked. The man really was horrible.

"With a little help from my old assistant Paula, yeah, I did. Like everyone else at that hellhole SNK, Paula was told about the accident and your memory loss and that no one was supposed to prompt you to remember. It was the perfect set up for me to step in and be the hero who brought you back home. A few bucks slipped to that old man Joseph in your building and I got in to clear out all the pictures and any other reminders of you and Baxter together. A few hours work and your life with him was wiped clean."

"But you had to know you'd get caught," I told him.

"That's true, and honestly I thought it would last a lot longer than it did, but it was worth it to see how pissed you are at me. That's only a taste of what I went through because of you, but still quite satisfying for me nonetheless."

The gall of the man astounded me. Deep down I always knew that Casey was right. He was evil and not to be trusted. The fact that I fell for his act for so long was a regret I would have to live with for a very long time, but this was the last time I would ever have to see his face.

"Because I will never have to see you again, I want you to know something. I wasn't involved in getting you fired. Mr. Nolan came to me and told me he had been thinking of letting you go for some time. He asked me directly if you had been involved in stealing clients from me and I told him I honestly didn't know. You got yourself fired and you were also the cause of my breaking up with you. You're self-centered and vain and arrogant without anything to back it up. You're a dismal excuse for an architect and even though I was the last one to figure it out, you can't be trusted. Knowing that your most recent firm figured that out in just a few weeks gives me more pleasure than it should."

"That's it? That's your big comeback for my pretending we were a couple?" he asked with a smirk.

"Not at all. You should also know that try as you might have to destroy my career, it didn't work. In fact, you're looking at the lead architect on the Basilica of St. Catherine's project."

David's jaw hung almost to the ground in a mixture of surprise and pure envy. Like me, he had desperately wanted to be even a small part of the project. It was the best kind of payback for what he had tried to do to me.

"And one more thing," I said as I slipped my hand into my pocket and pulled out my engagement ring, slipping it on my finger before flashing my hand at him. "I am going to spend the rest of my life being loved by a true man, a man of honesty and conviction, a man who knows the best way to get ahead in life is to work hard for what he wants. A man who I am sure will make me happier than I ever was with you. That, David, is what I call payback."

Without another word, I turned around to leave, putting David Dawson out of my mind and out of my life.

With that part of the story sorted, and filled with the excitement of my slowly returning memories, it was time to turn my attention to the only man that mattered anymore: Jake. Mr. Nolan, who, it turned out had a soft spot for romance, couldn't send me on my way to Jake fast enough, and by the early evening hours I was in the air on my way to Chicago. It seemed that once the flood gate of memories opened, more started to come through, and as I traveled I finally remembered the last time I went to Jake—when we were going to set our wedding date before the accident derailed everything in both of our lives.

Hailing a cab, I had a moment of fear. It was the first I had been in since the accident and my pulse began to race as I adjusted my seat belt tightly across my body before pulling my trusty clamshell suitcase onto the seat next to me...just in case. I had washed away all traces of the remaining blood that had been on it when Jake returned it to me, and only the small dents and scrapes that covered the case were left to remind me of the accident. As the cab picked up speed, I asked the driver to take his time, partly due to lingering fear about another accident and partly out of fear that I'd get to Jake's house only to discover he no longer loved me. Until I was certain, the engagement ring would stay securely in the front pocket of my jeans.

The cab pulled up to Jake's house and another returning memory of the first time I saw the house widened the smile on my face. Although it was late, Jake's truck wasn't in the driveway and it looked like no one was home.

"Paige, is that you?" came a familiar voice from next door. Mary was standing on her porch with Rufus in her arms.

"Hi Mary," I responded with a smile.

"Jake still hasn't come home from work," she said. "He does nothing but work since you left. If you ask me, it's not good for him to put in so many hours. He needs to learn to relax…"

I could tell her concerns for Jake would go on and on, but I didn't have time for chitchat.

"Do you know where he's working these days?" I asked to cut off her monologue.

"No, I'm sorry, but I don't," she told me. "But you can wait over here if you like."

As nice as her offer was, I didn't want to waste another minute.

"I know where he is," came a familiar voice from the sidewalk. It was Marcus!

"Marcus," I said when I recognized him. "Can you take me to him?" I asked.

"Sure. Let me get the car and I'll be right back to pick you up. Boy, is he going to be happy to see you," he said before racing down the street to where his car was parked.

"Mary, can you hold on to my suitcase until we get back?" I asked.

"Of course, dear," she said. "But can I ask you something?"

"Sure."

"You're really Jake's fiancée, right?"

"That's what I'm here to find out," I told her with a smile.

Marcus was back as quickly as he had left and within minutes he had deposited me at the project house. Only a couple of lights were on and it looked like Jake might be the only one still working. This house was more in the demo stage than the rehab stage, and I stood at the curb for a minute, trying to imagine what it would look like when finished before gingerly picking my way through the debris up to the front door. There was no bell to ring and I had no choice but to knock. There was no response. Had Marcus dropped me off at the wrong house? Knocking louder this time, I waited for someone to come to the door.

When it finally opened I expected to see Jake, but it was Charlie instead.

"Paige!" he said in surprise before I quickly put my finger to my mouth to silence whatever he had been about to say.

"Where's Jake?" I whispered. Charlie looked totally confused by my appearance.

"He's upstairs in the bathroom taking down tile," he said in a stage whisper that was less than quiet. "Do you want me to go get him?"

"No, I'd rather surprise him, if that's okay," I told him.

"Paige, do you remember that you're you now?" he asked with undisguised concern.

Even though that hadn't been my problem, I was happy to answer in the affirmative. "I remember you and I remember Jake and most importantly, I finally remember what we mean to each other!" I told him with a smile and a quick kiss on his cheek.

"Thank God," was his only comment before he walked away, mumbling to himself about things finally getting back to the way they should be. I couldn't have agreed with him more!

Making my way slowly up the stairs, I could hear Jake cursing loudly to himself. Apparently the demolition in the bathroom wasn't going as easy as it usually did. Maybe my news would help.

Turning the corner into the bathroom, I caught my first sight of him and my heart stopped. His back to me, his chiseled body drenched in sweat from the hard work he was doing, every bit of the love I had once felt for him washed over me in that instant and I couldn't wait to feel his arms around me.

"Jake?" I said softly before seeing his body tense as he recognized my voice.

Slowly he turned around as he took off the protective goggles he had been wearing and put down the hammer.

"My God, Paige. What are you doing here?" he asked in stunned surprise.

"Jake, are you in love with me?"

"What? What's going on?" he asked.

"I need you to answer my question. Are you in love with me?"

"I…" He started to answer, but then hesitated, as if he wasn't sure what the right thing to say was.

"It's not a trick question, Jake. Do you love me? Are you, Jake Baxter, head over heels in love with me and do you want to spend the rest of your life with me?"

Moving ever so slowly toward me, I saw my first hint of a smile from the man and I smiled back. He stopped just inches away from me as we stared into each other's eyes.

"You're the love of my life and I have loved you from the moment I first saw you. More than anything in the world, I want to spend the rest of my life with you, loving you and growing old with you."

"Then I have one more question," I asked as I put my hand in my pocket and pulled out my engagement ring. "Will you put this back where it belongs?"

Overcome with emotion as Jake realized I finally remembered, he closed the space between us in a flash before taking my face in his hands and kissing me softly. All of the pent up frustration and fear that each of us had experienced after the accident was gone and nothing in my life had ever felt as good as being back in his arms with my memories intact.

When we finally came up for air, he slid the ring on my finger and finally, all was right in my world once again.

Epilogue

$\mathcal{J}$ake and I spent the next two weeks talking about everything that had happened since the accident. Slowly but surely, my memories of the missing three years came back—some good, some not so good, but each one cherished because I could finally remember them. Relationships with Jake's family and friends were re-established and the story of how I finally remembered was repeated ad nausea.

Not surprisingly Jake didn't want to let me go back to Minneapolis without him, and with his mother and Holly's help, a small wedding was quickly arranged in his parent's backyard. Jen and her family, Casey and Bruce, and even Mr. Nolan and his wife joined us and after a short, drama-filled courtship, we became man and wife. It wasn't the wedding I had always dreamed of as a child, but that no longer mattered as long as I was with Jake.

As a married couple, we still had a few issues to decide, simple things like where we would live and who would give up their job. I knew I wanted to complete the church project before leaving SNK and for the next few months, Jake and I racked up an impressive amount of frequent flyer mileage in addition to spending hours and hours on the phone. Within a few months, the project design was completed, accepted by the Diocese, and Jake and my new in-laws joined my friends and family for the ground breaking of the church. The project would always be a feather in my cap and look good on my resume, but it was the last project I would do for SNK.

Mr. Nolan and the other senior partners accepted my resignation and quite graciously offered to pass on their recommendation of the new full-service design firm of Baxter-Cooper Design Renovations to all their friends and business associates in Chicago. I moved into Jake's beautiful home, and together we settled into our lives as business partners and, more importantly, husband and wife.

Our courtship was a wild ride, but these days, when Jake asks if I have forgotten something, we both smile knowing that the one thing neither of us will ever forget is the love we share.

Acknowledgments

$\mathcal{S}$pecial thanks to the friends, family, and others who have helped me get some of the important points of this work correct.

To my fishing experts Mike Reedy, Maureen and Steve Scholl, and David Luker for correcting me on the finer points of fishing for walleye and northern.

To the representatives of the American Institute of Architects for helping me learn more about their membership.

To City Engineer Jeff Domras for providing clarification about geotechnical engineering and soil standards.

I appreciate all your help!